FADING AMBER

Also by Jaime Reed

Living Violet

Burning Emerald

Published by Kensington Publishing Corporation

FADING AMBER

THE CAMBION CHRONICLES

JAIME REED

Dafina KTeen Books
KENSINGTON PUBLISHING CORP.
http://www.kensingtonbooks.com

DAFINA KTEEN BOOKS are published by

Kensington Publishing Corp.
119 West 40th Street
New York, NY 10018

All Kensington titles, imprints, and distributed lines are available at special quantity discounts for bulk purchases for sales promotion, premiums, fund-raising, educational, or institutional use.

Special book excerpts or customized printings can also be created to fit specific needs. For details, write or phone the office of the Kensington Special Sales Manager: Attn.: Special Sales Department. Kensington Publishing Corp., 119 West 40th Street, New York, NY 10018. Phone: 1-800-221-2647.

KTeen Reg. US Pat. & TM Off.
Sunburst logo Reg. US Pat. & TM Off.

ISBN-13: 978-0-7582-6926-3
ISBN-10: 0-7582-6926-9

First Printing: January 2013

10 9 8 7 6 5 4 3 2 1

Printed in the United States of America

To my sister Jade,
for all her love, support, and sacrifice.
I see it and so does God.
Thank you.

1

In regards to bad spirits, it's best to keep your mouth shut.

This is a handy rule of thumb, but secrets are unstable and require way too much maintenance. Every lie has to be reinforced by two more, and on it goes until eventually the secret implodes, and then everyone's day is ruined. It's a fitting punishment for dishonesty, just as long as you aren't both the liar and the person being deceived. That's when shit gets confusing.

So for the sake of honesty, I had to admit that these blackouts I kept having were getting worse. Much, much worse. They weren't daydreams anymore, or some momentary trance, but a complete displacement of time and space. Some sloppy editor had cut and pasted two separate scenes, hoping the audience wouldn't notice the lack in continuity. But there were some clues that gave away this manipulation.

The locale, for example, had changed. Instead of the child sweatshop known as James City High School, I was now at home, in my room, lying on my back on the ceiling. Yes, the ceiling. It wasn't the first time that I'd experienced the phenomenon of levitation, and my heart rate hadn't appreciated it then either. In fact, it was more alarming now since I had no memory of getting here.

I probably would still be asleep if it weren't for the sound of knocking on my front door. It could've been a neighbor, the UPS guy, or a Jehovah's Witness for all I cared. I needed a rescue, STAT. The knocking stopped and I soon heard a car start and back out of my driveway. I went into panic mode, desperately scrambling for control and some sense of reality.

My arms and feet dangled in the air, but my torso was trapped in some invisible harness. I rolled from one end to another and tried to use the corner wall to walk toward the floor, but my efforts were wasted. I had no power up here and I was just as afraid of floating as I was of falling. My entire body shook, my tears dropped on the floor below, and all my cries for help had gone unanswered.

Even if the person at the door had heard me, how would they get in? Even if they called the cops and they rammed their way inside, how would I explain why I was stuck on the ceiling? I could barely understand it myself, and I owned a higher knowledge of weird than the average person. Seeing as I wasn't going anywhere any time soon, I took in the aerial view of my room.

Four poster covered walls, two small windows, and the overflowing closet had never looked so alien, and the green color scheme added to the extraterrestrial feel. My computer desk and dresser sat on the opposite wall under an avalanche of books, soda cans, dirty laundry, and beauty products. I wouldn't have been surprised if something was living in my room making a nest for the winter, but I could sense no life energy in the house apart from my own.

In addition to my defiance of gravity, I was in pajamas and smelled of body wash. My hair hung around my face in wet, tangled clumps to where my fingers caught on the tight curls. It too had been cleaned, but managed by someone who had no skill in how to handle its texture. Since this was no doubt Lilith's fault, I didn't expect her to reveal full details of her deeds. My "internal roommate" went through a lot of effort to cover her tracks, but it was still a rush job, evidence that had to be removed quickly.

There lies the penalty of possession, what Cambions like me feared most. The sentient being living inside us was shady on a good day and could turn on its host if the wind blew wrong. I'd been told numerous times to be careful, to never lower my guard and never underestimate her power, but did I listen?

In my defense, I figured I'd have more time to adjust, to learn more about the Cambion world and the peculiar diet that came with it. After all, I wasn't born with this parasite like the rest of my kind, but got it as a crummy inheritance from a dearly departed friend. Her untimely death dropped a succubus on my doorstep along with a butt-load of responsibility.

Only my death could evict this evil tenant from her new abode, and I wasn't the suicidal type, no matter how bad my poetry got. It just wasn't how I handled problems; not how I rolled. Plus, my mom would kill me. But Lilith's recent stunt was enough to make me reconsider.

"How did I get here?" I asked her in a stern yet calm voice, not expecting an in depth answer. Lilith was a "Yes" or "No" kind of being, a ghostly Magic Eight Ball with limited responses. When she did respond, it would come in fragments of memories or a sharp zing up my spinal cord. But she remained still, tucked in her little corner at the base of my skull.

I struggled for composure, then continued. "Lilith, you need to stop doing this. I mean it! I'm sorry you got a raw deal in all of this, but you gotta let it go. This is *my* body, *my* rules, *my* choice."

Still no motion, which meant "No."

I rolled on my stomach and tried to do push-ups, belly flops, anything to demagnetize myself from the ceiling. No dice.

"Lilith! Let me down now!"

Before I could complete the command, gravity kicked in and my stomach jerked at the sensation of falling. The drop lasted longer than it should and the terror of weightlessness seized my heart. I could only manage a gasp as I drew further away from the ceiling, and the soft mattress broke my fall. Catching my breath, I pushed my hair from my face and noticed an important prop was missing from the set. My bracelet. It was gone.

It wasn't some arbitrary trinket, more like a handcuff with no key that required a band saw to remove. Its tracking system would've reported my whereabouts to my mom's laptop, and that security measure had now been breached.

I climbed out of bed and combed the floor in vain hope that I might have dropped it nearby. Pacing the floor, I recapped the last few moments I could remember, which consisted of a whole lot of nothing. What happened between 1:09 P.M. and 3:34 P.M. was a span that had no frame of reference. Only one person could fill in the blanks.

"What did you do?" I asked Lilith again.

That got her attention and she perked up. An image appeared behind my eyelids, a memory of me holding a jar of Caleb's "I love you" quarters that sat on top of my dresser. I remembered dancing and shaking the jar next to my ear like a maraca, one of the many embarrassing things I did in private while thinking about my boyfriend. Cake Boy and I were weird about the L word, so he allowed the accumulation of pocket change to speak for him. The image just popped in my head and I knew the vision was a clue from her.

I went to the dresser and checked the coin jar for anything out of the ordinary. Lying underneath was a note addressed to me on a white index card. At first I didn't recognize the handwriting—it was too sloppy. It reminded me of the way writing looks when you're learning cursive as a kid and using the lines on the page as a guide. At least I didn't have to worry about her forging my signature, although the bubble-like swoop of the *Ys, Qs* and *Gs* was spot on. Lilith had been living inside me for nearly six months with access to all my memories, so she was bound to pick up on a few things. I shouldn't have been shocked at her intelligence, her knowledge of the world around her, but I was. Even more so when I read the message on the card.

Samara,
I've hidden these memories from you.
Don't pursue this, don't question it.
Accept the peace that comes with not knowing.
You're safe now.
Forget it ever happened.
I'm sorry.
     Lilith

Was she for real? She really expected me to sweep this under the rug after reading a creepy haiku on a flash card? What was she trying to hide? Was it so bad that it was worth blocking out an entire afternoon of my life? Lilith made it clear that she wasn't going to budge on her decision, so I would have to do my own detective work.

But first, I needed to find that damn bracelet.

I checked the hall bathroom and found my clothes in the hamper along with my house key in my jean pocket, but no bracelet. In a frenzy, I searched Mom's room then went downstairs to check the kitchen and dining room. Unsuccessful, I crossed the foyer to the living room. My feet worked on their own accord as the rest of my body tried to drag out the inevitable. There was no getting around it now—it was the only place I hadn't checked.

I felt like that character in *Pulp Fiction* who had to get his father's watch back by any means necessary. My bracelet held a similar personal value, but without the really gross back story. Instead of a crime boss, I had a ghost to confront, a phantom by the name of Nadine Petrovsky, Lilith's former host.

I had no delusions that this part of the house was haunted, either by an actual substance or by a product of my neurosis. Seeing a close friend die in your living room will do that to you. Either way, bad times were to be had if I so much as stood in the entryway.

In a moment of courage, I rushed to the center of the room, looked for anything shiny, then jumped at the sharp chirp that broke the silence. Slowly, I turned to see the house phone sitting on the end table; the numbers of the incoming call glowing in the tiny display.

It rang again, and I could almost feel Mom's impatience on the other end of the phone. Just like the woman herself, the ring had a nagging persistence, demanding an answer whether I liked it or not.

I reached out as far as I could and snatched the phone off the charger, not moving any closer to the couch than necessary, and avoiding eye contact with the beautiful blonde sprawled on the floor. From this angle, I could see the length of her golden hair, the extended white arm, and the delicate wrist.

If I tried hard enough I could pretend that she was just taking a nap, the Sleeping Beauty after pricking her finger on the spindle. But Lilith knew better, I knew better, and a part of me hated Nadine for leaving me with this burden. Maybe this was her punishment, trapped in the plane of the living, forever beautiful, eternally young, and irrevocably dead.

Focusing on one mental meltdown at a time, I took a deep breath and put the phone to my ear. "Mom?"

"Hi, sweetie. I'm glad I caught you before you went to work. Your father just called my office and he said he's picking you up tomorrow to get your new car."

My car? It took a few seconds to decipher her meaning. "Oh! Yeah, right, thanks," I said when it finally dawned on me. "Wait, I have to work today?" I looked at the clock on top of the fireplace, which began to stretch and twist like saltwater taffy. The wall pictures and love seat joined the distortion, which was my cue to get the hell out of this room. I moved to the foyer while Mom ran off details about warranties and prices in my ear.

"Samara? Are you listening to me?" Mom asked.

"Yeah, cars are great. They go 'vroom,'" I replied, still trapped in my own thoughts. "This may sound like a weird question, but did you pick me up from school today?"

A long pause dragged through the line. "Uh, no. You called about an hour ago and said that you caught a ride from Caleb so you didn't need me to pick you up."

And she was cool with that? Ms. Julie it's-dangerous-for-the-two-of-you-to-be-alone-together Marshall allowed my boyfriend to take me home?

"Caleb?" I repeated.

"Yes, Samara. Caleb: tall, skinny, in desperate need of a shave, the boy you can't seem to live without," Mom said carefully as one would to a kid with special needs. "I figured since you both have to work today he can give you a ride. I'm a bit swamped here at the office. A lot of work piled up from the holiday and I need to play catch up."

I was still stuck on the 'Caleb taking me home' part. And the grim fact that I had to work today. Was he really at my house? Maybe he could give me some answers.

I raced to the door, and stopped at the security alarm. It was activated, which required a four-digit security code whenever the door was opened. I wondered what else Lilith had memorized. My locker combination? My Social Security number? My . . . real dress size? I shuddered at the thought.

I opened the door and flinched at the cold gust of air, a rude introduction to the winter season. The foliage was now brown, and most of it littered the lawn along with shattered glass and debris from the supernatural storm on Thanksgiving night. My next door neighbor untied a pine tree from the roof of his minivan. A woman in a pink velour jumpsuit jogged across the street with her enormous German shepherd. A group of kids strolled from the corner bus stop, hauling book bags and lunch boxes. On the surface, my quiet town seemed normal, yet everything was far from it. One only had to look hard enough.

To my disappointment, there was no sign of Caleb or his black Jeep, but I found what I was looking for. There, hanging on the doorknob, was my bracelet. I examined it for any damage, noting Lilith's name engraved on the gold plate. The chain was wet and dirty, and the link had been broken by something sharp, leaving a clean, even cut.

"Are you feeling all right, honey?" Mom asked when I didn't reply.

"Huh? What—no, I'm fine. I'm just a little out of it. I gotta go. I'll see you later."

I hung up and stared into space, feeling more confused than when I woke up. Lilith was right; there was a peace that came with not knowing, but there was also that gnawing, ferocious ache called "What the hell is going on?"

This wasn't fair! I had every right to know what happened to *my body*. Anything could've happened. I could've robbed a bank, murdered a bus full of nuns, or flashed the entire football team. For all I knew, somebody might have videotaped it, and the footage was now getting hits on the Internet. I couldn't, wouldn't let this go.

I slammed the door, no doubt scaring my neighbors in the process, and got ready for work and what I knew to be the beginning of another unpleasant holiday.

2

After a quick change, half a bottle of leave-in conditioner, and a smelly cab ride, I made it to work ten minutes late.

The Buncha Books sign glowed in the low afternoon light, the neon letters drawing the unsuspecting into its snare. I followed its beacon and trekked through the crowded prison yard of torture and overpriced retail.

The outlet center sprang to life this time of year and the bookstore was no exception. Everyone and their mother was taking advantage of the holiday sales. The company tech nerd stood behind his booth by the door, demonstrating the latest apps on electronic reading tablets. Children broke free from their parents' leashes and ran around the store.

The aesthetics appeared to have changed overnight at the J-O-B. Jazzy Christmas music blared through the PA system, red bows and wreaths decorated the floor displays, pillars, and bookshelves. A group of historical actors in their Colonial garb sat at a folding table, gift-wrapping presents for customers. The aroma of coffee grounds, pumpkin spice, and peppermint made the air so thick I could almost chew it.

I raced through the center aisle to the customer service desk with the hope of avoiding my superiors. Luck wasn't on my side today, because Linda, the store manager, stood behind the desk helping an elderly customer. While she was distracted, I slipped past her and clocked in on the opposite computer. Just when I was about to make my great escape, she spoke.

"Sam, you do realize your shift started at four, right?"

I paused mid step. I was *so* close. "Yes, I'm sorry. Something came up."

When the customer left the counter, Linda turned to me. "A lot of things tend to come up with you these days. The Christmas run is beginning and I need reliable people to handle the crowds. If that's a problem for you, then I'm afraid—"

"Her car got wrecked in a storm, Linda. Come on, you never had car trouble before? Cut her a little slack." A low voice said behind us, and I didn't need to see who it was. I felt his presence as soon as I entered the store, the second the cab pulled into the shopping center.

I turned around and saw Caleb leaning against the desk, with a bear claw doughnut in one hand and twirling his name tag necklace with the other. He wore his standard uniform: tan khakis, white polo shirt, and a cocky smirk. The five o'clock shadow around his jaw looked more like twelve-thirty. The light brown strands of his hair fell over his eyes, bending at the jaw.

Yep, Caleb Baker, king of extreme bed hair, was on the mend and back in action. Having influence over the opposite sex was one of the few perks of being a Cambion. He could look like fresh road kill, yet Linda's clouded vision only saw the man of her dreams.

"Oh sure, Caleb, naturally you would take her side." Smoothing her dreadlocks in place, she leaned closer to him in playful flirtation.

"Of course, but ten minutes never hurt anyone, has it?" He grinned, biting his lip.

Caleb never had much shame when it came to flirting, and waking up from a coma only three days prior hadn't weakened his game. However, that talent was getting me out of the hot seat right now, so I kept quiet.

With a blink, Linda looked at me as if surprised I was still there. "Well, go on, Sam. Don't be later than you need to be."

I slid by Caleb while our eyes locked for an eternal second. "Thanks," I whispered.

"No problem," he replied, and our fingertips connected for the briefest touch.

Though I saw Caleb yesterday, it felt like much longer, maybe due to all that had happened during the turkey day of doom. Things were tense between us now because of obligations and secrets we had to keep, and being this close to each other was nothing short of sweet torture.

Our empathic link had turned us into a pair of conjoined twins, moving in sync to a beat the beings inside us orchestrated. We were even beginning to dress alike, or maybe that was due to the employee dress code at our job.

By the time I reached the café, I was past the respectable limit of tardy, and Alicia Holloway, fellow serving wench and classmate, had no qualms about telling me about it. She had every reason to be stressed out. Our very pregnant café manager only showed up to work every lunar eclipse, leaving us baristas to man the battle stations on our own.

Angry as Alicia was, it was hard to take a person seriously who looked like a brown Precious Moments doll. Not that I had room to talk, but I just wanted to pinch her cheeks and play with her twisty braids.

I'd been acting suspect to everyone and I needed to make amends somehow, so I might as well start with her. She recently got her learner's permit and I used that fact to my advantage. Promising her driving lessons smoothed back some of her ruffled feathers, and we were able to work in civil harmony.

"You know Malik Davis ran away from home," she prompted, pulling gingerbread cookies out of the oven.

"I heard," I grumbled.

"I saw the police come by the school, but no one's seen him," she added.

In actuality, *no one* had seen the *real* Malik Davis in over three months, but that was something only Caleb, Tobias, and I knew about. I doubted anyone would find Malik's body—Tobias was good at making things disappear, including himself.

Thinking of Tobias made me thankful for the memory loss. Just for a few glorious minutes, I could forget the Big Bad who hid in the shadows, namely a shape-shifting incubus with a score to settle. I hadn't seen Tobias in hours, but it didn't mean he wasn't around. He could be anywhere, *become anyone*, what with being the ultimate master of disguise and manipulation and all. If he could go so far as to disguise himself as my dead classmate and live with his family, then nothing was off limits.

"I'm sure he'll show up eventually," I assured as I chugged down a shot of espresso.

"How are you holding up?" she asked. "I mean, I know you and Malik were close and all that."

I almost spat out my drink. "What? No we weren't. Malik was always pushing up on me, not the other way around. If you haven't noticed, I already have a boy-friend." I pointed in the direction of the music department.

"I've noticed, but have you?" she asked, and I didn't ignore the venom in her tone. It threw me off guard to have this usually happy little cherub catch an attitude, so I called her on it.

"Don't tell me you have a crush on Malik, do you?"

"No!" she said a little too quickly.

I gasped. "Omigod, you do!"

"Shut up. I do not." Her face bunched in an adorable pout as she continued wiping down the work area.

Oh, Tobias was gonna pay for this. Not only had he been masquerading as one of the biggest man-whores on campus, he managed to enchant every female in school, including the trusting sophomore who was now giving me the side-eye. At least I knew the root of the problem wasn't entirely my fault, so I could work with a clear conscience.

After we shut down, the employees piled up at the entrance while Linda did the last minute sweep of the store.

We huddled in the vestibule, watching the lights in each department go out one by one. My eyes stayed glued to Caleb who spoke to me in code without moving his lips. I understood every word; I could feel the energy, the unexpressed emotion rushing off his body in waves, and being in cramped quarters with a dozen other people made the vibe that much more naughty.

His hands rested at his sides, clenching and unclenching in a strange rhythm. Color drenched his eyes, the sentient being behind them adding his two cents in our nonverbal conversation. Caleb was having a time making Capone behave, if the constant fidgeting was anything to go by. My own sentient being was eager as well, and if Lilith had her way, Caleb and I would be mated officially by now instead of this song and dance we had going on.

When Linda returned, we all filed out into the cold night. The crew scattered to their cars as I stood under the awning, waiting for the blue Chrysler that wasn't there. Julie Marshall was a bona fide soccer mom, but her chauffeuring duties were getting rusty these days.

Soft flurries fell at a slant across my vision and the world blurred into patches of gray. It wasn't cold enough for the snow to really stick, but a thin overlay of white covered the empty parking lot.

Alicia's dad waited in his SUV by the curb and the engine revved to life when he spotted her.

"Remember, driving lessons!" Alicia yelled, or rather threatened, as she climbed into the passenger's side. The van pulled away and more cars fled the premises before I could ask for a ride.

As I was on the brink of losing all feeling in my toes, Caleb drifted next to me. Flurries speckled his hair and his ears and cheeks were glowing bright red. Tall and lanky as he was, Caleb was a cutie, although a few minutes inside a tanning bed wouldn't kill him. If I squinted, I'd lose him in the snow.

"You coming or what?" he asked.

"I'm waiting for my mom," I answered.

"She's not coming."

I flinched, and not from the cold. "What?"

"I called her an hour ago and told her I was taking you home."

"Did you now? And she agreed?" That didn't sound like Mom at all.

"Yep. She trusts me with you. She knows I won't do anything reckless. Plus, she's got us clocked." He pulled up his coat sleeve and checked his watch. "We have fif-teen—no, thirteen minutes before she's coming after me with a pair of hedge clippers and a can of kerosene. 'Homemade birth control,' she says."

Now that sounded more like Mom.

"Come on. It's cold out here. Second-guess all this in the car." He led me to his Jeep, which sat in the far end of the shopping center. His hand slipped over mine; his thumb working the circulation back into my fingers.

"You all right?" he asked.

I glanced up to a pair of violet eyes that spoke of con-cern. "Not really," I mumbled. "Did you pick me up from school today?"

"No. Why?"

"I'm trying to figure out how I got home."

He looked confused. "How did you get to work?"

"I took a cab," I said while my mind continued to work in the reverse gear. "I don't know much before that, because I blacked out again. I woke up in my room, on the ceiling."

He stopped dead in his tracks and stared at me care-fully. "Really? Is Lilith okay?"

I shrank back, appalled. "*Lilith*? Shouldn't you be worried about *me*?"

"Yeah, I'll get to that in a minute. Did she tell you what hurt her?" Before I could ask, he continued. "The last time Capone was out on the town, he did the same thing." To show his point, he pushed the hair out of his face and revealed the bruised lump on his forehead, one of many battle scars from the Thanksgiving demon war. "You know when you're feeling hurt and vulnerable you curl up in a ball? Well, the spirits tend to climb and do this weird perching thing when they're really scared. They like being in high places and observing. Gives them a sense of control when something goes wrong. So, I gotta ask, what went wrong with Lilith? What freaked her out?"

"I don't know. She won't tell me." I rubbed my face in large circles. "Oh, and how about this, my bracelet was cut off. I found it on my front door. Angie's gonna be so pissed. And Mom is gonna kill me." I showed Caleb my wrist and the twist-tie I stole from the breadbox to fasten the bracelet back together.

Caleb appraised my craftwork then centered his attention on me. "What's the last thing you remember before the blackout?"

"I remember sitting at my table at lunch then I saw . . . ugh, I can't remember. It's like right there on the tip of my tongue." I scrunched up my face in concentration, almost straining my muscles to get one flash of a memory. Then one hit me. "You put olive oil around my school. When did you do that?"

"Oh. Yeah, right," he admitted. "Saturday night. Got my brothers to help me out. I even covered the area around the store so we won't have to worry about Tobias showing up here. Are you mad?" His plump bottom lip pushed out in a pout, begging me to crush it between my teeth like a ripe grape.

"No. One less problem for me to worry about." With that thought in mind, I surveyed the parking lot. Everything seemed fine, but that was always when weird stuff happened. "We have to be careful. Tobias is still out there."

While he opened the car door for me, I noticed a huge dent on the side that reached all the way to the front bumper. The curve around the wheel was crushed inward; the black paint had flaked off, exposing the metalwork underneath. "Somebody got you good. That sucks; you just got your car back from the shop."

He looked to where I pointed and frowned. "Yeah, I have to take it in for another paint job."

"Did this happen today? Do you think Tobias is wrecking cars again?"

He stared off for a minute, his brows furrowed in deep thought. "No. This time I think it was my fault."

"And you want to drive me home?" I joked, but there was nothing funny about his answer, or the lack thereof. I knew his evasive tactic by name; the vague responses, the omission of important information. When he climbed into the driver's side, I asked, "Were you drunk?"

"When have you ever seen me drink, Sam?"

"Then what happened? Stop being so secretive."

He put his key into the ignition then stopped. "Your blackout, it was sometime after one o'clock, right?"

I paused, then replied, "Yeah. How did you know?"

"It was around the same time I got a weird feeling while driving." He started the engine then pulled out of the parking space, leaving me staring at his profile with a slacked jaw.

Sick of the suspense, I blurted out, "What feeling? Did you have a blackout, too? Did you have an accident?"

"I'm not sure. I was on my way to work, and when I got out of the car, that dent was there. I have no idea how it got there, and it wasn't there when I left the house. I arrived on time, but something was off, you know?"

"Why didn't you tell me?"

"I'm telling you now, and I'm still freaked out about it, especially after what you told me. You know what this means, don't you? We're sharing experiences now. Our link is building, growing stronger, demanding completion. We'll have to make a decision soon about our future."

Whoa! Now was not the time to talk about something so . . . forever. Less than a year ago, the thought of having a steady boyfriend gave me hives, but now I had something far more dangerous to avoid. There would come a time where we would complete the bonding process by mating, but the effects were irreversible. There would be no trial separation for us, no divorce, no irreconcilable differences. Caleb and I were in it 'til death or demonic madness, whichever came first.

"Do we have to do this now?" I asked.

"No, not now, or tomorrow, or next week. Just letting you know that the topic will be coming up again very soon and we need to address it. I need to know where your head's at."

"*My* head?" He was the one acting sketchy with his repetitive, "It's dangerous to be near you, but I'll drive you home" nonsense. Duplicity, thy name is Caleb.

"It's not about you anymore and it's not about me," he said. "It's a plural thing now. Every decision has to be for the benefit of both of us. We may not like it, it may not be what we want, but it's what we need."

"Stability," I said.

"Stability," he parroted. That was the one thing he craved more than food, more than human energy, more than me. He never had it growing up and attaining a semblance of it was now his life's mission. After everything that's happened between us, I couldn't blame him one bit.

Keeping in the spirit of stability, I caught him up on the three weeks he missed while he was in the hospital. I rambled on about school, the Malik scandal, and how everyone, including my best friend hated me and Caleb listened attentively. The tension melted away and we behaved like a normal couple again with no outside interferences. When he pulled into my neighborhood, I wished I lived farther away from work, maybe out of state. I wasn't ready to let him go.

Christmas blossomed to life on my street. Flashing lights outlined houses, and plastic ornaments populated the lawns. It would only be a matter of time before my mom turned from the loving and somewhat paranoid guardian into the holiday-crazed psycho who came with the season. I could see the beginning signs of the transformation as we pulled up to my house.

Phase one: the door.

The wreath over our door was a hand-crafted monstrosity that she ordered from one of those home shopping channels. The thing was the size of a life raft with enough lights on it to cause seizures. Staring at that blinking eyesore from the street, I knew that the fever was quickly setting in.

A black sedan parked in front of my house. We recognized the make and model, and the tinted windows and New York license plate were a dead giveaway.

Caleb and I groaned simultaneously, and our joint reaction would've been cute if it weren't for such an ugly circumstance. David Ruiz had been sent by the higher ups in the Cambion world to keep tabs on Caleb and his brothers. His presence reminded me of the conflict we would soon face with that powerful family.

Caleb focused straight ahead, drilling a hole into Ruiz's car with his embittered glare. As unhappy as Caleb was to have a run-in with the private eye, I was even less enthused to see him snuggling up to my mom. No wonder she agreed to let Caleb pick me up. She got a little distracted when a guy was in her life, a rare occasion, but one that had proven dangerous in the past.

Caleb parked behind Ruiz's car and cut off the engine, leaving an overwhelming silence between us.

He checked his watch. "Forty seconds to spare," he said with forced humor.

"Good. Let's use our time wisely." I removed my seat belt, leaned in and kissed him before he could stop me.

"Sam," he moaned, but I could tell he was enjoying the affection. He needed something to take the edge off, too. Soon, he gave up the fight and placed his hand on the back of my head and pulled me closer.

The kiss deepened and with each caress of his lips, hot electricity sizzled on my tongue like Pop Rocks. Words could never properly describe the act of feeding. Our lip-locks alone were atomic, but the transfer of our energy made each kiss straight supernova. I could feel its current pass from his mouth to mine, the give-and-take; the dizziness of being drained and the high of drawing new life into my system.

I didn't understand the consumption process, nor could I understand how I could now see events that Caleb was too young to remember. I simply enjoyed the ride and watched his past flash behind my eyelids in a highlight reel. It came in no particular order, but I understood them all, because Caleb knew what each moment meant to him when they happened. There were some memories that I could've done without, like the faces of girls who shared his company . . . and his bed. I tried not to dwell on those moments and allowed them to pass once the energy burned off. However, the ones of him taking a shower were forever in my secret stash.

Just before the windows began to fog up, he pulled me away. "Okay, Sam. That's enough for now."

"Sorry. I'm just . . ."

"Hungry?" he guessed.

I nodded. I hadn't consumed energy in who knew how long and I didn't want to feed on any strangers tonight. Caleb was a safe food source, equipped with an intimacy reserved only for me. Munching on random males still made me feel grimy, so I only did that in emergencies.

"Come on then. Our time is up." He unhooked his seat belt and climbed out of the car.

I did the same and we walked side by side across the crunchy grass to my door. When we made it to the porch the door flew open and Mom stood on the other side, wearing a pair of old sweats. Her brown curls stuck to her face, blood rushed to her pale, freckled cheeks, and she sounded out of breath as if she ran to the door. My stomach lurched at what she could've been doing, especially with Ruiz inside. And she thought *I* needed supervision.

"Right on time. I'm impressed. Come on in. You can give me a hand." Mom waved us inside and hurried to the dining room to our right.

Caleb and I stared at each other for a brief moment, shrugged, then stepped inside. The foyer was flooded with boxes in various sizes, no doubt taken from the spare room that doubled as a storage shed. Words like *fragile, outside lights,* and *garland* were etched across each box in black marker.

"What's going on?" I asked.

"I'm getting the house ready for company. Need to make sure everything is set."

"Christmas isn't for another couple of weeks," I argued.

"I know, but I'm feeling the itch. I want a whole new look this year and I'm going for something more traditional. A Norman Rockwell theme."

I wasn't sure why the change bothered me, but it did. We always had the same theme every year, a constant I could rely on. "No Santa's workshop?"

"Nope. I figured it's time for a change. It was nice when you were a baby, but I want something a bit more sophisticated. Also, I want the house to look presentable for Evangeline when she comes to town. I spoke to her this afternoon, and she says she's coming to see you and was thinking about staying for the holiday. You know how flashy she is."

"Angie's coming?" I stopped and looked to Caleb, who had been admiring a snow globe from the opposite side of the table. Our eyes met knowingly. Mom might've been thrilled to play hostess to a legion of Cambions, but Nadine's mother was a complex woman and there was more to her sudden visit to the States than implied. As much as I was dying to see my 'fairy godmother,' so to speak, I didn't anticipate the fallout that would come with her arrival.

"She sounded really anxious to come down," Mom continued and reclaimed my attention. "She was thinking about bringing her daughters with her. You haven't met them, have you?"

"Not face-to-face. But I know them." Having full custody of Lilith gave me a VIP pass to Nadine's entire life history, from education, to language, to friends and family. The thought of Nadine's sisters coming along to sip eggnog didn't settle my stomach at all. How would they react to me? I wasn't a blood relative, but Lilith and their spirits came from the same succubi, making us spiritual siblings.

As Mom went on about window treatments and square footage, I felt the impulse to look up. Caleb watched me intently, as if trying to get my attention by eye contact alone. When he got it, he tipped his head toward the kitchen.

"Be right back." I scooted my way to him through the dining room.

"Don't go too far. I need you to help me hang these bows," Mom called behind me.

In the quiet of the kitchen, before I could get in the room good, Caleb turned to me with a stern expression. "Don't freak out."

"It's a little late for that, don't you think? Like say . . . six months?"

Caleb sighed. "Evangeline's just coming to visit and update us on what's going on."

"Do you really think she's coming alone? You think the Cambion mafia isn't coming with her? You and your brothers are on their hit list. They already have Ruiz shadowing you. What if they find something wrong?"

"Then I'll have to convince them otherwise," he answered.

"How? They think you're turning into an incubus. Do you know what they do to full blown demons? I'll give you a hint—it's not a game of foosball."

Caleb stiffened, a little stunned. "And you know this how?"

I looked to the dining room to see if Mom was listening. "Ruiz told me last night. Mom knows that Angie sent him here to protect me, but not the part about the witch hunt for you. If you're found guilty . . ." I stumbled over my words. The penalties were too hideous to verbalize.

"One thing I know about the family is that they're sticklers for rules. One of those rules being never to kill a Cambion's mate. To go against their own law would make them look bad with the other families in the U.S. and abroad."

"Uh, hello?" I waved my hand in front of him to wake him out of his delusion. "We're not mated yet."

"We're close enough, and whatever happens to me happens to you, and Evangeline won't let you die. Lilith is her only connection to Nadine."

I nodded slowly. Angie was the one thing in our corner,

but did she have enough pull to save the both of us? "What about Tobias?" I asked.

His face twisted into an ugly frown, mimicking nausea. "One crisis at a time, Sam."

I understood his reluctance to talk about him, but Tobias was still an immediate danger that could make things a whole lot worse if Ruiz caught wind of it. Caleb was right; we needed to prioritize in order to keep the BS in our lives to a minimum.

I was about to reply when we heard footsteps coming down the stairs. Ruiz appeared, holding a huge box of Christmas lights. The Cuban Necktie, as he was nicknamed, had forgone his usual suit and tie for some jeans and a T-shirt, but he still had a clean-cut air of authority that went with any outfit. It made sense—if you're going to stakeout someone's house, you might as well be comfortable. Judging by the armpit stains and sheen of sweat against his tan skin, I'd say Mom had certainly put him to work.

"Okay, I think that's the last of them. You shouldn't have so many wires in one place, Julie. That's a fire hazard." He placed the box with the rest in the foyer, then stood up straight to stretch. By doing so, he caught us watching him from the kitchen.

Wearing a smug grin, he approached us. "Hello, Samara. I'm glad you made it home safely." His smile faltered when he looked at Caleb. "I take it you're staying out of trouble, Mr. Baker. Have you curbed your eating habits?"

"Within reason." Almost instinctively, Caleb pulled me into the safety of his arms.

Ignoring the icy reply, Ruiz said, "Your level of consumption is no laughing matter, Mr. Baker. I've reported the incident with the three nurses you fed from on Thanksgiving night, and my superiors aren't pleased with what's taking place in this town. You're unpredictable and I'm not comfortable with you being alone with Samara."

"I'm not comfortable with you talking about me like I'm not in the room," I jumped in. "I'm also uncomfortable with you courting my mom while plotting to kill my boyfriend. So what's your point?"

For the briefest second, he looked insulted. "Samara, I'm not the bad guy here. I don't make the rules. I'm just following orders."

I rolled my eyes. "Whatever. Why are you in my house?"

"Your mother needed help decorating, and she's very persuasive. She would've made a very powerful Cambion. Too bad Cambions are born, not made." He stared pointedly at me. "For the most part."

Any other day, any other time, I would've let the comment slide, but too much had happened to me in a matter of hours and there were too many sharp objects in the kitchen. I stepped away from Caleb's hold and got in the detective's face.

"I get it; I'm a freak of nature. But here's the thing, you're not my daddy, and I won't even let *him* tell me who I should date. I'm not scared of you or the people you work for. You're not a Cambion, and I doubt anyone will care if you go missing. So, as long as you continue to have these little activities with my mother, I get to spend time with Caleb. 'Cause frankly, I trust you as much as you trust him, possibly less." I folded my arms and waited.

Both men remained silent, gawking at me with open mouths and blatant astonishment.

I was on top of my game when it came to telling someone off, a trait that I inherited from both sides of my family. My dad taught me to learn a person's weakness and attack at the proper time.

I knew Ruiz held a very soft spot for my mom, which put him in a compromising position. One wrong word to his superiors could lead to Caleb's execution, in turn, killing the only daughter of the woman he had the hots for. This was just another reason why people in general should never, ever date. It was just too complicated.

"All right," Ruiz said. "But the rules still stand. No feeding on others, no leaving town. And if I hear so much as a whisper of an attack on another female . . ." He didn't need to finish his threat; his point had been made.

"Fine," Caleb agreed.

"Fine," I grumbled.

During the final round of our epic staring contest, Mom called from the living room. "David, can you help me with these lights?"

At the sound of Mom's voice, Ruiz's muscles relaxed. There was a flicker in his dark eyes, worry maybe, and then he quickly returned to his usual robotic pretext. He was a hard-ass who kept his emotions on ice, but for a split second, he dropped his shield. Caleb and I looked to each other, silently discussing the ripples of energy emitting off the detective's skin. Each vibe varied with a person's mood, but Caleb and I knew this particular emotion by heart. Desire.

I fought to keep my dinner from coming back up. Thankfully, I wasn't telepathic, so I was spared from having to read the sick thoughts this deviant had toward my poor mommy.

Trying to play it off, Ruiz upped the threat level in his tone a few more notches. "Don't forget what we discussed." His glare bounced between the two of us as he walked backward to the living room.

When he left, Caleb stared at me with awe. "You're so . . ."

"Hood?" I guessed.

"Please." He scoffed. "Try as you might, no one living in the suburbs can be hood. It's scientifically impossible. Actually, I was going for 'extraordinary'. I've never met anyone like you."

I shrugged, refusing to acknowledge the heat in my cheeks. "What can I say; I'm a rare and unique snowflake."

"That you are, Miss Marshall." He bowed his head like a gentleman. "I'd better go. I need to tell my brothers what's going on."

On the way out, Mom stopped us at the foyer. "Caleb, you leaving already?"

"Yeah, I gotta get back to the hotel."

Mom looked genuinely disappointed. "Oh, all right. I could've used the extra manpower. Drive safe."

"Yeah, Caleb, drive safe—don't want any more accidents." I stuck my tongue out at him. Thinking of transportation sparked an idea. "Hey, Mom, since Caleb brought me home in a timely fashion tonight, can he take me to school tomorrow?"

Mom frowned. "I don't know. Don't wanna press my luck with the two of you."

"Oh come on! It's not like we're gonna run off and elope. It's just a ride to school. Plus, you get to sleep in." I looked to Caleb. "Be here at seven-twenty sharp."

"Seven-twenty? In the morning? I'm rolling over right about that time. Why don't you take the bus?"

I stood stunned as if I'd been slapped. Caleb was nineteen and had gone to half a dozen schools in Europe, but even he had to know the universal code of high school politics. "Because I'm a senior, and riding the yellow Twinkie is social suicide. I know it's early, but it's only for one day—I get my new car tomorrow afternoon. Aren't you supposed to be all loving and supportive, do or die and all that noise?"

"Not at seven in the morning. Is the sun even up then?"

Omigod, I had the worst boyfriend ever! Keeping my voice low, I said, "This would be a great way to make sure I'm safe. The house and my school may be shielded by oil, but the six miles in-between are not. Didn't you say you would protect me no matter what?" I batted my eyelashes.

He tightened his lips, looking like a petulant ten-year-old. "Be ready when I pull up." He grumbled, then began the walk of shame to the door.

"You'd better get used to losing battles if you continue dating my daughter," Mom called after him. "Samara's prone to getting her way."

"I wonder where she gets that from," Ruiz mumbled behind her while unpacking a box of extension cords.

I walked Caleb to the door, not willing to let him go just yet. Call me selfish, call me needy, but I just got him back. We had faced a lot of obstacles this past month, three hammers hitting us at the same time. From Caleb's recent stint in the hospital, the war with Tobias, and the Cambion royal family breathing down our necks, I craved one moment of normalcy.

I stepped outside with him and closed the door behind me. "Do you still think we're safe?"

He zipped up his coat and looked at me. Keeping a straight face, he said, "Yes."

"That makes one of us," I replied as he gave me a hug that I desperately needed.

His fingers burrowed into my hair and his chin settled on top of my head. "It's gonna be okay," he whispered, his tone confident, full of a certainty I wished I had.

I took a huge gulp of air and held it and my eyes burned with unshed tears. Though I was dying for another explosive make-out session, I needed his comfort a whole lot more. I needed him to hold me and chase my fears away, to take me back to a time where I was ignorant of real harm. As long as he held me like this I could stay in that place and allow time to stop.

That was one thing Lilith and I could agree on.

3

I woke up at o'dark-thirty to get ready for school. Mom was still asleep, drained from all the decorating that went on long after I went to bed. Despite the energy I took from Caleb last night, I was surprisingly tired. I almost fell asleep in the shower. At least I didn't wake up on the ceiling this morning, so that was progress.

Wiping the steam off the mirror, I took a look at my reflection and found nothing noteworthy to report. My skin was a few shades lighter and now had an ashy tone of old cardboard. The red and white streak in my hair was fading, and I made a mental note to retouch it. I also needed a wax—my eyebrows looked like two caterpillars trying to mate. My face refused to lose its baby fat, my small, puffy lips needed ChapStick, and my chin was there only in theory.

Lilith never sleeps, but she seemed more awake today, vibrating down the length of my torso and filling my eyes with an emerald shine. Maybe she thought I'd forgotten the mishap yesterday. Yeah, fat chance of that happening.

My investigation may have been postponed, but not canceled. I pulled out a fresh pack of brown contacts and placed a lens over each eye, hiding Lilith's presence and everything that came with it.

The Thanksgiving holiday was murder on my waist line and each pair of jeans laughed at me as I tried to zip them up. Normally, our "internal roommates" burned energy pretty quickly, so one would think that would include calories. Oh no, not in my case, because there was no justice in the world and in general, I failed at life. Caleb ate more than the average sumo wrestler, yet he rocked a six-pack while I sported a kegger.

I thought of Caleb during my meager breakfast of dry toast and self-loathing. But I wasn't too depressed to appreciate the next phase of the holiday madness.

Phase two: the house.

Mom's decorations had really brought the Marshall Residence to life. Strings of garland hung around the entryways, and bows and holly were set in shrewdly placed areas around the room. The whole house smelled of apple pie from the candles in the living room. It was subtle and tasteful with careful splashes of color, proving that less really was more.

I had just finished a glass of orange juice when I heard a horn honking outside. He hadn't even bothered to come to the door? What a piece of work.

On my way out to meet him, I grabbed my jacket and Caleb's winter coat that he'd let me borrow the other day then looked around for my book bag and purse. Then I remembered that they were still in my locker at school. This whole blackout thing was throwing off my rhythm, but it helped to keep me focused. I was on a mission now and I wouldn't stop until I got answers.

A thin layer of frost dusted over the cars and rooftops. The early sun winked through the trees and caught the icy surfaces in a glassy shimmer. I dashed across the crisp grass to his Jeep. It was a good thing, too, because it looked like he was ready to take off at any minute. I climbed inside and withstood the hot blast of air from the heating vent.

"Morning, sunshine!" I said, all bright and full of pep just to annoy him.

He grumbled something and stared out to the street ahead, a pair of black aviator shades shielding his eyes. My Cake Boy wasn't a morning person by any stretch, which explained where my sudden fatigue came from. Him.

He had the "fresh out of bed" look, but then he always looked like that. It was kinda sexy the way his tousled hair naturally fell around his head and stuck up in the back. What people spent hours and a gallon of hair gel to accomplish, Caleb managed just by rolling over. "Oh, don't be that way. Consider it a labor of love." I leaned in and pecked his cheek.

More grumbles came from his side of the Jeep as he put it into drive. "This is one thing I don't miss about school. This is inhumane."

"Ain't it the truth," I said with a sigh.

We didn't say much during the journey to school—we were both still trying to wake up. He turned into the student parking lot and pulled next to Mia's red BMW that had stopped in the third aisle. As if he didn't own enough nerve, Caleb waved from his window, trying to get her attention.

I stared out of my own window, sulking. "Can you be any less subtle?"

"Can you be any more petty?" he replied.

My head whipped in his direction. "Me? She's the one who won't talk to me."

"So now you two need to kiss and make up. You've

been friends for over a decade. There's no need to ruin that over a misunderstanding."

"Why don't you tell Mia that?"

He paused, his head tilted to the side, in quiet debate. "I think I will."

"What?" I jumped, and he was out of the Jeep before I could stop him.

As Mia came around the front of her car, Caleb crossed her path. As usual, she dressed to the nines: a cream turtle neck sweater, some tight, I-can't-breathe-but-I-look-hot skinny jeans, and knee-high suede boots that matched her jacket. Her dark hair had been pulled into a high pony tail, and the up-do showed off a flashy pair of gold hoop earrings.

Just looking at her made my chest ache. I wanted my friend back, my partner in crime. We had been besties since the sand box, but you wouldn't know that by the way she was mean-muggin' the hell out of me right now. This Cambion business—the secrets, the lies—were destroying every relationship I had, and Mia was one of the many casualties. Something told me it was going to get worse before it got better, and I could only hope Mia and I didn't kill each other before then.

Seeing as Caleb didn't go to this school, or any for that matter, it took a minute for Mia to recognize him. Once she was able to match the face with the location, she almost dropped the gourmet coffee in her hand.

"Omigod! Caleb!" she squealed and jumped into his arms.

"Hey stranger! How've you been?" Caleb swooped her up and spun her around.

When he set her down, she asked, "When did you get out of the hospital? Are you okay?"

He pushed the shades to the top of his head and

smiled. "I, um, checked out Thanksgiving night. It was a bad food allergy, but I'm good now."

"So I heard." Mia's eyes narrowed at me, and then her stare settled to my wrist. Instinctively, I pulled my coat sleeve over my bracelet. Angry as she might've been, Mia was a jewelry snob and had probably appraised its retail value from across the lot.

"Anyway, I'm glad you're okay," she said to Caleb. "You gave us a good scare on Halloween."

His gaze dropped to his boots, and his dimples dug into his cheeks in a way that would appear bashful on anyone else. But for Caleb, it was a loaded weapon in the hands of a child, ignorant of the devastation he could cause. "I know, but I'm okay, really. So what is this I hear about you and Sam not getting along?" he asked.

The question ruined the good-natured mood. She folded her arms and looked away with her chin high. "I don't know what you're talking about."

"I have it on high authority that you're ignoring her. What happened?"

"Why don't you ask your girlfriend? I mean, she's still your girlfriend, isn't she, or did Malik Davis snatch her up?"

Whoa! That was about a nine on the bitchmeter. One side effect of having our allure with the opposite sex was the display of hostility by those of our own gender. Mia was no different, but she was never this rabid before, never to me. What was bringing this on?

I stepped between them, but Caleb pulled me back. "I told you, there's nothing going on with me and Malik. I wish you would believe me."

She rolled her eyes and turned to our mediator. "Caleb, you're a good guy and I think you have a right to know what's been going on while you were in a *coma!*" She stressed the last part for my benefit. "Did she tell you about how she was creeping with another guy? You should've seen how she was throwing herself at him."

"It wasn't even like that and you know it. Caleb knows that I'm not interested in Malik. Why don't you worry about your own love life and get your big nose out of mine?"

Mia gasped and her hand shot up to cover her nose. That was one of her most hated body parts, a feature that attested to her Filipino heritage. I didn't mean it in the literal sense, but the mere suggestion had her ready to scrap. "You got a problem with my nose? How about you do a few sit-ups before you start talking about somebody, jelly roll?"

I stumbled back in shock. Oh, she went there.

Caleb made a T shape with his hands. "Whoa, ladies, time out. It's not that serious. Mia, it's just one big misunderstanding—no need to fight over it. Speaking of love lives, how are you and Doug holding up?"

"They're not, and she's taking it out on me," I answered in a huff. This whole argument was ridiculous. How old were we again? And Caleb, bless his heart, was trying to be the adult in the situation.

"Whatever. Look, you guys do what you want—I don't care. Just stay away from me, Sam." With a dramatic toss of her ponytail, she stomped away.

"Okay. I guess I'll see you in those *three classes* we share! Love you!" I called after Mia, who flipped me off in reply.

Great! Another hole in my life I needed to patch up. I'd have to wait until we both cooled down to talk to her again, or else we'd end up scratching each other's eyes out.

"That went well," Caleb said cheerfully.

"Just another day at James City High," I whimpered and rested my head on his chest.

"This is a sign, you know. Our draw is at its strongest with the broken-hearted and desperate. She's obviously miserable and that misery makes her highly sensitive to us."

I knew what he was saying was true, but it didn't make the pain go away. I wouldn't give up, though. Not on her.

While Caleb held me, I noticed our theatrics were drawing a crowd, that of the female variety. Girls drew closer, riveted by the tall boy at my side.

"Um, I better go. The wolves are circling and I haven't fed today. I don't want to have all these teeny boppers after me," he said and lowered his shades.

"Yeah, you better get lost, you dirty old man. Leave the young'uns alone."

After a quick peck on the lips, I marched toward another day of education with a side of abuse. I barely made it to my locker before the circus began. The Courtneys, all three of them, strutted down the hall holding clipboards and passing out flyers. They wore matching V neck sweaters and pleated skirts with blue ribbons in their hair. Leading the march was Courtney B., the redheaded stepchild that I wanted to slap silly. The thought was extremely tempting given my current mood.

I hid my face in my locker, praying that they would just walk by me and pretend I didn't exist, as usual. By doing so, I was pleased to find that my book bag and cell phone hadn't moved from where I last placed them. That was one problem solved. Only ninety-nine more to go.

"Sabrina, I was wondering if you would be interested in signing this pledge. We're doing a fundraiser. Since you two were pretty close I'm sure you would like to contribute to the cause."

Coming to terms with the fact that Courtney still couldn't remember my name after six years, I braced myself for another helping of insults. Slowly, I turned around to face the trio. "What fundraiser?"

"The Malik Davis foundation. We're offering support for his family while the police continue the search for him." Courtney B. turned to her left to the blonde with a short pixy haircut. "Courtney G. is working on a fabulous collage with all of his pictures." Then she regarded the brunette at her right whose skin was one big freckle. "And Courtney C. is setting up a talent show type deal to raise awareness. The principal already agreed to have a little performance for the pep rally next week."

"Fabulous," I said with no emotion. Envisioning a musical number in the middle of the day didn't inspire any.

With wide eyes, Courtney G.'s head tilted to the side like a confused collie. "Your hair is really thick. Do you wear weaves?"

I stared the girl up and down. "No. Do you?"

"Can I touch it?"

"Not if you want your hand back," I answered quickly.

Courtney B. stepped closer and showed me the sign-in sheet on the clipboard. "So anyway, I need you to sign here and there, and there's a box you can check if you want to donate money to the gift basket."

I stared blankly at her. "Gift basket?"

Courtney B. nodded. "It's really nice. All the students are chipping in and—"

"Just give me the form." I snatched the clipboard and scribbled my name on the empty space next to fifty other signatures. I didn't ignore the fact that most of the names were females. Tobias had definitely left his mark on the girls in my school.

When I handed it back, I expected our little exchange

to be over, but she continued to stand there watching me with what appeared to be sympathy in her cold, gray eyes. But I knew differently.

"This must be hard for you, Sonya, not knowing if your boyfriend is alive or dead. This is the second time you've had a guy meet a sudden misfortune. How strange. But we're all rooting for Malik to come home safely. Just know that you're also in our prayers." The three of them made the Catholic sign of the cross at the same time.

Holding the clipboard to her chest, she leaned in and said, "I hear Caleb is out of the hospital, so you might not want Malik to come home too soon, am I right? I understand." She gave me a sly, just-between-us-girls wink.

I was getting really sick of repeating myself. I had the urge to blurt out that an incubus was now the captain of the basketball team, and that we might actually have a shot at winning regionals this year. Though it would certainly make *me* feel better, it would just confirm the rumors of my flakiness. After all, I had no proof to back me up, none that would hold up in court.

In a true act of mercy, the bell rang.

"Oops, gotta go. Thanks again, Simone." With a wave, Courtney skipped away with her two trusty lapdogs at her sides.

First period went by without incident or my full attention. I had other things on my mind and a list of questions that needed answers. Number one: where the hell was Tobias? My concern wasn't brought on by fondness, but a basic survival tactic while in battle, to always be one step ahead of your enemy.

I kept looking over my shoulder in government class, staring at the empty desk in the back row. A part of me expected him to materialize out of vapor, or roll up late in his Malik costume. The way I saw it, if you were going to steal someone's identity, then at least have the decency to follow through with it and show up to class.

I was on edge by the time lunch rolled around, my curiosity growling louder than my stomach. Instead of the loners that I usually sat with, I wandered past enemy lines to the more popular side of the cafeteria, prowling for spiritual sustenance. My lunch mates hadn't expected my seating change, but I assured them it was a temporary transfer. I moved from table to table, taking in that thin film of vitality that covered each living creature in a yummy aura.

You would think I rolled up to the lunch room in see-through lingerie the way the guys were staring at me. Even the ones who had girlfriends (plural). I got bum rushed by every type of the Y-chromosome, from that really close talker guy, the dude with the breath that could curl lashes, that player that always grabbed at his crotch. They were all food for me, much like how a cow was nothing but a cheeseburger with legs.

As a rule, I try to avoid people who make lewd comments about me and my genitalia, so I skipped over those and headed to my main entrée. The real heartbreaker was the painfully shy guy who conjured every ounce of courage to talk to me. These are the ones I actually give the time of day and in turn, made *their* day with a kiss on the cheek. And even with this level of discipline it was still a challenge not to feed directly or take too much from one person. Temptation would always be there.

Now that my hunger was sated, my curiosity needed fuel. There was no better source of intel than the eyes and ears of the school.

Dougie, along with his teammates, gawked at me as I sat next to him. He snuck a glance around the cafeteria for someone else I might be staring at, then asked, "I'm sorry, have we met?"

"Yeah. That one time in the fourth grade." I patted his hair and almost got impaled by the short black spikes glossed with gel.

Once the shock of my presence wore off, he dove into the pyramid stack of burritos on his tray. The muscles in his arm flexed under his thermal undershirt. Though he was about five-eight, Dougie was filling out in all the right places, thanks to his spot on the wrestling team and the excessive appetite that rivaled Caleb's. "So, you makin' up for your shadiness and finally gracin' us with your divine presence?"

"Shut it, Dougie. I'm here on a mission." I craned my neck over the heads of students and scoped out the entrance.

"What kind of mission?" He wolfed down the rest of his burrito in one bite.

"For one: I have an appointment with Jason Lao and he won't meet with me at my own table. Some crap about social boundaries. So you're neutral territory."

"Right," he drawled with his mouth full, salsa dripping down his chin.

"And two: I want to ask you about Mia, specifically which type of bug crawled up her ass and died. You know, just so I can classify what species of crazy I'm working with here," I said.

Keeping to her word, Mia continued to avoid me in class, proof that the "silent treatment" wasn't just for fifth graders anymore. It was high time that I got to the bottom of this before a fight broke out on the monkey bars at recess. If anyone knew what was up, it would be her estranged other half and part-time stalker.

"You got me." He shrugged; a hopeless gesture of a

man who had given up on life. "She's got nothin' but attitude these days, but it's time for her to grow up. Anyway, I'm done with her."

I shook my head and made a tsk-ing sound. "Dougie, you know good and well that you'll never really be done with her."

"As long as she's actin' stank, I am. I'm officially on the market."

"Did you put out an ad yet?" I joked.

"As a matter of fact, I posted a full spread on Jason Lao's site. Got two hundred hits already—even got a reply from a forty-year-old lady in Norfolk. She looks hot for her age." He winked, and the mischief in his eyes made them twinkle with greens and browns that changed to match whatever he wore.

God, I hoped he was kidding, but knowing Douglas Emerson III, I doubted it. Talking with him like this reminded me just how much I missed my friend, the privileged anti-prep with an obsession with all things hip-hop. He embodied everything normal in my life, and I clung to each nuance. Warm and fuzzy memories came with Dougie, and Lilith noted each one and stopped targeting him as food, which was another reason I enjoyed hanging with him. He was the only non-virgin who didn't want to jump my bones. Telling by the hungry stares by his teammates, he was also the only guy at the table who wasn't imagining me naked. Refreshing.

Jason Lao scurried to our table, wearing a white shirt, a tweed blazer, and a permanent note of urgency. Of the four years I've known this kid, he always dressed like he was going to a job interview, and always searched his surroundings in case the feds were after him.

"You rang?" he asked, sounding annoyed at our secret meeting.

"Yeah? What's the latest on the web-a-sphere?" I asked.

"A whole lot. There's a Secret Santa thing going on and it's causing heavy traffic and slowing down my site. Oh, Doug, you had a few more hits on your personal ad. I checked out some of the girls' profiles, and whoa—HOT!" Jason fanned himself, then continued. "And I just set up a dedication page on Malik Davis. The comments are piling up pretty quick."

I rolled my eyes. "Isn't this a little too much? We don't even know where he is? Didn't you say he ran away?"

"Yeah, but tell that to his groupies on the pep squad," Jason replied. "Just this morning, a girl bursts into tears in the middle of class. Man, I wish I had that kind of power over the ladies."

Trust me, you don't, I thought.

"Besides, the police aren't so sure that he ran away," he added.

Dougie and I exchanged glances. "What do you mean?" I asked.

After a quick peek over his shoulder, Jason leaned in and said, "Well, Patricia Hughes works in the main office after school, answering phones, sifting mail, and all that crap, right? Well, she was there when the police came in yesterday, and she heard that his truck was found on a side road in the Colonial Parkway. It's really weird. That's Malik's second accident. Remember the one in September?"

Dougie scoffed. "He wouldn't shut up about it. And we had to sit through that dumb ass assembly about drinking and driving. Malik might wanna lay off the sauce and practice what he preaches." He unwrapped his third burrito.

"That's cold, dude!" Jason exclaimed, but still found it funny. "He could be dead for all we know. The parkway is no joke. I won't even drive through there in the daytime."

I kept quiet as the guilt of what I knew rode me hard. Malik had died in that first accident and my continued silence only piled on to this growing mountain of suck. This latest development only made me hate Tobias more. His sick game was prolonging the pain of an innocent family and denying them closure.

The bad news just kept on coming as Jason went on with his story. "She said the cops found the truck abandoned in a ditch. There were scratches on the driver's side, like he might've hit something. But anyway, Malik wasn't with the truck, so wherever he is, he's on foot, or . . ." he let the sentence hang, but every grim possibility filled the blanks.

I wouldn't have been surprised if they saw smoke coming out of my ears—my brain was working overtime. Had Tobias gotten hurt in a car accident? Maybe he was in a coma. It would serve him right, a true stroke of karma after what he did to Caleb. But Tobias was virtually indestructible, well able to walk away from a simple fender bender. More importantly, I would've sensed his reactions to the collision, his pain, his alarm. But I couldn't feel him anymore. In fact, I hadn't sensed him at all since yesterday just before . . . my blackout.

"So, Sam." Jason leaned in with intrigue; the local gossip hound still on duty. "How do you feel about the latest development? You guys were sort of an item, right?"

"No. We weren't, and let me go on the record by saying that I was never, ever with Malik. Put that in bold print for everyone to see." I rose to my feet.

"What's with her?" I heard Jason ask as I left the table.

"I dunno, man. Girls are all messed up in the head 'round here," Dougie replied.

In the quiet of the hall stairwell, I leaned against the wall and controlled my breathing. There was too much going on; too many unanswered questions. Tobias had suddenly dropped off the face of the earth, roughly around the same time I lost consciousness for two hours. Maybe Tobias had a similar effect, but he seemed fine the last time I had a blackout. He mentioned that he preferred me that way, pliant and at his mercy. What happened in those two hours to cause Tobias to disappear? More importantly, where was I when all this was going on?

"Lilith," I called. "You wanna help me out here?"

No response.

It was worth a try. With a heavy sigh, I pushed off the wall and moved toward my next class, though the only subject I had on my mind was Tobias.

4

A shiny new quarter slipped through the coin slot as I gave the metal dial one good turn.

At the end of the rotation, five measly pieces of candy fell out the dispenser and tumbled into my waiting hand. Quarters didn't amount to much these days, but I alone seemed to appreciate their value. I frowned at my pitiful rations and saw it as a prelude to a much bigger rip-off.

Popping a Skittle in my mouth, I strolled through the sitting area, past the car showroom to the bank of windows that overlooked the dealership. BIG LARRY'S END-OF-THE-YEAR BLOWOUT SALE was written on a red banner at the entrance.

I'd seen this sign all over town, along with the corny commercials on TV. It was hard to forget a three hundred pound white guy dressed like a pimp and a dancing bulldog. Thankfully, there were no half naked women on the grounds; however, the dog, also named Larry, was an active part of the buying experience. At the moment, he circled around me, sniffing my legs while wearing an elf hat and bells around his collar.

To my left was a closed office door where my dad stood on the other side, filling out paperwork and doing what he did best. Negotiate.

He picked me up after school and brought me here to get my new ride since the old one bit the dust Thanksgiving night. My Nissan Juke had been turned into scrap metal, thanks to Tobias's violent display of love and jealous rage. Dangerous and gorgeous as he might be, the hotness level drastically declined after that stunt.

Though I was furious about losing the car I spent years saving for, being a pedestrian for three days taught me to count my blessings. I didn't care what kind of car I got as long as I escaped the ill fate of parental and public transportation.

I was sure Dad didn't buy the whole "freak storm" excuse about the car, but at least the insurance covered enough to get a replacement. Being a corporate lawyer, he could smell BS from a hundred yards, and the odor was coming off thick from my direction. It didn't seem fair that Mom knew my dirty secret, yet Dad was left to question my eye color change and strange behavior. He was set in his ways with deep beliefs, and I couldn't bear to have him look at me with fear or contempt. I was his first born, his Baby Girl, and I wanted to stay that way a little while longer.

Before little Larry decided to mark his territory on my leg, I took a walk outside to do some wishful thinking. I drifted from car to car, stroking each glossy veneer and wincing at the price stickers on the windows. Tearing my eyes away from a Mustang that I could never have, I spotted a black Jeep at the end of the row similar to Caleb's. It was fascinating to see what his Jeep looked like in its initial state, free of mud splatter and a huge dent on the right side. Cake Boy really knew how to wear down a car, and as of late, he was spending more money on repairs than the original purchase.

Staring at the front grill of the Jeep reminded me of his accident. It seemed odd that he would have a reaction to my blackout while behind the wheel. My previous trips into the abyss hadn't seemed to affect Tobias's ability to drive, so what made Caleb so different? Why couldn't he remember how he got the dent in his Jeep?

"Okay, baby girl. You ready to check out your new car?" Dad asked behind me.

I turned around and smiled up at the tall man in the tailored suit with a proud strut of victory. Mr. Keith Watkins, esquire, had apparently worked his magic, ensuring I was leaving out of here on four wheels with cash to spare. Big Larry himself fell in step with Dad, looking just as greasy as advertised. His gut fell over his belt and the buttons on his white shirt held on for dear life. His sagging jowls and droopy brown eyes seemed to support the myth that people look like their pets.

"We got you a great deal on an O-five, little lady. It's a bit old, but the mileage is impeccable." Big Larry smiled down at me, showing a row of straight, tobacco stained teeth. "Your daddy is a tough nut to crack, but I'm willing to make a few concessions for such a pretty customer." He winked.

What a flirt. Whether it was his sales tactic or Lilith's influence, I didn't care. Hell, if I played my cards right, I could roll out of here in that Mustang I had my eye on, but I didn't want to push my luck. The power I had over men wasn't a toy.

Big Larry led the way as we moved to the side of the building to where a green Maxima waited for me. It wasn't my Juke, but it was in my favorite color, which earned a ton of cool points in my book.

I wrapped my arms around Dad's waist and squeezed as hard as I could. "Thanks for doing this, Daddy."

"No problem, although it appears you go through cars faster than clothes these days."

"It was a storm. I can't control the weather." *Or the crazy demon that compelled that weather*, I thought.

"So how's your mother?" he asked me on our slow approach to my new whip.

"The same as when you asked me on the way over here." That question was just as random the second time around, and I had a feeling it's been sitting on his tongue long before today. This little father-daughter trip had taken an awkward turn as he continued to pry into Mom's personal life, specifically her relationship with a Cuban detective from New York. Knowing I would be too grateful to deny him info, he picked this exact time to launch his interrogation. Well played, old man. Well played.

"For a married guy, you seem awfully interested in what another woman is doing," I said. "Does Rhonda know about your side hobby?"

"I'm just concerned for Julie's well-being, nothing more," he replied indignantly. "She is after all, the mother of my child."

"So is Rhonda," I countered. "You remember those two six-year-olds that live at your house, don't you? Dad, you have a whole other life and Mom deserves a chance at that too. Let her move on."

Not to sound gross, but Dad looked good for his age, and why he married a hateful gargoyle was one of life's many riddles. I got my baby face from him, and very few people believed he was thirty-four, with not one wrinkle or blemish marring his mocha skin. I wasn't sure if it was out of anger or something else altogether, but he seemed to age twenty years in a matter of seconds. "Yeah, well your mother's judgment has been cloudy lately. You do remember that last man she tried to date." His dark eyes narrowed at me, drilling his point with deadly precision.

Of course, this wouldn't be a proper argument without bringing up past mistakes. And Caleb's father, Nathan Ross, was a fatal mistake, one that I singlehandedly removed from the earth.

"Mom's fine. She knows how to take care of herself," I assured.

"And what about you? Your taste in men is a little questionable as well."

I was about to comment, but the words fizzled in my mouth. I knew Dad disliked Caleb, but that didn't make his statement invalid. Caleb was cryptic—that was what drew me to him—but that mystique can get old real quick when enemies vanish, vehicles get wrecked, and people wake up on the ceiling. It's hard to fully trust a person and doubt him at the same time, but not impossible. I did it every day. Telling by the skeptical look Dad was giving me, I wasn't the only one.

After dinner, another game of twenty-questions, and yet another petition for me to consult a therapist, Dad and I parted ways with the promise of meeting up before the Christmas madness kicked off. Too many people had died around me this year and Dad wasn't sure if I was dealing with my grief properly. He was right; I wasn't, hence the dead girl in my living room that no one could see but me. A shrink couldn't help with my particular issues and being labeled a head case might ruin my chances of getting into law school, so I could tough it out for a while.

I didn't go home right away; instead, I made a pit stop at Caleb's hotel across town. He and his brothers were staying there until Caleb could either find a new apartment or salvage the old one from the wreckage that Tobias left behind. Caleb never told me at which hotel he was staying and with everything going on, I hadn't bothered to ask, but I didn't need a name or directions. I would always know where he was and vice versa.

In my experience, there was no such thing as a broke Cambion; their charm afforded them many luxuries and allowed them to get away with murder, quite literally. Caleb came from money, but he lived humbly; slaving through the grind like the rest of us indentured servants. So imagine my shock when my Spidey senses led me to the gated palace of the Charlotte Hotel.

A massive water fountain stood on a thatch of grass in the center of the circular driveway. The place was a throwback to the roaring twenties set under the soft glow of antique lanterns. All that was missing was a bell hop, a couple of flapper girls, and some gangsters with machine guns. The place screamed of good living, from the cheerful valet who took my car, the openly gay concierge behind the check-in desk, to the piano jazz playing in the lounge near the lobby.

This wasn't the place that took kindly to loiterers, so I rushed to the wall of elevators as if I knew where I was going. I stepped inside and punched all the numbers, much to the annoyance of the elderly couple in the car with me. The doors opened on each floor, and I poked my head out in search of any trace of Caleb. The empathic pull grew stronger, thicker, all-encompassing the higher we climbed, so I knew I was getting warm.

The couple got off on the fifth floor as a young man with dark shades stepped in. Not that I was checking him out or anything, but the guy was well-built and dressed even better with a leather jacket, turtle neck, and black gloves. Definitely from out of town. He reached to push his floor of choice then paused at all the lit buttons on the panel.

"Kids." I shrugged and gave him room to stand.

He stared at me, not saying a word, and grew more fascinated than deemed appropriate for such a small space. Through the cover of the shades, he stared at me with a level of intensity that gave me chills. I glanced up at the tiny security camera in the corner and hoped it wasn't placed there just for show. I had half the mind to get off on the next floor and take the stairs when I felt that familiar tingle gain pressure against my spine. I leapt out on to the eighth floor as soon as the doors opened.

I sucked in a deep draft of air, reaching out for Caleb's essence on my way up the hall. I looked to the passage to my left, then the one to my right, and decided to keep moving straight ahead, following the remnant of French toast and conceit in the air. It would be just like Caleb to request breakfast at night. His brothers were no better when it came to food and I was sure they were giving the room service staff a run for their . . .

Why was that guy still staring at me? He must've gotten off the elevator when I did, and he now stood in that stoic manner that gave me the heebie-jeebies. The dark shades hid his eyes, but not the creepy vibe he was giving off. The feeling only got worse as he took a step and then another, gradually picking up speed.

Maybe he had a room on this floor. Maybe he was one of those crazy killers on the news that Mom kept going on about. Or maybe Lilith was using her mojo again.

Being male catnip, as Mia once called it, had a nasty disclaimer where the attraction could turn violent quickly. I was smaller than him, so I couldn't fight him off if things came to blows, but I was more concerned for his safety than my own. Lilith would shrivel this guy to dust before he so much as copped a feel, but I'd seen my share of dead bodies to last a lifetime.

He wasn't shy about his pursuit, but took his time as if knowing he would catch his prey eventually. I walked to the end of the hall until there was nowhere to go. No emergency stairs or freight elevators offered an escape, and the solid wall ahead seemed to mock me.

I turned around to face my opponent head on. My heart pounded in my chest, my muscles clenched while I waited for him to make the first move. To my surprise, he simply turned to the hallway to his left, but his stare stayed locked on me as he disappeared around the corner.

I lifted my head to the ceiling and pushed out the breath I'd been holding. My bag fell from my shoulder and my limbs relaxed under the rush of relief.

"Sam? What are you doing here? What's wrong?"

I jumped and clutched my aching chest. My heart was seriously getting a workout today. Caleb stood inside the opened door behind me, looking annoyed and very damp.

"Don't scare me like that!" I yelled and swung my bag at him.

"From what I can tell, you were already scared," he replied, ducking the blow. "I felt you while I was in the shower. What happened?"

"There was a guy by the elevator. He made me nervous."

Caleb poked his head out of the door and searched the hall. "Where?"

"Nothing, never mind. Did I catch you at a bad time?"

Caleb looked down at the towel hanging low around his hips then smiled at me. "Depends on how you look at it."

I took that moment to check out the merchandise, and

what an eyeful. Water dripped from his hair and trickled down his chest, and a glob of shaving cream clung to his right ear. My gaze journeyed south to the hills and valleys of his stomach, counting the smooth knots of muscle that stood in bas relief under his skin. He wasn't weight lifter material, nor did he achieve underwear model status, but he had a little somethin'-somethin' going on, subtle, and well proportioned. A healthy beige tint covered his skin, and he no longer looked like a walking corpse. He must've fed recently, allowing Capone to munch on something other than his host for a while.

Checking my mouth for any drool and dodging his wolfish grin, I barged into the room. Caleb didn't bother to step aside, but let our bodies graze each other intentionally. The smell of soap wafted off his skin and water soaked the front of my sweater as I passed.

Caleb's room was actually a ginormous suite with a window that stretched the entire left wall and overlooked the pool area below. It had a modern look with funky art deco furniture and bright colors, but it was hard to drink in its full scope with luggage, boxes, and Caleb's music library cluttering the room. I would figure that half this stuff would be in storage with the rest of his furniture until he got his place fixed. His long bow and extra arrows weren't exactly dire necessities, but to each their own.

It would seem that I had suddenly rolled up to the club without knowing. Electronic rock music played in one of the bedrooms in the back of the suite—some trendy, obscure European band only Caleb would appreciate. Music snob that he was, he had remarkable taste and could easily make a career out of mixing if he applied himself.

I stepped down into the sunken living room and plopped on one of the red couches. "This is a bit swank for your taste," I commented.

"Yeah, I was staying at the motel a few blocks from here, but got moved to this place."

"Moved? Why?"

"After I took you to school, I found a bunch of moving guys in my room bringing all my stuff here. Evangeline set it up—no notice or anything. She booked the top floor for when she comes to town. She wants to keep all her ducks in a row."

"And keep you and your brothers on a short leash," I added.

Snapping his fingers, Caleb perfected the image of absurdity: A pale white guy getting his groove on wearing nothing but a towel. The sad part was he was actually good.

"I'm not paying for it, so I don't mind being a pampered prisoner," he said. "Michael and Haden have those two rooms over there, and I got the master bedroom." He did a little shimmy dance as he strolled inside said room. As the youngest, it was a rare occasion for Caleb to one-up his older brothers, so any small victory was momentous.

Thoughts of the dynamic duo inspired my next question. "Where are Michael and Haden anyway?"

"They went out on an errand, but they'll be back later tonight," Caleb yelled from his room.

I craned my neck to see his bedroom door. "What kind of errand?"

"They didn't say. Probably off to get some beer. They're not big fans of the local selection around here. They only drink Smithwick's and Beamish."

Beyond the cracked door, a white towel hit the carpet and my train of thought took a detour into forbidden territory. Staring at laundry had never felt so dirty.

"So what brings you to my not-so-humble abode? Does your mom know you're here?" he asked.

"Who? Oh, right. No, I just wanted to stop by and tell you that your taxi duties are officially over. I got my new car."

"That's great. I'm not in the habit of getting up at seven. A guy needs his beauty rest." He entered the room again and pulled a gray t-shirt over his head.

My stare moved toward his freakishly long and jacked-up feet, which were covered in bandages. He had escaped the hospital and walked six miles to his house barefoot as a result of Capone's hostile takeover. If anyone knew the extent of damage a wayward spirit could cause, it was Caleb, so I'd come to the right place.

I tucked my feet under me, getting good and comfortable before I dove into the real reason for my visit. "I wanna ask you about your blackout. Did you have any memory lapses or lost consciousness?"

He joined me on the couch, but made sure there was plenty of space between us. "Why do you ask?"

"Humor me," I said.

His stare drifted to the far end of the room and considered his answer. "No. I had a type of déjà vu, *Groundhog Day* feeling, like I'd lived the same day before. I'm driving to work, but the weather's different—sunny. I'm wearing a different shirt, and a different song is playing on the radio. Then I get out of the car and it's snowing. I'm in my work shirt and there's a big ass dent in my car. You say that you lose time, but there was no time gap here. All I know is I never want to go through that again."

"Maybe you have a different type of blackout. Maybe you were dreaming and you had a memory implant, like that Dicaprio movie."

He gave me a skeptical look. "Right. Well, your guess

is as good as mine, and to tell the truth, nothing about what we are surprises me anymore." Caleb stretched and slung his arm over the back of the couch. "Do I have permission to leave the witness stand, Counselor Marshall?"

"Not yet. I'm trying to figure something out." When I told him about Malik Davis, aka Tobias's disappearing act and the abandoned vehicle found on the parkway, he finally understood why I was so disturbed. Since each of us were connected by a three-way link—and a really sick twist of fate—it was possible for us to share a reaction in different places. Caleb had his alibi, but where was I when all this vehicular damage was going on?

"God, Caleb, you have no idea how much this bugs me. Two hours of my life are missing and I can't get an answer from her. She won't even explain the whole 'climbing the ceiling' thing. You were right about her being traumatized and scared, but she's shutting me out of her feelings." I grabbed my bag on the floor, dug inside, then passed him the note that Lilith wrote to me.

Caleb scanned down the index card, grimaced, then handed it back. "Well, at least it doesn't rhyme."

"Ha-ha. She's out of control and I'm getting sick of the guessing game. I think my blackout has something to do with Tobias's disappearance. He's following me one minute, I blink, and then poof, he's gone. I haven't felt his presence all day. Have you?"

He shook his head, then asked in a tone dripping with bitterness, "Do you miss him?"

"I miss being able to make my own choices," I answered just as tartly.

"Sam, you're still new to the whole Cambion process. You're gonna feel like you're not your own person, but you're still you. Lilith is just along for the ride. Don't let her drive." His voice rolled around me, warm and potent. The sound along with his dominating presence made my eyelids droop. I wanted to kiss him so bad . . .

I shook out of my daze and I was about to respond when a knock broke the silence. "Housekeeping," a thickly accented voice called from the hallway outside.

Caleb looked to me and then back to the door. "Sam, um, I don't think it's a good idea for you to be here right now. I was about to eat before you got here."

"I don't mind," I insisted. "I could really use your input on this blackout thing. What did you order?"

"Vietnamese," he answered, then moved to the door.

When the woman stepped into the room, it dawned on me that he wasn't talking about Asian cuisine. She was a young, petite thing with black hair pulled into a bun on the back of her head. She wore the typical cleaning lady uniform, pristine white and starch-stiff with matching sneakers. It was easy to detect her shyness around males by the way her stare dropped to the floor and how she clutched the stack of folded towels to her chest like a shield.

Caleb ushered her to the living room and bid her to sit. She readily obeyed, and I could tell her compliance wasn't from her duties to serve the clientele. One look, one fleeting glimpse from the corner of her eye was all it took, and she was his.

He knelt in front of her and eased loose the towels she held in a death grip. "It's okay if you want to leave, Sam. I know how you get when this happens," he warned from over his shoulder. "I already ordered before you came by. I wasn't expecting you."

I squirmed in the seat across from them, certain that this type of room service was not mentioned in the hotel brochure. The comfort level had dropped by two hundred percent, and it didn't help that Caleb regarded this poor woman as an item on a take-out menu.

"Uh, Caleb, can I have a word with you for a second?" I stood up and marched to the small kitchenette area. Caleb followed, cursing under his breath.

In the privacy of the kitchen, I rounded on him with clenched fists. "Have you lost your mind? Ruiz said you weren't allowed to do this."

He leaned against the counter, clearly miffed that I interrupted his meal. "Ruiz isn't here, and I can't starve myself. That would cause more problems that neither of us are ready for. You of all people should know that."

"Then here . . ." I shook off my jacket and rolled up the sleeves of my sweater. "Feed from me. It's safer."

His gaze traveled the length of my body, considering the option for just a second before he looked away. "No, it's not. I shouldn't have let you feed from me last night. I don't want you to get the wrong idea. Capone wants to claim you as his, and so do I. Once I start, I won't be able to stop, and I won't risk going too far with you. We will bond on our own terms, no one else's."

"Meanwhile, the cleaning staff is a free-for-all," I argued.

Caleb sighed irritably. "It's different with strangers. I'm not connected to them, I'm not emotionally invested and none of them tempt me like you do. She's not the first donor I've had today and she won't be the last. I know what I'm doing."

There were more women? What the hell? "Look, I get that you're hungry, but—"

"I can't have you, Sam, not in the way I need, so I have to settle for the next best thing. It's enough for now."

I crossed my arms over my chest, standing my ground. "Fine. I'll just stay here and make sure you don't go overboard."

"Suit yourself, but I'm sensing a serious lack of trust in this relationship," he said with a mock grin then left my side. He returned to the sitting area where the docile cleaning lady waited as instructed.

He sat next to her on the sofa and gently pulled her closer to him. Whispering comforting words, he reached behind the woman's neck, and her head tipped back in eager submission. I was quite familiar with that response. I'd felt the shivers whenever he looked at me, the way he would lure me closer to him. I recalled the heat of his mouth dance over my skin as he left sipping kisses on my throat.

I shouldn't have been watching this. It was wrong on so many levels, forcing me to reevaluate the dynamic of our fated union. Were we going to be one of those weird swinger couples that traded off spouses at dinner parties? I should've broken this up, cussed Caleb out, and told this woman to run for her life, but my feet remained planted where they were.

Moreover, it looked really good, similar to watching someone eat a juicy burger with all the fixings and not offering me one bite. I just came back from dinner with Dad, but Lilith rolled and churned within like I hadn't eaten in days.

The maid returned the kiss, spine arching, head tilting back in a romance novel pose. Her fingers clawed at his shirt and hair, fighting to get closer. Her lips parted again and that silvery thread of light passed in to his mouth. The moment he breathed it in, an ice-cold splash hit my stomach, and my knees buckled. I braced the wall for support, hugged my waist, and tried to ignore the heavy breathing coming from the couch.

"Caleb, that's enough. Check her pulse." I couldn't believe I was actually coaching this madness. I was truly a sick individual, one who found a strange excitement by watching my boyfriend feed from another woman, a thrill that I was too ashamed to address. At the very core, our kind were incubi and succubi, and not even centuries of adaptation could dilute that dominant gene.

He didn't seem to hear me at first, but his fingers reached up and pressed the hollow dent near her throat. When he felt her heartbeat, his eyes flew open and purple heat shot in my direction. He stared at me with a blank expression, not really seeing me, but only the power lust that struck him blind. His hand slipped from the woman's neck and she tumbled back to the sofa cushion in a boneless heap.

Caleb rose to his feet and moved toward me, slow and deliberate. He never looked so dangerous, so wild, and the sudden tremor rocking my body wasn't from fear, but anticipation. He continued to stare as if I were a sheet of glass, his intense gaze keeping me in place. Just when he was about to walk right into me, he stepped to the right toward the wet bar. Stunned, I watched him pull a small bottle of orange juice out of the minifridge, then he snatch the bottle of aspirin waiting on the countertop.

Shaking the liquid in his hand, he returned to the couch where the woman lay sprawled on her back, gasping for air. He sat her up and handed her the juice and pills. He checked the pulse on her wrist while she chased each tablet with a swig of the drink. Between sips, she thanked him in both English and in her native language, her eyes glassy and on the brink of tears.

The room fell into silence while he waited for her to regain her senses, but he and I knew the woman would never be the same after tonight. Part of her life, her history was now in Caleb's possession. She would wake up tomorrow with a migraine from hell and spend the rest of her days chasing a high she could never catch again. We not only took lives, but we ruined them for those who survived our touch.

When she was able to stand, he escorted her out and slipped a twenty-dollar bill into the front pocket of her smock. At least he was a good tipper.

"Are you satisfied?" I asked when we were alone again.

He leaned against the door with his eyes closed, still shaking from the rush of the intake. He was virtually glowing with power. "Are you? I told you what I was going to do, but you insisted on staying. As usual, you never listen to me. It's food, and a guy's gotta eat."

"Yeah, but do you have to be all triple-X about it? You don't have to feed directly."

Violet light slipped between his slightly parted lids. "Are you critiquing my table manners now?"

"No, I'm just saying—"

"What *are* you saying, Sam?" He pushed off the door and met me halfway to the center of the room. "We're Cambions. We feed on human life. Nothing, not even our bonding will change that. There's nothing personal about it, not on my end. I'm not cheating on you."

"Oh please, your fidelity is the last thing on my mind right now," I lied. "Your food regimen; however, is another story. You know what will happen if you feed too much, too often, so why are you doing it?"

"My stay in the hospital took a lot out of me, and I need to build up my strength and get back what I lost."

"At the risk of being caught by Ruiz? At the risk of turning into an incubus? And you talk about me needing to control my spirit. How about you put the leash back on yours." I marched to the door, bumping his arm in the process.

My hand held the doorknob when he called after me, "Sam, wait."

I spun around. "What?"

He stepped forward and extended his hand with my shoulder bag dangling from his fingers. "Don't forget this."

I snatched the bag from him and stormed out of the room, regretting ever coming there in the first place.

5

"**S**eventeen, eighteen, nineteen, twenty!" I collapsed on the floor and stared up at the ceiling, wheezing like an asthmatic.

My stomach muscles burned and cramped, my sweaty T-shirt clung to my body, I smelled like complete ass, but I sure felt good. Exercise was a great outlet for aggression, and nothing served that purpose better than Tae Bo. I punched and kicked for over an hour, imagining the open air touching my fist was Caleb's face.

That little stunt in his room really ticked me off, which caused profuse swearing and excessive road rage during the drive home. Each mental replay of the incident made me angrier, but I couldn't quite pinpoint why. I had two options: either curl into a ball and cry all night or invest that energy on something constructive, so I decided on a late night workout.

Plus, Mia's little comment about my spare tire struck a nerve. She was, as my guidance counselor would say, acting on her feelings, but the truth often came out through anger. All the same, it was time to push away from the dinner table and get my fitness on. Just because I was a preternatural man-magnet didn't mean I could let myself go. I did, after all, have a boyfriend to look cute for. Or at least I thought I did.

I opened the window to air out my room, which now had the dank odor of an old gym sock. While getting ready for a shower, everything around me went black. The power went out and all the faint background noises that came with electricity went with it, making the silence more acute. I could see the streetlights outside, so I knew only my house was affected. Normally, I would've freaked out, but since this was the third time tonight that this had happened, I was just annoyed.

I flung my door open and yelled out into the hallway. "Mom!"

"Sorry, honey! One second!" she called from the bottom floor.

Staying close to the walls, I relied on memory and repetition to guide me downstairs. "What are you doing?" I asked.

"Just trying to get these lights to work. One of the bulbs is broken and now the whole thing won't light up." Mom stood at the front door holding a string of bulbs and a pair of binoculars in her hands.

I groaned and met her by the door, knowing that this was the third stage of the holiday madness.

Phase three: the lawn.

Mom never did anything halfway, so if it blinked, chimed, or twinkled, it was probably in our yard, blinding those who drove by our house. Since she was going for something less gaudy this year, she had to downsize, which was driving her crazy. Her obsession with having the perfect holiday was interfering with me and a hot shower, and that just wasn't going to fly. "Mom, you have got to stop doing this. Just let it go."

"Shh!" She stepped onto the porch, letting all the heat out of the house while spying on the neighbors across the street. Mom placed the binoculars in front of her eyes and scoped out the competition. "Look at them. They think they're so much with their halogen lights and surround sound."

I followed her gaze to the yard across the street. Their landscape was always perfectly groomed and stayed green all year, and I had to admit that their display was quite impressive. Baby Jesus and the gang stood on the lawn under a soft glow from inside the manger. A pair of eight-foot angels guarded the scene, their halos blinking in time with the tune of *Silent Night*. "The Cunningham's have a new theme this year, too," I noted.

"The nativity scene. How original," Mom sneered. "All of a sudden they decide to get a new concept. Did they tap my phone or something?" She spied through the binoculars again. "They're not gonna win. Not this year. Oh shoot, I think she saw me! Duck, honey!" Mom dipped behind the railing on the porch.

Refusing to cater to the crazy, I waved to my neighbor like a sane person. "Hi, Mrs. Cunningham!"

The slim brunette, wearing fuzzy earmuffs and a skin-tight snow suit that made her resemble a ski bunny, paused on her way to her car. She was what Mom often described as a trophy wife, due to being twenty years younger than Mr. Cunningham and having been under the knife more than a Butterball turkey. "Hello, Samara. Looks like you guys have power trouble. Are you all right?" she said.

"Yeah, just a tripped wire. I just need to hit the fuse box."

She treaded across the lawn and moved in for a closer look. "Julie? Julie, is that you?"

Swearing under her breath, Mom pulled out of her hiding place. "Debra, hi! How are you?" she yelled cheerfully.

"Oh, I'm wonderful, thank you. I notice you have a new theme, too. Minimalism, I see. It's cute, very practical for those on a budget," Mrs. Cunningham said with a smile so wide I could see it from the street.

"Yes, but less is more, you know." Mom threw her head back and laughed, sounding super loud and extra fake. Waving back, she mumbled through grinning teeth, "I hate you."

"Um . . . yeah, I'm gonna go turn the lights back on." I left Mom to her obsession and entered the kitchen. After clicking on the circuit breaker, the house came alive with a blast of music from the radio, blinking digital clocks, and the soft whirl of electrical appliances.

With that accomplished, I returned upstairs and took a shower, where Caleb continued to intrude on my thoughts. I still couldn't believe he fed off a woman with me right in the room. More to the point, I couldn't believe I stuck around to watch. Neither of them were naked or anything, but the whole exchange was just as pervy as if they were.

Maybe I was reading more into this than I should. Sucking the life force out of people didn't have to mean anything personal. Caleb didn't seem to have a problem turning his emotions on and off, so what was my issue? It was only food, right?

I dried off and entered my room with a new resolution: to cut loose and stop sweating the little things. I was sick of being cautious and worried all the time, and it was the Cambion motto to celebrate life as long as we could.

While digging in my drawer for some pajama bottoms, the lights went out again.

"Mom!" I yelled.

When I didn't get an answer, I turned and noticed the hallway light leaking under my door. I looked to my night stand and saw the glowing red numbers on the alarm clock blinking in the dark. I opened the door and poked my head out to find all the lights on in the house except mine.

Confused, I stepped back into my room and closed the door.

The scream that followed didn't travel far. Mom was probably still outside fighting with the lights and the neighbors. The radio in the kitchen blasted old Christmas tunes, which would likely drown out any noise I made. But I was pretty sure the lack of sound had to do with the leather-clad hand trapping my mouth.

A hard body pressed against my back—I could tell by the woodsy cologne and the prickly stubble that grazed my cheek that it was definitely male. His hot breath covered my ear when he whispered, "Don't be scared."

It's pretty damn late for that, buddy! I thought as I tried to wiggle free. I gave him a good jab in the gut with my elbow and the heel of my foot struck his shin.

"Samara! Stop! It's me!"

I kicked and squirmed in his hold. My teeth worked through his glove until I caught the fleshy meat of his hand, then bit down hard. He yelped and pulled his hand away, and I seized my moment of escape. I punched blindly in the dark, aiming for anything solid.

"Mom! Get the gun!" I yelled and reached for the door, but a pair of strong arms trapped my waist again and pulled me back.

I kept screaming and stomped the floor, hoping, praying that Mom could hear the noise. I kicked my feet up until they lay flat against the wood of the door, then pushed backward with all the strength I had in my legs.

The force made him stumble, and he tripped over books and clutter scattering the floor. Being a slob had come in handy tonight, and my room was a death trap for those unfamiliar with the rugged terrain. What followed was a long, clumsy tumble to the floor and I fought my attacker all the way down. Hands and feet flew everywhere as we rolled on the carpet. My nails clawed at skin and hair, but as hard as I tried, he was just too strong.

He rolled on top of me, straddled my hips, and pinned my arms over my head. "Stop! I'm not gonna hurt you. It's me, Flower. I had to find you," he said.

I stopped struggling and searched for the face in the darkness. "What did you call me?" Only one person called me by that name, the only one who had eyes that shimmered like brass. The color began to change from bronze to gold, his emotions turning the dial on high. If I had any doubt who he was, Lilith's reaction closed that deal. Instead of flips and jitters in my belly, she seemed to bristle with aggression. I could feel her rising to the surface, ready to attack as if all her past efforts to be with him meant nothing. My enemy was now hers, and for the life of me, I couldn't understand why.

"I can't talk long, but I need your help," he said. "I'm trapped. I can't get out. I need you to find me. I'm locked away somewhere not far from here, but I can't move."

"What? I-I—"

"Listen to me!" He shook me to attention. "You have to find my body. It's weak and will decay if I don't return to it. It will die. I don't have much time. Please, Flower, help me."

"Your body? I don't understand. If your body is trapped, then what am I looking at?" That really was a legit question, because it was too dark to see anything, nothing but the familiar amber glow that hurt my eyes.

As an answer, light from the hallway poured into the room as the door flew open. Mom stepped in, holding her trusty Louisville slugger with every intent on using it for murder. When she spotted the man hovering over me, the world had officially come to an end. Heaven had poured out the deadly plagues out onto the earth and landed dead center in my bedroom.

Letting out a battle cry, Mom swung the bat, and almost knocked his head clean off. That one strike was so hard; the air that whooshed past my head felt like a slap. The man slammed into the wall by the opened window from where I suspected he entered. I jumped to my feet and went for the light on the lamp by my bed. One click explained the sudden darkness. He must have turned it off when I wasn't looking.

"Samara, go downstairs and call the police. Now!" Mom ordered and aimed her bat at the intruder.

There was no way I was leaving her alone. Was she nuts? "Mom, wait, you don't understand—"

"Go, Samara!" she commanded.

"That's Tobias!" I pointed to the body.

Mom barely seemed to register my words, but when she did, she looked at me. "What? How did he get in here?"

"Through the window, I'm guessing."

She stared at the open window and then back to me. "You said blessed oil would keep an incubus out. How did he get in here?"

Good question, one of many I didn't have the answer to. We both looked to the unconscious man sprawled on the floor. Now that I had a good look at him, he didn't look like Tobias at all, but his face was very familiar.

From the hulky build to the turtleneck sweater, I knew him as the creepy guy in the elevator earlier tonight.

Possibilities ran through my head in quick-fire succession. Maybe he was overtaken by the Cambion draw and followed me home. But that wouldn't explain why he had golden eyes or why he called me "Flower". That was Tobias's pet name for me and no one else knew about it. Maybe Tobias was playing chameleon again and was passing himself off as this poor guy, but that wouldn't explain how he broke the protective shield around my house. My mental process came full circle, returning to the original question: How did he get inside without detection?

I stepped forward and kicked his foot, which limply fell back into place. The guy was out cold and wasn't about to get up anytime soon.

"Get away from him! We don't know what he'll do." Mom pulled me behind her.

"There's something wrong," I said. As if to prove my point, the body moved.

Mom and I screamed at the same time and retreated toward the wall. In that same instant, my cell phone rang, which made us scream even louder. I inched to my desk and grabbed my phone, knowing immediately who it was. No doubt he could feel my distress and was checking on me. Whatever issues I had with Caleb had fallen to the wayside, and hearing his voice right now became my only salvation.

"Sam, where are you? What's going on? Why are you scared?" Caleb kept spouting off questions, each one making his voice climb a higher pitch.

"He's here. I-I don't know how, but . . ." I looked to the body lying on the floor, which was still twitching. His chest jerked up and down, and his stomach flexed as if he was about to throw up. This man obviously needed help, but all I could do was watch in stunned horror.

"Sam! Talk to me! What's going on? Who's there with you? Sam, can you hear me?"

The man's torso lifted into the air to where only his shoulders and feet remained on the floor. His head turned to the side and he parted his mouth slightly, preparing to yawn. But instead of air going in, something came out. Small at first, a trickle of drool, then it expanded into a fountain of inky fluid. It took a few blinks to understand that it wasn't blood, or even liquid, but vapor.

I clutched the phone in my hand, almost breaking it, while Caleb announced, "I'm coming over! Stay where you are!"

"Samara, run! Go and call the police." Mom crept toward the door, never taking her eyes off the body.

"Sam, I'll be there as soon as I can. Don't move," Caleb said.

"Get out of here now!" Mom screamed at the same time Caleb ordered, "Stay there!"

"Will you two make up your minds!" I yelled to both of them.

Meanwhile, the dark substance pooled around the man's head. On and on, it poured out of his mouth, spilling over his face and bleeding into the carpet. After what felt like twenty-four hours, the last of the eerie mist left the man's mouth and proceeded to move on its own. This living mist danced over surrounding objects before crawling up the wall toward the window's ledge.

"Sam!! Tell me what's going on!" Caleb continued to scream through the phone.

The air moved fast in the room and papers and debris fluttered around us. My throat closed up as I watched this thing slither up my window. It hovered on the sill for a long moment, blending in with the scenery and consuming all light and matter within reach. The thing itself was the total absence of light, a portal that had punched its way into our dimension. It swirled and rolled into itself in the way a black hole robbed a galaxy of its stars. Planted deep in the eye of this storm was a tiny point of ocher light breaking through the darkness, a beating heart pulsing in an uneven rhythm.

This thing, wondrous and terrifying as any dream, appeared to be breathing and taking up space in a plane it had no business occupying. Beautiful as it was, I had no doubt that what stood in front of me contained a whole lot of evil, and anyone who looked directly into it would be swallowed. Yet I couldn't look away, I couldn't move, and I could barely speak. I wasn't the only one, because Mom stood in a daze in the middle of the room.

"Tobias," I whispered.

It wasn't an earthly creature that owned ears, but it heard me and understood its name. It wasn't a human that possessed a mouth or a tongue, yet it spoke with the voice of many people. Thousands of them, mostly female, blended together to create one unified cry of torment. It was whisper-soft at first, but quickly grew louder as the golden speck of light operated as its voice box and trembled with each flux of sound. Of all that had happened within these few frightening minutes, those voices were what made my blood run cold. So many lives. So many victims.

"Find me," it had said over and over, the low vibration of its voice shaking the floor beneath us. In an eruption of sound and broken glass, it disappeared into the night, taking half of my window and any hope of a sound sleep with it. I soon realized that that wasn't all it took.

The room was quiet again. Mom and I stared at the broken glass and the man lying motionless on the floor. He lay at an odd angle, legs bent and joints all wrong, an abused life-sized doll that had been tossed in the corner. His eyes were closed and I could tell he was no longer breathing. His pale cheeks and eyes were hollow, his skin as dry and delicate as the sheddings left behind from a snake. Every last sliver of energy had been snatched from this man's body and in seconds it began to show signs of decay.

"What . . . the hell . . . was that?" Mom asked, still unable to move.

I didn't answer right away; I was still trying to figure it out, or rather convince myself that what I'd seen and heard had really happened. It was many things, actually: a warning, a distress call, and a glimpse into my future if I didn't get Lilith under control. It was the corruption of something sacred, a crime against nature and humanity, all for the sake of immortality.

I didn't notice I was crying until the tears were halfway down my cheek. Wiping my face with the back of my hand, I said, "That was Tobias's soul, Mom."

6

"**O**kay, let's just pause a minute to take stock of how many people have died in this house," Mom began, holding a mug of herbal tea in her trembling hands.

"First, there was Nadine in our living room." She gestured to the sitting area across the hall. "Then there was Caleb's father in my bedroom, and now a total stranger in your room. All we have left is the dining room and perhaps the kitchen and we'll have a full set, like a game of *Clue*. Who done it, and with what weapon? Will it be Miss Scarlet in the library with the lead pipe, or Colonel Mustard in the laundry room with a lint roller?"

I sat across from her at the dining room table and watched the nervous breakdown unfold before my eyes. It was bound to happen eventually and I was surprised it hadn't come sooner. To her credit, this was the first death she'd seen live and in person, and she was handling it pretty well. Though only by extension, she was part of the Cambion world now, and finding the occasional dead body came with the lifetime membership.

Needless to say, the past four hours had been a mad house. The police had done crowd control while the paramedics tried in vain to revive the victim, who we discovered was a tourist from out of town. They had attributed his cause of death to a heart attack or stroke, as was the effect of too much life energy taken from our donors. However, the fact that the man's skin looked like he'd been dead for days instead of hours went beyond the realm of forensic science and straight into *The Twilight Zone.*

I'd seen many faces of death this year, a few by the hands of Cambions, but this method of consumption was—for a lack of a better word—overkill. Someone had drained that dude dry to the point of mummification, and only Mom and I knew who that someone was.

The police had taped off the house, and I was once again the star of another crime scene. There had been no evidence to prove any foul play outside of self-defense, but there were too many weird coincidences to overlook in the once quiet town of Williamsburg. Knowing the drill, I had kept my answers precise while Lilith worked her "mojo" on the young officer who took my statement. The mere sight of me had him fumbling through the interview, and the conversation had veered off topic more than I would've liked.

"So, what are you doing later? Did you need someone to watch the house tonight, just to be on the safe side?" he had asked in a low, husky tone so only I could hear.

The question hadn't surprised me at all. Only the strong-willed and chaste were immune to the Cambion allure, but the lovelorn or emotionally bankrupt didn't have a prayer. Cute as he might've been, now wasn't the time for romantic pursuits, not with the local coroner wheeling a body bag through the foyer.

"Um, sir, just so you know, I'm seventeen and have

plenty of people looking out for me. My *boyfriend* will make sure I'm safe." I tipped my head to Caleb, who stood in the kitchen entryway, looking ready to commit capital murder.

He had arrived around the same time the police did, but it was best that he stayed clear while the investigation was in full swing. Caleb already had a reputation for being at the wrong place at the wrong time and he didn't want more suspicion drawn to him by interfering. Seeing Officer Pedo Bear make a move on me could very well ruin that plan. It was hard not to find his jealousy adorable. I had to deal with women practically hump his leg every day at work, and it seemed fair to turned the tables on him for a change.

As soon as the parade of emergency teams left, we had settled in the dining room for some tea and some much-needed reflection. Somehow, perhaps by divine intervention, I made it through the ordeal without a complete meltdown. But I was sure it had something to do with my other half refusing to leave my side.

Caleb rested his elbow on the table, listening to Mom's rant as he stroked my back. He had said very little in the past hour, but I could tell his brain was working behind the scenes. I was sure his legs had fallen asleep by now, but he wouldn't let me move off his lap, and I could tell that it was more for his benefit than my own.

"A lot of household accidents happen in the kitchen," Mom continued. "Or maybe the stairs. Someone could easily fall and break their neck or even slip in the shower—the tiles can be pretty slippery. Better yet, the house could catch fire. It's the holiday season and there are Christmas lights and wires everywhere."

"Mom, maybe you should take some of your anxiety medication," I suggested.

Mom's head shake looked like a twitch. "It makes me

drowsy and I need to make sure the house is secure. Someone could try to break in again. There's no telling if that . . . *thing* is watching the house. And I need to go to the store and get more olive oil. The house is tainted now. Didn't you say a corpse will nullify anointing oil? We need to purify your room and board up the window, but you might not want to sleep there tonight. You need to get to bed soon. You have school in the morning. Oh gosh, I need to give you a ride tomorrow, don't I?"

I watched her warily. "Uh, no. I just got my new car today, remember?"

Mom rubbed her face with her hands. "Oh right, right. Well, I should probably call Evangeline. She'll want to know what's happening."

"I'm sure Ruiz told her by now." I looked to the living room where the detective paced the floor and talked on his cell phone.

"You don't have to leave, Ms. Marshall. I have olive oil in my car. I don't go anywhere without it these days," Caleb offered.

"That's the thing. I don't think olive oil works anymore," I said. "The house was secure before, but that didn't stop him. The intruder was human; he could pass through the barrier just like we can. Tobias can't, though, not with his own body."

"But you said anointing oil worked as a deterrent for your kind," Mom spoke up.

"It still is, but only if a Cambion drinks it. It'll harm the spirit inside. A demon body can't even touch it or enter a house covered with it. But Tobias wasn't using his own body."

"I don't think it's him." Caleb pressed his fingers to his temple and stared off in deep concentration.

"How do you know?" I asked.

"I just do," he said quickly. "It could be another Cambion in town. I'll have my brothers look into it."

"How can you be so sure that it's not Tobias? He told me things only he would know about. He called me Flower. No one else calls me that, and Lilith recognized him—sort of. She didn't seem happy to see him."

"Flower? Is that code for something?" Caleb asked.

Not wanting Mom to hear, I whispered the meaning in his ear. This did not improve his mood; the stiffness in his posture and the cold disconnection to his eyes made that point clear.

"Why couldn't Lilith sense him before? You're linked to him too; he wouldn't have made it up the block without Lilith knowing," he asked in a calm voice that was not only misleading, but unsettling.

Angry as he was, he brought up a good point. My connection with Tobias would always give his identity away whenever he went incognito. That power didn't seem to be working too well tonight. But I knew what I saw. I wasn't crazy. Not completely.

"How should I know? Maybe Lilith's blocking him," I answered. "Nadine made her do it once before; that's how she hid from Tobias all these years. But when I fed from him at school, Lilith recognized his energy and that must've broken the barrier. It's like the connection is reinforced by the energy the two shared."

I didn't like the look Caleb was giving me, so I decided on redirection. "All I'm saying is I'm just as confused as you are. Something bad happened to Tobias, and I need to find him before he hurts any more people. If his body is really missing or trapped, then he's using possession as an outlet. Yes, he can do that—he's a demon," I said before Caleb could interrupt me. "He told me he can shed off his body like a coat and possess human men at will.

That's how incubi can reproduce. They're sterile or biologically incompatible or something so they need to do it through a human if they want offspring. Anyway, I think he's more interested in using that body snatching talent to warn me. He said he needed me to find him."

Mom got up from the table and went to the kitchen for more tea. She was hitting it hard tonight and I wondered if her drink was spiked with rum. I wouldn't blame her if it was—knowing this much about the netherworld would drive anyone to drink.

Alone in the room, Caleb continued to hold me close and caress my back. "Look, try not to worry about—"

"Are you serious? I saw a man die in my room and you want me to brush that off?" I snapped. "You're not even in the least bit curious what happened to Tobias? Why I can't sense him, better yet, why you can't either? Why everything in my life has been turned upside down in a matter of hours, hours that, by the way, Lilith won't tell me about?" I rubbed my throbbing temple. "I can't shake the feeling that it's all connected somehow."

"Sorry his well-being isn't one of my top priorities. I'm more concerned about what you're dealing with. Are you sure there's no way you can get Lilith to open up?" Caleb pressed.

Before I could reply, Lilith took that particular time to make her presence known. A jolt of electricity zapped my back. If Caleb weren't holding me, I would have fallen out of the seat.

Capturing my waist in his hands, he pulled me up straight and settled me back on his lap. "Whoa. What was that about?"

"I don't think Lilith likes that idea. I guess I'm on my own. With or without her, I'm gonna find Tobias before it's too late."

"You're not putting yourself in danger," Caleb said,

sounding all hard and authoritative, like I was going to listen to him. Perhaps knowing me way too well, he added, "Don't try anything foolish, Sam. You're hot-headed and trouble knows your name, address, and phone number."

I gasped. "You've. Got. Some. Nerve."

The side of his lips curled in a delicious smile. "And then some. Promise me you'll wait until we learn more. We can't run in guns blazing. We'll need to plan."

It took a minute to get my temper in check, but I nodded. "Fine. But I'm telling you now, when we do, the gloves come off."

As promised, Caleb went to his Jeep and grabbed some olive oil and covered all the entrances and windows, then disappeared upstairs to do the same. Though we both knew that it might not do any good, I was sure he needed to keep busy.

Ruiz also stayed behind to talk Mom off the ledge, but his bedside manner needed work. I walked in on them speaking in hushed tones in the kitchen. Instead of pointing the finger at Caleb as usual, his suspicion was aimed at me.

"I just spoke to Evangeline and she said she's coming next week. It's the earliest that she can arrive. We agree that it's a good idea that you have a Cambion elder around for counsel."

Mom turned and leaned her hip against the counter. "What does that mean?"

"Samara is a young Cambion with little knowledge of her power and even less discipline. Men are naturally attracted to her. For them to resort to violence is a sign of something off balance with her spirit."

"Are you saying that what happened tonight was *her* fault?"

"That man seemed pretty desperate to get to her. Had

you not intervened, there's no telling what could've happened. Is there any other explanation for his heart to stop, for his body to look like that? Self-defense or not, his life energy was taken, by a Cambion. The police in this town aren't stupid, Julie. Bodies are popping up like crazy. This is creating more attention on this town and Samara, the wrong kind of attention."

"She's my daughter, David. A man came into our home and tried to hurt my child. What would you do in my position? I'm sure Evangeline will understand. She's a mother, too. I'll talk to her."

"I'm sure she already understands. She's concerned for the both of you."

Mom turned and saw me standing in the entryway. She ducked her face behind Ruiz's shoulder, hiding her tears from me, but I already saw them. I hated being the cause of those tears, but I was willing to take the full blame for this screw-up, just as long as Ruiz didn't find out about Tobias. That would be a death warrant for all of us.

"Is there a problem?" I asked, glaring at Ruiz.

"No problem, sweetie. Everything's fine," Mom answered in a weak voice. "Go ahead to bed. You can sleep in my room. I don't plan on going to bed tonight. I need to clean up."

I kept staring at the detective as a soft green tint coated my vision. Lilith didn't like the situation either. Ruiz kept his android posture, but I could tell he understood the silent threat: You hurt my mom; your ass is mine.

I left the two downstairs and followed the sound of banging to my room. It was the first time I'd entered the room since the attack, and though the place was a wreck, I was relieved to find no blood or chalk outlines on my floor. In the middle of a pile of shredded cardboard, Caleb stood, wielding a box cutter in his hand.

"What's up?" I called out.

"Boarding up your window," he mumbled and ripped off a strip of duct tape with his teeth. "It's all I could find, but it should keep the cold out until you can get a replacement."

"That's fine. I don't think I'll be sleeping here for a while." I leaned against the wall and watched him work.

He seemed completely engrossed in his task to the point of obsession, but his emotions were too jumbled to read. Our link was growing stronger with each passing day, becoming more physical. I could feel his excitement, his pain, his fear, which were all turned on full blast right now.

Maybe he would finally take the threat of our meansome threesome more seriously. Tobias wasn't playing around when he said he had unfinished business. He was a demon, and by profession human life meant little to him, and Caleb's meant even less. This feud wouldn't end until one of them stopped breathing and the winner claimed me as the prized trophy piece.

I drew deeper into the room, searching Caleb's face for answers, but he kept his back to me. "You okay?" I asked.

"Sure. Why wouldn't I be okay?" He placed the final sheet of cardboard over the window frame. "I should be used to dead people popping up and being helpless to stop it."

"Helpless? Why?"

It took a long beat for Caleb to answer. He was too busy taking his anger out on the board that kept slipping from his hand. He bit off another strip of tape and slapped it over the border, almost pounding the adhesive through the wall. "I try to protect you, but it never works out, does it? No matter what I do, you always get hurt; you're always left to fend for yourself."

I just stared at him and struggled to piece together his

scattered logic. "So . . . you're mad because you weren't around to rush in and save the day? I'm sorry, what century are we in?"

He stopped moving and braced himself against the wall. "I can't afford to have something happen to you. If he hurt you . . ."

"He didn't. Tobias won't hurt me. I'm too valuable to him."

"You're valuable to *me*!" His sudden outburst made me jump. "I couldn't help my mom, or my dad. I couldn't save Nadine. I've lost too many people in my life and I . . . I can't lose any more. When I heard you on the phone and felt your fear; I lost it. I've had too many close calls with you already. I-I can't . . ."

I touched his shoulder, then drew my hand away when he flinched at the contact. "Hey, I'm all right. I'm not going anywhere. Whatever game Tobias is playing, we won't let him win. You. Are. Not. Weak."

Caleb didn't seem to hear me, but stared at the wall ahead of him. I recognized the blank expression, the deadened look in his eyes. It was his coping device, an escape hatch for when emotions got too big to handle. Bad things always followed that detachment, and this would give Capone the perfect opportunity to take over.

"No. Don't do that. Hey, stop. Don't shut down on me, not now. I need you with me. Come back, please?" I hugged his waist and rested my head against his back, which felt as solid as a brick wall from all the tension. "It takes strength to cope with loss. I envy you, because I haven't dealt with my grief at all, and I'm due for a psychotic break any minute now. I saw how you fought Tobias on Thanksgiving night and it was all kinds of awesome. I could never do that. I'm too small."

"That was Capone. He fought Tobias, not me." He took a deep breath and spun around to look at me. "And you're not that small, Sam, and from what I hear, size doesn't matter. I wouldn't know anything about that, though."

That made me snort, and we broke into a hearty laugh that we both needed. This was a good thing. Caleb's ego demanded some inflating, and I needed to remember what it was like to laugh until my eyes watered.

We locked eyes for a long moment as the humor began to die and something wicked in the air came to life. There came the heaviness again, gravity pulling us together, a force that had become second nature. He leaned into me and brushed away the tear from my cheek with his thumb. His finger moved lower and traced the outline of my bottom lip.

"Anyway, I'm saying it's not a crime to be scared."

"I'm not scared of Tobias or anyone else. I'm afraid of what I'd do if anyone tried to take you from me. There'd be no stopping me." His expression darkened, his eyes taking me in with a fierce heat that could burn right through my skin. "I *will* keep you safe."

Under different circumstances, I could've walked out of the room and gone to sleep without any problems. But the night's excitement had lowered my guard, heightened my senses, making me painfully aware of his scent, his warmth, his presence.

Being this close to each other was a volatile combination. My mom was downstairs and she could walk in at any minute. The fact that a man just died right where we stood did not make for a very romantic atmosphere. But the second I saw that lavender glow, the hypnotic swirl of lights in his eyes, it was over.

Caleb grabbed my waist and yanked me to him. Our mouths met in a clash of desperation and repressed energy. My arms wrapped around his neck in the process to climb up his body. His hands slipped under me and lifted my legs to mold around his hips. We tumbled until my back pressed against the wall. His mouth plundered mine, stealing my breath, all reason, and any impulse to stop. But Caleb's will was stronger than mine.

He pulled his mouth away and rested his forehead against mine. His breath fanned over my face, hot, shaky, and uneven. We stayed propped against the wall, locked in a tangle of limbs until our breathing calmed. Slowly, carefully, he loosened his hold around my legs and allowed my body to slide down his. Even the act of setting me down was a physical challenge that involved every ounce of his concentration.

He backed away with his head bowed and his eyes to the floor. "We can't keep doing this."

"I know," I agreed, not moving a muscle. It wasn't a good idea to make any sudden moves with his eyes still glowing like that. I wasn't afraid of him. In fact, I was pretty sure I could take him in a fistfight—judo classes be damned. I was afraid *for* him. I knew his limits and he was skating the edge of reason. I knew, because I was right there with him.

He paced in front of me and gripped hunks of hair with his fist. "It will only get worse from here on out. Our spirits will crave more than what we can give them. It's getting harder to restrain Capone." He met my gaze, wearing a hard mask of sobriety. "And I *don't want* to restrain him. I told you I'd protect you no matter what, even if it's from myself. And I mean it."

He made it sound like fire would rain from the sky if we ever got pelvic. "Shouldn't this kind of morning-after regret come much later?"

"I'd rather regret it now than months, years down the road. I don't want you resenting me for something you had no choice in, and I sure as hell don't want to have to *feel* that resentment coming off you for the rest of my life. You couldn't smile and fake it—I would always know. We could live miles away in different states and I would still know. The one thing we need most is the one thing we don't have. Time." He crossed the room and sat on the edge of my bed. "It's past your bed time, Miss Marshall. We've had enough excitement for one night."

Was I being dismissed? His mood swings were getting all over my nerves and all the anger from earlier tonight came back with interest. "Dude, if you're gonna clam up every time we make-out, then we should probably end this now. I know the risks, and the only real fear I have is being a teen mom and that can be prevented. Being bound to you forever will not put an end to my world, but it might be the end of yours if you keep up the grown-man bitching, so cut it out!" I looked around the room to the messy accommodations. "If you wanna sleep here, go right ahead. I'll be in Mom's room."

While leaving the room, he called after me. "While I'm here, do me a favor before you go to bed? Not just for me, but for your sake, too."

I stopped with my back to him. I didn't need to see the hurt look on his face; I could hear it in the strain of his voice, and I felt his heart breaking in my own chest. "What?" I asked.

"Lock your door."

Those were the chilliest three words I'd ever heard, spoken with the desperate voice of a prisoner condemned. A last request. I nodded and closed the bedroom door behind me, aching for rest that I knew I wouldn't get tonight. And neither would he.

7

No one really knows how it all started, but what little knowledge survived the ages was as absurd and disturbing as a ghost story told around a campfire.

Three different versions of what were known as *The Origin Tale* were recorded in Angie's family memoirs, all amounting to the same horrifically detailed outcome: death and lots of it. I had trouble sleeping after reading these entries; however, I'd love to see a Disney version of this grim fairy tale, uncensored and in 3D.

I was three-fourths into the first volume of this epic saga and couldn't put it down; not so much for historical curiosity, but because it was the juiciest soap opera ever put to paper. Obsession, jealousy, and violence drowned the pages in blood, as each female in Angie's line bared their souls for future generations.

Though these records were for genealogical purposes, I also believed that these Cambion heroines wanted those like me to learn from their mistakes. They whispered words of warning from beyond the grave, begging me to maintain my humanity or else lose my soul forever. For their sake, for their sacrifice, I owed it to them to listen.

More to the point, Angie's flight would arrive in a matter of hours and she would demand a full book report as soon as she saw me. She'd given both volumes to me to read and I'd been pushing my duties aside until the last minute. Could anyone really blame me—each book consisted of almost two thousand pages, single spaced, with a ten-point font size. But now, with the clock ticking and two pots of coffee running through my veins, it was crunch time.

School, work, and Caleb's extended trip to "jerk-istan," were put on the back burner for the past week in order to meet this deadline. Wherever I went, volume one was tucked under my arm while everything faded in the background. These leather-bound grimoirs didn't help my popularity at school and rumors of my use of witchcraft were in heavy circulation. Everyone around me knew better than to talk to me, which was why no one knocked on my bedroom door all weekend.

Mom kept busy downstairs doing last-minute finishing touches on the house and yelling at the neighbors. I figured the Christmas lawn wars were still in effect, but as long as there were no shots fired, I left Mom to duke it out on her own.

The funny thing was that I felt I'd read these books before. The stories, the cast of characters came back to me, jogging my memory somehow. It then became apparent that the memory wasn't mine, but Nadine's. An image of her sitting on her bed reading this book flashed in my head. Long, blond strands fell over her eyes as a white hand turned the page. She had been sentenced to read both volumes as well and forced to memorize sections to recite for her mother at dinner. I sensed a type of urgency with the request, as if Nadine's life depended on her study of these books. It was a civil duty, a royal obligation to learn her Cambion roots, and now the responsibility had been passed down to me.

By the time I pulled my nose out of my book, it was dark outside and I had twenty minutes to meet up with Angie for dinner. I'd talked to her hundreds of times over the phone and I pretty much knew her life story, but that didn't stop my hands from shaking and sweating. Most women had that reaction when it came to the grand dame of Cambions. Angie was pretty high class, and mingling with us country bumpkins had to be a step down for her. The thought made me self-conscious and forced me to change my wardrobe twice.

I settled for a simple blue knee-length dress with an empire waist and ruffled shoulders. Wearing my hair in a loose bun with curly tendrils framing my face, I looked like someone out of a Jane Austen novel. Not my usual taste, but the Wonder Twins were sufficiently covered and that was the best I could do as far as modesty.

This was an intimate meet-and-greet for Cambions only, which meant no outsiders allowed. So Mom stayed behind, but not without updating me on the latest child abduction on the news.

"... and all the police could find were human bones in the wood shed behind the house." Mom concluded, holding a wrapped plate of peanut butter cookies. "And don't forget to give these to Angie. It's always good to bring a gift to a party."

I shook my head and took the plate, though secretly thankful that her time with Ruiz hadn't lowered her guard. Then again, she couldn't afford to in the Cambion world, even if she was a quiet observer. I might be spiritually connected to Angie, but I was Julie Marshall's baby, and woe to anyone who messed with that.

After a hug and kiss, I hightailed it to the Charlotte

Hotel. I knew I was in for a formal event when I found Caleb's brother, Michael in the lobby. His tall, gangly body settled into one of the high boy chairs as he played a game on his phone. His long brown braid fell over one shoulder and touched his belly. He didn't wear his usual Silent Bob trench coat, but a white dress shirt, black slacks, and one bright yellow checkered sock.

Michael was the oddball of the Ross clan, but he was the smartest and sweetest of the brothers. He was also the spitting image of Caleb, minus a good twenty pounds.

"Hey, Michael!" I called.

He lifted his head and I was greeted with the same colored eyes that all the males in his line owned. But unlike Caleb's, Michael's were wide, bloodshot, and shifty, never quite making direct eye contact with those of the fairer gender. He tucked the phone into his pocket and stood.

"Ah, you made it. I was hoping you were going to run late," he said, the slight hint of his English accent creeping through the syllables.

"Why? Trying not to go upstairs yet?"

"Pretty much, yeah." He nodded. "Evangeline's been barking orders since she arrived. She instructed me to wait here to meet you while she changed."

"What a loyal man-servant you are." I patted his shoulder. "You shouldn't be afraid of Angie. She's cool people."

I could tell Michael wanted to comment, but he didn't. "Right, well, let's go then. Don't want to keep her waiting. Did your mum make those?" he asked, ogling my cookies.

"Yes, and they're for Angie. Back up, you heathen!" I held the plate close to my chest as he escorted me to the bank of elevators.

Keeping my eyes peeled for any weird guests, I leaned in and asked, "Any news about, you know, Mr. T.?"

He glanced sideways at me. "Isn't that the bloke with the Mohawk and chains around his neck?"

"No. I meant Tobias," I whispered then scanned the lobby again. The name seemed cursed now, where unspeakable horrors awaited anyone who said it three times in front of a mirror.

Michael pushed the button on the elevator and motioned me to enter first. "Sam, he's an incubus, not Lord Voldermort. You can say his whole name."

"I know, but he can be anywhere, listening in on us."

"Not here. We've sealed the building with oil."

"That didn't stop him before," I argued. "Did Caleb tell you about the man who broke into my house?" I gave Michael the lowdown in case his brother left out details. He looked sufficiently worried, especially after learning that I now slept with the lights on in my room.

When I finished, he said, "That's very unfortunate. Seems everything's gone all Pete Tong, hasn't it?"

Since he didn't follow up that random comment with an explanation, I searched the elevator car for one. "Who's Pete Tong?"

Michael looked away with a quick shake of his head. "Oh. It means 'wrong.' It's a Cockney thing for slang to rhyme," he explained. "But I'm not entirely sure Tobias is involved."

"Why does everyone keep saying that? Am I missing something?"

"Probably, but I wouldn't worry about it too much. We've got bigger problems at the moment. Let's focus on surviving the night, shall we?" he said as the doors opened.

Angie rented the entire top floor, which was one oversized apartment with two levels. We stepped through the glass French doors to the foyer that seemed to go on for miles. A black and white marble floor led to a grand staircase in the center. Beveled mirrors and oil paintings accented the cream walls and oversized palm leaves gave life to the room.

"Hello? Angie, we're here!" I called out.

Angie's head popped around the corner, her ash blond hair swinging over her shoulder. Letting out a girlish squeal, she clapped her hands and raced to my side. The clink of her numerous bracelets provided a song for every movement.

She wore her forty years better than the black cocktail dress that clung to her like a wet suit. She had an oval face, a long, pointy nose, and full lips that on anyone else would throw off the symmetry, but with Angie it only seemed to enhance it. She reminded me of one of those femme fatales in old black-and-white detective movies. From her tall, ramrod posture to her feline stride, she epitomized elegance, yet she had a bit of sass that leaned toward the obscene, the dangerous.

"My little warrior, you are finally here!" she cried and squeezed me tight.

"Yeah, I almost didn't make it though." I rocked from side to side in her arms.

"Nonsense. You had to come. You would not dare leave me here alone with these savages." She winked at Michael who looked away sheepishly. It could've been the way Angie stared at people, totally engrossed, like they were the most captivating creatures on Earth. It stood on the left of flirtation and just shy of creepy. A popular Cambion trait.

"Thank you so much for greeting Samara," she told Michael. "Now would you be so kind as to bring your brothers. Dinner will begin shortly."

At her command, my stomach flipped. For a second, I had forgotten that Caleb would be joining this little get-together. I hadn't seen him since that stunt in my room and I wasn't in the mood for more drama. Actually, I had seen him plenty of times at work, I just didn't want to. I was still raw and bitter, and talking to him would just lead to more words I'd regret later.

Keeping in good spirits, I presented my gift. "Here, Mom made you some cook—" I paused at the plate that now had three lonely cookies and a pile of crumbs. "Michael!" I whipped my head around to see the thief fleeing the scene of the crime. I couldn't believe it. I'd been holding the plate the entire time and didn't even notice. Oh, he was good. Munching on his prize, Michael disappeared behind the sliding elevator doors.

Angie lifted a cookie from the plate and motioned me to the sitting room. "As I said, savages, dear."

"So what have you been up to?" I asked.

"Well, I sold four paintings and have two commissions. My next showing isn't until February, so I'll be free to handle business here."

Knowing what type of business, my muscles tightened. Did she have any news about the Cambion big wigs? Were they still after Caleb?

Sensing my unease, she said, "No politics before dinner, Samara. It's bad etiquette. Let us enjoy our time together. Come, the others are waiting."

I wasn't expecting the red carpet and fanfare, just something a little less awkward. One thing about the Petrovsky progeny, or Cambion children in general, there was no need for a blood test. Dressed in their Sunday best, they lined up by height in the living room, looking like the Von Trapps from *The Sound of Music*. They stood with hands behind their backs, their postures displaying regality and years of boarding school discipline. Sore thumb was not the right analogy to describe my presence. I squinted my eyes, blinded by the glare of all that blond.

"And these are my darlings. I told you about them, yes?" With a graceful sweep of her hand, Angie pointed to each replica of herself, starting with the sixteen-year-old. Of all three siblings, she resembled Nadine the most, not just in appearance, but in attitude. She oozed apathy, a world-weary detachment that took years to master.

I extended my hand to the tall girl. "You must be Olivia, right?"

A nod was her only reply. With chin lifted in the air, she scrutinized every square inch of my person. Her eyes were keen, hooded with heavy lids as if she were about to doze off at any minute. In that instant, I knew I was working a tough crowd, so I decided to move on to the thirteen-year-old.

"This is my son, Szymon, and my little mouse, Mishka," Angie said.

I bowed my head. "Nice to meet you."

Szymon shifted from foot to foot, unsure where to look. Though he had Angie's features, his light gray eyes excluded him from the group.

Mishka, on the other hand, seemed more curious than the others and a bit more eager to break the ice. All curls and rosy cheeks, the ten-year-old stepped forward and curtseyed. Her emerald eyes widened as if I were something shiny. "Are you our new sister now?"

"Uh . . ." I looked to Angie for the right answer, but she was out of ideas.

"Don't be stupid, Mishka. Of course she's not. She's just a carrier, that's all," Olivia said with tight lips.

Ouch. "I'm a little more than that," I replied. "But,

I'm not here to replace your sister. Nadine was a good friend of mine, and I'm honored to have a part of her with me."

She shrugged. "If you say so."

"Olivia, that is enough. You are being rude," Angie admonished.

"No, that's okay. This is tense for everyone. The last thing anyone needs is to be fake around each other." I stood a foot away from Olivia and said, "I'm not a bad person, and I hope you'll realize that throughout your stay. I'm not expecting us to be best friends, but your mother wants me here, so please respect that and respect me. Otherwise, this holiday is gonna be very uncomfortable for both of us."

Olivia glared in rebellion, her eyes flashing with jade sparks. Not wanting to be upstaged, I allowed Lilith to make herself known and the world around me took on a green tint. The girl jumped back, startled, then pulled her brother behind her. "Not when he's around," she warned.

Immediately, I closed my eyes and turned my head. "Sorry."

"It's all right, Samara. He needs more time with you." Angie stepped to her children. "Olivia, take Szymon upstairs. I will be there shortly."

The girl nodded, then ushered her brother out of the room, holding him close in a motherly, almost possessive fashion. Mishka skipped behind them, her spiral curls bouncing around her head. Szymon bent his head toward the floor, never lifting his gaze, not even as Caleb passed him in the hall and ruffled his hair.

"What was that about?" Caleb asked.

Maybe it was because I hadn't talked to him for a few days, but damn, he looked good. Leaning by the entryway with his hands tucked in his pockets, he seemed to agree. The cuffs of his black shirt were rolled up to his elbows and the top three buttons were undone. His freshly washed hair was combed back, revealing a deceptively boyish face.

"I let Szymon see my eyes glow," I explained and turned my back to him.

His footsteps drew closer. "You have to be careful about that. Only the girls are like us. He's pure and immune to our draw, but we don't want to scare him more than we have to."

"Uh, yeah, my bad." I could feel him staring at me, seeking eye contact, but I wouldn't give in. My heart pounded double-time and all my body weight traveled toward my feet.

No doubt sensing the tension in the air, Angie said, "Please, get comfortable and enjoy the refreshments while I check on the rest of the food. Room service should be here soon."

While the waitstaff placed the food in the dining room, I was left to mingle and dodge the hungry glances that Caleb shot my way. We kept to opposite sides of the living room in a slow dance around furniture and strategically placed easels in the living room. Whenever I worked up the nerve to look up, there he was, stripping another piece of my clothing with his X-rated vision. My skin prickled, laid bare to the hot static in the air while Lilith rattled in her cage to break free. Trying in vain to ignore them both, I steered my attention to the artwork on display.

Angie was a critically acclaimed painter, and her provocative, ultrafeminist pieces captivated the art world. She was also illusive, only doing a show every five years in select cities, and she presented a sneak peek of her collection as a conversation piece.

I walked by portraits of people in cages, or shoved through a meat grinder and other kitchen appliances.

Some pictures were simple and elegant, while some looked like an epileptic fit with paint.

"It's so complex. Look at the angry brush strokes, and the composition; the symbolism of the red across the man's torso," an accented voice spoke next to me.

I tilted my head sideways and tried to interpret the chaos on canvas. "That's a man?"

"I hope so," he replied.

I stared up at the second oldest of the Ross clan and self-appointed big brother and watch dog. Naturally, Haden arrived unfashionably late, looking as uncomfortable as I felt. He cleaned up nicely in a gray suit and jacket, his black hair slicked back, touching his neck.

"Don't look too happy about being here," I said.

His indigo eyes made a quick sweep around the room. "I'm not here to be festive. I just wanna know the latest about my brother and leave. Brodie's been in New York for weeks and he hasn't called in days."

I rubbed his arm. "I'm sure it's nothing. I wouldn't worry. Angie will protect him."

Haden's thick brows pinched together, as if he was trying to convince himself to agree. Though big, rugged, and abrasive, he was the peacemaker of the four brothers, the glue that held it all together, but even he had his breaking point. "Yeah well, I want all this over and done with. Michael and I have lives and jobs to get back to."

"What is your exact job title, Haden? I know Michael's some software nerd, but . . . what do you do?" I asked with almost frustrated curiosity.

"A little of this and a little of that," was his only reply. He tipped his head toward Caleb, who stood by the wall, talking to one of the female servers. "So why are you angry at Caleb now?"

The change in topic made my taste buds go numb. "Why don't you go ask Caleb yourself?"

"Already have. He didn't say much."

I blinked. "What did he say?"

"You sound concerned."

"Not really."

"Right." A boyish smile stood in contrast to Haden's hard, scar-ridden features. "Denial is not a good look for you." He leaned in and kissed my cheek, and a warm sensation spread over my entire face. "Go talk to Caleb," he whispered and left my side.

I did another lap around the room, holding a napkin loaded with finger food and wondering what lay in store for us this evening. Angie had news for us, I just knew it, and the wait was killing me. The head of the Cambion family had all but put out an APB on Caleb, and Angie was the only ally we had. I just hoped she had a good plan.

"You look nice tonight," Caleb said behind me, his breath fanning the back of my neck. I half expected him to kiss me there as was his usual endearment, but he didn't, which was more devastating than if he had.

"Thanks. So do you," I replied. "It's amazing what a bar of soap and a comb can do."

"Life's full of many wonders. So, are you still mad at me?"

"Heavens no! Why would I be mad?" I said immediately, almost yelling the words. "You are what you are. Who am I to change you?"

"Just so we're straight here, you're angry with me because I prefer to feed on random strangers instead of you, or are you mad because you think my diet is out of control?"

I had to think about that for a minute. "Can't I be both?"

"No, because both reasons are stupid," he countered. "I'm careful of the energy I take and not one woman has died on my tab. You know I'm crazy about you—I don't even have to say it; you can feel it and know I'm more than just talk. Every second with you takes a painful amount of restraint, but even that will break at some point. What we share will consume us; it's not a matter of if, but *when*. So if it's okay with you, I want to keep my sanity a little while longer."

And he walked away, leaving me on edge with a snappy comeback that came thirty seconds too late. I hated when that happened. Every nerve ending on my body was fried, not from his words, but the heat behind them. Why did he have this effect on me? Or maybe what I was feeling was my effect on *him*. This empathy business was just plain freaky, the constant back-and-forth of emotions, to the point that I was lusting after myself through him.

Not knowing what else to do, I crammed my face with more crab puff thingies, praying for the night to end quickly.

Dinner was a strained event, and the first ten minutes were brief lapses in conversation and several sideways glances in my direction. The Petrovskys idealized the typical family who sat down for dinner every night and discussed the day. They were a very affectionate family, always smiling and touching, as if in need of constant assurance of the others' presence. Tragedy will do that to people, but I had a feeling that they were always like that.

Another round of food passed about before things began to pick up. The kids seemed a bit more talkative, and Olivia finally stopped glaring at me, put down her steak knife, and focused on her meal. While the kids ate, I could see their hands and the gold band identical to mine hanging on each child's wrist, even the boy's.

Though this served as an heirloom and security caution, I couldn't shake the impression of being collared.

"So, Samara, have you been reading the journal entries?" Angie asked.

"Yes."

"And what did you learn?"

The room grew silent as all eyes fell on me. I couldn't believe that I was getting a pop quiz at dinner. "In short, Lilith is a succubus, but was once human, and one of many ancient tribe women who breathed in some bad smoke. The smoke being from the charred remains to this giant angelic being that the villagers decided to tear in half and burn. You know, typical family tree stuff. The moral of the story: when around malevolent spirits, keep your mouth closed."

With a snort, Szymon covered his nose to keep his drink from escaping. Being far less amused, Olivia slapped her brother on the back of the head. When he recovered, he continued to eat, his body shaking with suppressed laughter.

"I am happy that you find our lineage amusing," Olivia snapped. "At least we know where we came from."

"Obviously you don't if you have three different versions of it." She must have assumed that I hadn't heard her, so it shocked her when I answered in her native tongue.

"English, ladies," Haden intervened as he looked at the two of us. "Not everyone here can speak Polish."

"Thank you, Haden," Angie said, her stern tone bringing the room back to order. "They are just legends, Samara. No one takes them seriously, although the origin story is celebrated in some cultures. Actors even put on performances retelling the event."

"With or without the citywide massacre?" I asked.

"With." She smiled. "My main concern is the family line. Have you gotten to the three sisters of Antioch?"

"Uh, sorta. They're the ones telling it, right?"

"The first half, yes. When you reach the part where they hide in the Carpathian Mountains, let me know. So, what are your plans for the holidays?"

"Well, um, I was hoping you all would come over Christmas day and exchange gifts and have dinner."

"We're Jewish," Olivia said with a flat note.

"I know, but I was just throwing some ideas out there."

Resting her chin in her palm, Angie leaned closer to me. "It sounds marvelous, dear. I've brought plenty of gifts for you and your mother."

Looking around the table, I noticed there was a key person missing. I'd expected him to show up at some point, but the chair at the head of the table remained empty. "Where's Mr. Petrovsky?"

Angie dropped her fork and stared down at her plate. "I'm afraid he is ill and staying with his family for the holiday. It appears that the years are catching up with him."

Confused by her statement and her ominous tone, I asked, "What does that mean? Aren't you two the same age?"

The room was silent again and the mood shifted to one normally felt at a wake.

"We'll discuss that later. That is part of the reason why I'm here and why I need you to study the journal entries. You need to know what is expected of you as an extended member of our family."

The loud clank of silverware got everyone's attention. Olivia pulled out her chair and stood. "Mama, please excuse me." She quit the room before her mother could respond.

"Forgive her, Samara. You must understand, Olivia and Nadine were very close," Angie implored.

I understood perfectly. I was a stranger, one who threatened the nobility of her bloodline. To make matters worse, she was forced to break bread with the sons of the man who murdered her big sister. If those weren't grounds for resentment and angst, nothing was.

I took a swig of water before saying, "Look, I don't want to reopen any old wounds for you guys. And I know you have a ton of questions, but this is all new for me, too."

"Don't let this discourage you. No one blames you and we have come to terms with what has happened," Angie assured.

I looked to the entryway where Olivia passed. "Not everyone," I said as stomping feet resounded upstairs with the slam of a bedroom door as the grand finale.

8

After dinner, the Petrovsky offspring were banished to the solitude of their beds while the rest of us gathered in the private office for coffee and tea.

Forest green print covered the walls and the dark wood furniture made the room a masculine study. The place screamed of luxury: the tall fireplace and plush leather chairs and heavy oak desk in the corner. My grandpa had a lair like this, but more books and decapitated wildlife occupied the walls.

Angie nestled into a fancy armchair by the fireplace and got right down to business. "Tell me, Samara, how many head Cambion families are there?"

Wow, it was quiz time again. Taking timid sips of my drink, I did a mental head count. "Um, thirteen altogether, including three in North America."

"So you know who the Santiago Family is?" she prodded.

I searched the room for aid, but the brothers became

suddenly interested with different points around the study. Caleb sat on a chaise across from me with his arms crossed. Yep, I was on my own.

"Yes, they govern parts of Canada, the entire East Coast all the way to Puerto Rico," I answered.

"Very good. And you're aware that you were born under their jurisdiction and you must obey the laws within their region?" When I nodded, she rose from her chair and said, "As your elder, I'm obligated to explain Cambion law and specify how we differ from our predecessors."

"I kinda know the difference between succubi and Cambions," I said.

"Yes, but you need to understand the history. The thirteen families are very old, but that is not what makes them powerful. It is their discipline and their persistence to destroy all demons. It has been a quest, a competitive one, for over a thousand years. We want our bloodline free of further corruption so that no more demons populate the Earth. To do that, certain rules must be put into place that no family can overturn." She paced around the room with a smooth, graceful glide, balancing a tiny cup on a saucer.

"If a Cambion suffers the loss of his mate, or is even rumored to overindulge in feeding, he is to be reported and observed by his appointed leader. If he is suspected of converting to his demon counterpart, he is to be executed. Simple as that." Angie's gaze stopped on every male in the room as she spoke. The brothers bowed their heads, like misbehaved boys sitting in the principal's office.

"As a law, those who know that such a Cambion is on the brink of transformation and failed to report it must be punished as well. The method varies with every region, but it usually leads to death. Not only was your father a convert, but he murdered the heir of one of those head families. This is a capital offense."

I wasn't sure why I raised my hand like class was in session—it was just reflex. "This may sound harsh, but it was your daughter Nathan Ross killed, not theirs. If anyone, you should be the one to convict the brothers."

She offered me a look a mother would wear when her kid said something cute. "It is a matter of principle and reputation. The offense occurred on Santiago territory, and having a rogue Cambion right under their nose makes them appear incompetent to the other families, not only in this country, but those around the world. Their title could be challenged if they show weakness."

"Why do the other families have to know? Can't you just cover it up by saying it was a freak accident?" I asked.

"Sam, you have no idea how notorious the Petrovskys are in the Cambion circuit. They're the historians, holding one of the oldest records of our existence," Haden explained. "Word of Nadine's death went global. All eyes are on America, and they're hoping to see blood spilt."

"Well, Nathan Ross is dead. There's your blood," I replied.

"That would be enough if Caleb were not under investigation. The Santiagos feel his feeding habits will become a similar problem in the future. Since Caleb is American, born under their territory, he is of special interest," Angie said. "As the oldest, Broderick has gone to New York and offered to intercede on your behalf."

"You mean take my place at the guillotine," Caleb said.

"We can only hope it doesn't come to that. But the deaths reported in this state have put quite a stain on their reputation," Angie said grimly.

"Are you serious? They could kill Caleb just to save face? They can't do that!" I cried. "This is illegal! These guys are going to jail for murder."

"Secular law doesn't apply to Cambion dealings, Sam. The family has their hands in every position of office. If they want someone to disappear, they disappear. It wouldn't be the first time," Haden intoned.

"This isn't fair!" I slammed my cup on the table. "I will blow the lid on this whole thing before they kill an innocent man. I will go to every news station and expose them."

"And tell them what?" Michael jumped in. "That incubi and succubi exist? Most people don't even know what a Cambion is, Sam."

"There's gotta be a way to stop this."

"There is no need to be upset just yet. This is only an inquiry," Angie chimed in. "Their primary concern is Caleb, but killing a Cambion's mate is forbidden under any circumstance. Your bonding will overthrow the ruling based on a technicality." After taking a dainty sip of her tea, Angie's gaze settled on me. "Now that that is established, I think it's time to discuss the extent of your relationship."

I suddenly grew fascinated with the shadows on the floor. "Angie, I think that's a little too personal."

"That may be so, but your decision could determine how this investigation will end."

Once again, it all boiled down to the big to-do. Our bonding was inevitable, but I was hoping for something romantic and a lot more private. This may not be a big deal for anyone else, but I was the only inexperienced person in the room, and to put it mildly, I was terrified. But if it meant that no one else had to die, I was willing to take one for the team.

Caleb, unfortunately, had other ideas. "No," he growled. "We've already been over this. If we bond and something happens to me, Sam will die too."

"How about we cross that bridge when we get there," Haden disputed. "Why don't you think about someone else for a change?"

"I am!" Caleb bellowed. "I will not be pressured into something that might not even work. Our personal lives shouldn't be up for public debate. It's bad enough that I have to cater to a demon spirit, now I have to be told who I should—" He pursed his lips and breathed through his nose, quelling his temper. "First my free will, then my privacy. Is there anything that belongs to me? I'll control my own life." Caleb rose from the chaise and headed to the door.

"Caleb, if you don't wish for that life to end tonight, I suggest you sit down. Now," Angie called after him, her eyes glowing with blazing emerald light at Caleb's back.

He stopped abruptly. In that same instant, a sharp pain hit my chest, a strike of panic that left me breathless.

Haden and Michael got to their feet slowly, taking care not to make any sudden movements. The two studied Angie keenly, their bodies tensed, ready to jump into the line of fire if necessary.

Caleb spun around and met Angie in defiance, but quickly turned away with evident pain. His gaze met the floor, blinking rapidly, struggling for sight.

Not daring to look her in the face again, he said in a shaky voice, "If you kill me, you'll just be doing Tobias a favor. Am I the only one who remembers him? He's also connected to Sam. I'm sure the Santiago family would love to hear that a demon could be an heir to the Petrovsky dynasty." Keeping his head low, he left the room, letting the door slam behind him.

Angie closed her eyes and massaged the bridge of her nose, conjuring composure. Michael and Haden glared at me as if this was all my fault.

"We should go after him." I began to rise, but Angie lifted her hand to stop me.

"No. I need to speak with you alone, Samara. Michael, Haden, please keep an eye on your brother. Make sure he doesn't leave his room for the rest of the night."

The brothers backed out of the room, only turning away when they reached the door.

The study went quiet again with only the cracking of firewood to break the monotony. I too had trouble looking at her at the moment, so I played with my hands, picking at the hangnail on the right thumb. "Caleb has a point, you know. The powers that be won't be too happy about Tobias."

"Yes, which is why they will not be told, not until you and Caleb are mated."

"You think that's why Nadine didn't tell you about Tobias? She was afraid how you would react? I mean, she was mated to an incubus, her sworn enemy. He might've tricked her or she did it willingly—I don't know—but Tobias and Lilith are connected now."

"What a tangled mess, little one. I'm so sorry you were left with this burden. Had I known . . ." She covered her face with her hand, pushed back the tears that tried to escape. "When was the last time you saw him?"

I told her everything that had occurred in the past week, from my blackout, Tobias's disappearance, to the intruder in my house. The last straw came when I showed her my bracelet and the severed chain covered in duct tape. I'd been using different tools to hold the link together—paper clips, hair barrettes, rubber bands—but they would rust or slip off in the shower.

Angie wasn't the swearing type. It was bad etiquette.

But she seemed to be making up for lost time in the span of two minutes. Once her tirade was over, she moved to the fireplace and retrieved a small, flat box and a lighter from behind a vase on the mantel. With a flick of her wrist, a cigarette settled between her fingers.

"You promised me you'd quit," I mumbled.

"Did I?" She lit the end and took a drag.

After thinking about it, I realized she was right. "No. You didn't promise me. You promised Nadine."

"Yes, well it's only a recent lapse. Suffice it to say, it's been a very stressful month." Her free hand stroked my hair. "Gets a bit confusing up there, doesn't it? It's hard to tell where Nadine ends and you begin."

"Sometimes."

"And your feelings for Tobias are conflicted, yes?"

"Not just Tobias, Caleb, too," I answered.

She nodded and took another deep pull of smoke. The cherry at the end of the cigarette glowed bright and ran in close competition with the fire in her eyes. "Caleb is hurting. Don't take it personally. Despite everything that may be happening, he loves you."

"What makes you so sure?"

"Don't you feel it? It's all over this room as thick as fog. It's all over the furniture, seasoning the food at dinner. I understand that he doesn't like to be pressured, but what is your reason for not sealing the bond? You two can finally be together, and this would solve all of your problems."

"And create new ones," I disputed. "I don't think I'm ready for that step. I'm pretty messed up in the head. My parents had me when they were still in high school and I don't want one careless act to ruin my life. I get where Caleb's coming from, the need for control, and these . . . *things* in our bodies are fighting us at every turn."

She was quiet for several excruciating moments, and

even in heavy concentration, she looked stunning. She circled the room again before she put out her cigarette and sat next to me. "Do you know the real reason why my husband is ill? Because I'm slowly killing him."

I hadn't expected that at all, and the light, conversational tone made it more disturbing. "What?"

"He's not like us, but we are linked and my spirit requires that I feed from him regularly. He brings me so much joy, Samara, I could simply burst. But he's getting older and doesn't replenish his energy as quickly as he used to. His immune system suffers because of it and he will worsen as the years go on. And when he dies . . ."

"Your spirit will go through withdrawal and you may go insane," I finished. "But didn't you say that those who lose a mate have to be reported? Does that mean you might be killed?"

Her silence answered that question for me. "Do you see how fortunate you are? You and Caleb are both Cambions, equals who can bond completely. There is a mutual exchange where you strengthen one another."

"If we don't kill each other first," I mumbled.

There went that motherly smile again. "You are in love. You are going to fight and pester each other. It's a certainty. But the connection you share, even now, will help you survive where others would have died. My husband and I are not as fortunate and I must prepare for his passing, which is why I need to make sure my family is in order. There must be someone to lead the Petrovsky name and guide my daughters."

"What about Olivia?"

"She will be appointed if you refuse the title. But if you refuse, you and Caleb won't have my name as protection and you will be back where you started."

"Great." I needed another heavy responsibility on my shoulders, I really did.

"This is why I've come to see you, to explain what is in store for you," she continued. "Your bonding with Caleb is one of many concerns."

"Yeah, about that . . ." I began, fighting the sudden nausea. "Doesn't our empathic link count for anything in all of this? Caleb's drink had been spiked with olive oil on Halloween, and he wound up in a coma for a month. We may not be bonded, but the link that we share almost drove me insane. As far as I'm concerned, we're already screwed—no pun intended."

"I've considered that." Angie nodded. "Cambions rarely mate with other Cambions and when they do, it's done immediately. The link you and Caleb share was meant to be a temporary phase, in the way an engagement precedes a wedding. How you've held back for this long is remarkable, given what we are, what's in our nature. Which makes sense that the family believes that you and Caleb are already bonded, and who are we to make them believe otherwise?" she said.

I stared at her sly expression, weighing what she implied, but even more so to what she didn't say. "You mean you made them *believe* that we were? So basically we just fake it until we make it."

"These are very unusual circumstances that never had to be addressed before. Lilith is a mature spirit trapped in a child's body, and you are too young to make a decision so permanent. This is the best option for you right now."

"How will they know if we're not lying? Is there a test? A secret handshake?" I asked.

"Not likely if there are those who can attest for you, someone they trust to give a sound witness."

It took me a second to catch on. "Ruiz," I said.

She nodded. "He reports everything to them. If you can convince him that you are bonded, there will be no reason for further investigation," she said. "Allow the detective to observe you together as often as possible. Once he is convinced that you are a bound pair, he will report it and the family will have no choice but to close the issue."

I shook my head, dumbstruck. "How on earth will I pull that off?"

"Be creative. I trust your judgment on this." Angie winked.

"What about Tobias?" I asked, afraid to know the answer. Whatever it was, it was going to be bad for all of us, but I had to know what I was up against.

"Quite simple, little one," she began with a gentle smile, her words honey sweet laced with poison. "The demon must die."

After I left the hotel, I drove around for a while to clear my head, because Angie's words kept scrambling my thoughts.

"The demon must die. The demon must die."

The phrase played over and over, the repetition digging grooves into my brain. I didn't want Tobias to die, not if it meant Caleb and I would go with him. My concern was entirely selfish and I was completely comfortable with that. Though I was sure Tobias could survive just about anything, I still needed to find him before Angie did.

I took the city tour through Tobias's path of destruction, the demon walk of ill-fame, as it were. I cruised past my house, my school, Merchant's Square where Tobias took me to feed, then I finally parked in front of Caleb's townhouse, which was under construction. Apart from the blue tarp covering the roof and the boarded windows, the outside looked fine. Most of the damage was inside, and it had to be gutted and renovated.

Whether it was a woman or a solid building, nothing

was left standing after Tobias was done with it. I doubted he would have the nerve to show up in Caleb's neighborhood again, so I ventured to my next destination.

The spray bottle of olive oil that I always kept in my bag now rested on my lap, just in case he decided on another sneak attack. And as always, Lilith worried my spine, in full knowledge of the damage anointing oil could cause. Caleb almost died when a few drops were slipped into his drink at Courtney B.'s Halloween party. Naturally, Lilith would fear for my own safety, and as far as she was concerned I was a child playing with matches.

Staring out to the road, I remembered the costume party all those lifetimes ago. What I would give to go back to a time where a party was just a party, and not a prelude to tragedy. I remembered my green fairy wings, the candy apple on my head and Caleb's nifty trick with his bow and arrow. Then I recalled the masked man on the dance floor who I now knew was Tobias. I followed him around the party, just as mindless and desperate to reach him as I was now.

All thoughts led back to him, and I had to admit, he was a beautiful distraction as well as a despised habit. Even in thought, he wouldn't leave me alone, and Lilith's flaky behavior only aggravated this rash. I wouldn't give up the search for him and there was one last spot that I hadn't checked.

The Colonial Parkway was the one place you didn't travel after dark unless surviving the dawn just wasn't your thing. The unsolved murders over the years made the parkway notorious throughout Williamsburg, but only the stony path and ancient forest edging its border knew the real story. Of course, this was the route I chose to take, the path of truth.

With high beams glaring, I scanned the road for any sign of wreckage, though the police had cleaned up the area by now. Thirty minutes into my search, I found shiny fragments of glass on the road. I slowed my speed and found more debris ahead—some shards of metal, a small piece of rubber, but there was no crash site. I was about to give up when I caught something bright and colorful on the right shoulder.

I was alone on the road, so I put the car in reverse and parked right next to the marked point. On closer inspection, I noticed that there were old flowers, candles, and personal notes grouped in a neat little pile. No doubt Malik's friends and loved ones had visited this spot before me. I didn't bother reading the thoughtful words on the weather-beaten sheets of poster board; I knew they would all say the same thing and I had enough guilt riding on my back.

I grabbed my bag and climbed out of the car, keeping my eyes peeled for anything out of the ordinary. Despite the dictates of common sense, a strange boldness guided my steps. No one could truly hurt me without feeling Lilith's wrath. No one *human,* anyway.

I strolled a few yards from the crash site and found ridges of dirt bulging up through the stripped grass. Tire marks had molded their print in the cold mud. There were no skid marks on the actual road, but if there were, it would likely follow the same arcing path the mud tracks made toward the ditch.

Going into detective mode, I tried to replay the scene. Maybe something jumped out, making the truck swerve to the right. It could have been a deer. They were pretty crazy around here. I moved farther down, my heart pounding with excitement as I searched for the next clue. I walked until there was no more glass and the trail went cold.

"It must have happened here," I said to the glittery concrete. "Tobias, what happened to you?"

I listened for movement, any odd shift of leaves, or the presence of anything alive. Roaming possums and raccoons were my only company, the moonlight reflecting in their eyes in a sinister glow. It appeared that even *they* knew I shouldn't be on the parkway at night. As I went back toward my car, I noticed that one particular light was too big and too bright to come from an animal.

I squinted my eyes, following the light as it moved through the trees in a sweeping motion. It drifted low to the ground, swinging from side to side then swooping up the trees. They weren't eyes at all. It was a flashlight.

There were no houses in this area, and there were no other cars on this road from what I could see, but it was clear I wasn't the only one here looking for something. Suddenly the light went out and I could hear something moving closer, the snapping of twigs and the crunch of dry leaves. I stood motionless, powerless as another noise carried on the breeze. It was an unusual sound for wind, not quite a howl but a sharp whine of an injured animal.

As soon as it began, it stopped.

Had I imagined it? Fear tended to play tricks on the mind, but I was clear headed enough to know I wasn't alone here. And if paranoia served me correctly, I was being watched. I could feel the deep penetrating stare of something dangerous and hungry. I felt the stare before I saw the dark figure through the trees. It reminded me of a bird of prey, the way it perched on a branch, guarding its home from invasion.

A crawling sensation ran up my back and I jumped and looked behind me. When I saw no one there, I felt stupid for not remembering Lilith was around. She was always around, all-seeing all-knowing, and forever irking my nerves. To my surprise, she wasn't afraid. If anything, she seemed conflicted and a little sad, unsure whether to stay or leave. So I made the choice for her.

Reason finally arrived, and I almost broke into a run to my car. I didn't look to see if the thing was following me. Past experiences taught me to never, ever look back.

Approaching headlights forced me to abandon the main path and walk on the shoulder. I reached my car, jumped in, and locked the door behind me as the car pulled alongside mine.

The tinted window slid down and a dark head leaned in from the driver's side. It would probably be the only time in my life that I would ever be glad to see the detective.

"Samara?" Ruiz called. "Is that you? What the hell are you doing out here this time of night?"

I took my time rolling down my window, thinking of a good excuse. Then I remembered the flowers by the ditch. "A classmate of mine wrecked his car here and I just wanted to pay my respects." I pointed to the flowers and candles on the road.

"You couldn't do this in the daytime? Does your mother know you're out here?" he asked.

Uh oh, not the mother card. "It's not that late. What are *you* doing out here?" I asked, trying to get him off the topic. The last thing I needed was him ratting me out.

"Have you seen Haden or Michael Ross? I saw them come this way, but I lost them."

They were on the parkway too? Was this a Cambion rest stop? "No. Haven't seen them," I said.

He leaned in, his expression hard and brooked no nonsense. "If you're trying to protect them from something, don't. They are in enough trouble as it is, and running off like this is only going to make it worse."

"I haven't seen them, I swear!" I said. "Last time I saw them, they were back at the hotel. Have you checked the bars in the area?"

"Yeah. They do like their alcohol. It's a bit out of the

way just for a drink, though," he said more to himself then to me. "You should get home, Samara. This isn't a good place for you to be alone. I've heard stories about this area." He looked around the woods. "I'm sorry about your friend. How did he die?"

"Uh, not sure. When the police find his body, I'll let you know. They only found his truck." I started the engine and took one last look to the woods to where I saw the strange figure. Of course it was gone—creepy things always left the scene when other people were around just so you would look crazy. But I knew what I saw, and I knew it had to be another piece to the puzzle. I just wished I knew what it meant, and I wasn't brave enough to find out tonight.

"Yeah, it's not safe out here at all," I said to myself.

9

It was a ridiculously cold Friday, partly cloudy with a high chance of mortification.

One of those days when your pillows started talking, bargaining with you to stay. *Fifteen minutes, ten more minutes, just five more minutes.* School let out yesterday for holiday break, so I didn't bother to set my alarm and even with the extra three hours, I had to peel myself out of bed.

I didn't get much sleep last night for two reasons. One was that I stayed up watching Christmas specials with Mom. It was our tradition and the year couldn't end without viewing commercialized cheer. And on those rare occasions when the planets aligned, the great trifecta of holiday cinema would show in the same day: *It's a Wonderful Life*, *A Christmas Story*, and *National Lampoon's Christmas Vacation*. Mom saw it as a sign of good luck for the new year, but I wasn't holding my breath.

The second reason for my fatigue was what I'd like to

call "naughty sleep deficiency." Real talk, was it normal to have vivid, raunchy, X-rated dreams about your boyfriend? Five nights in a row? I knew girls had fantasies about getting married or going to the prom, or being swept away by some guy on a white horse trotting all sexylike along the beach. But my nocturnal experience was straight scramble porn nasty. I wasn't sure I could look at Caleb in the eye after what I'd seen, which was unfortunate because I had to see him at work today.

I had no doubt Lilith was giving off some subliminal vibes. She'd done it before with Tobias, but now Caleb was the star of the show and the imagery had never been this hard-core, never this real. I would wake up in a cold sweat with half the sheets on the floor, and I could swear on a stack of Bibles that he was in the room with me. Lilith was pulling out all the stops to get her point across, and she wouldn't let me rest until she got a slice of some Cake Boy.

In addition to the skinamax movie that played in my head, my waking hours were no better. I was getting it from all angles—home, school, and work. The paranormal world bled into my everyday life, its virus infecting everyone I knew.

In summation, Mom was losing sleep and had to up her meds, Dad kept calling me every day in order to guilt-trip me into getting therapy, Ruiz kicked his stalking duties into overdrive, and Tobias was on the warpath and his whereabouts remained unknown.

Lilith wouldn't talk about my blackout and kept jabbing my back whenever I broached the issue. Angie was chain smoking and conducting lengthy conference calls behind closed doors. Michael and Haden kept slipping from under Ruiz's radar and disappearing for hours at a time for "beer runs."

Dougie had become a gigolo overnight by dating five

girls in one week. Mia still refused to talk to me in class, Caleb was still acting shady, and Malik Davis was still dead and kinda missing.

But all that had been put on pause for one grand announcement.

Robbie Ford was back in town.

It began with a text that I got while getting dressed for work.

ROBBIE: Yo Sammy! Off for Xmas break. Tell Ur boy to call me ASAP. New Year's party @ my house. Be there. Clothing optional. :p

Robbie was an evil genius in every respect—the Brain with no Pinky—and voted most likely to blow up the planet with one stroke of the keyboard. He just finished his first semester at MIT, but according to his spastic e-mails, college wasn't all it was cracked up to be. I guess he figured a little drunken debauchery would do everyone some good, and I couldn't agree more. Robbie's parties were what made the world go round, and it boosted my ego to be one of the first to know about it. But his direct correspondence might've had to do with Caleb and his musical expertise. With Caleb as the deejay, it was bound to be the jump-off of the season.

Having an idea in mind, I texted Mia. If anything could get her to open up, a kick-ass party would.

ME: ROBBIE FORD NEW YEARS PARTY! COME WITH ME!!

I waited for her to reply while eating a bowl of cereal. Draining the bowl, I almost choked when I saw her message.

MIA: OMG! What R U gonna wear?

I started break dancing in the middle of the kitchen—no joke. The line of communication had been opened. It was a step in the right direction and I would take what I could get at the moment. I was going to get my friend back no matter what it took.

After texting back that I had no idea what to wear, I grabbed my coat and bag by the door, busting a move the whole time. I could already hear the bass pumping through the speakers, feel the sweaty bodies on the dance floor, and savor the freedom of not thinking, just for one night. This small glimmer of hope put a much-appreciated spring in my step.

That was until I opened the front door.

"What the . . . ?" I gaped at the blonde standing on my porch.

Olivia turned around and faced me. She appeared to be in mourning, wearing a black funeral dress and a permanent frown.

"Hello, Samara. I'm glad I caught you before you left. I plan to join you today," she said, all droopy-eyed and taciturn.

I stood frozen in place, still holding the door. "Join-what-where?"

"Mama is occupied with business. Mishka and Szymon are annoying. I'm bored, and I want to accompany you to work, as a guest, of course."

"Good lord, why? I don't even wanna go."

"I'm curious and this would be a good way to get to know each other. It doesn't seem fair that you know so much about me where I know virtually nothing about you. I would like to explore and see how the other half lives."

"You mean slumming?" I rephrased.

"More like broadening my horizons," she corrected.

I regarded the seven-foot wall in the expensive suit

standing next to her. He reminded me of a German gym-nast action hero on steroids with his buzz cut, square face, and cold blue eyes. "Who's this guy? He looks vaguely familiar."

"This is Gunner. He's my driver and personal guard. Pay no attention to him."

Was she kidding me? The guy was as wide as my door. I thought Haden looked intimidating with all his scars and bulk, but this guy looked like he ate Haden. "There's no way he can come to my job. He's too obvious. People will think he's Secret Service or a hit man or something."

"We must have a guard with us at all times, especially while in this country. You won't even notice him, I promise. The bookstore opens at ten, yes?"

"Doesn't matter 'cause you're not coming with me." I stepped out onto the porch.

"What's going on?" Mom yawned on her way down the stairs, wearing a fuzzy bathrobe and a night mask on top of her head. After rubbing her eyes, she screamed on sight of Nadine's clone at the door. "Holy crap! Is that a ghost?"

"No, Mom. It's Nadine's little sister," I answered. In all fairness, "clone" wasn't a precise description, because unlike Nadine, Olivia actually knew how to smile, and did so with relish as she poked her head inside to address Mom. She also spoke better English than Nadine did; I just didn't like what she had to say with that vocabulary.

"It is nice to meet you, Ms. Marshall. I'm Olivia Petrov-sky. I was hoping to accompany Samara to work today."

"Oh. How exciting. Come on in." Mom motioned for our guests to enter, then tipped her head to the heavy for hire. "What about Tony Boom Boom over here? Is he go-ing, too?"

"Yes, he has been instructed to keep watch over Sa-mara as well," Olivia explained.

"Well, that's nice. Isn't that nice, honey?" Mom asked me.

"No. No it's not. I have enough drama going on and you want me to add more to the mix? She's a—" I lowered my voice so the bodyguard couldn't hear. "She's a Cambion, Mom, and she's pretty, and she's mean. That's a triple-threat. She's gonna get her butt kicked, or worse, she'll get me fired. I've got enough on my plate as it is."

"Samara, it's only for a day and this would be a great way for the two of you to connect. You are Cambion siblings now." Mom tried to reason, but I wasn't having it.

I glanced at Olivia, who spoke to her watchdog by the door. I noted their body language: their closeness, the assuring touches on the arm and shoulder and the immersed stares between one another. It was very intimate given the two-decade age difference, but I didn't feel any seedy vibes, so a quick call to the police wouldn't be necessary. It seemed more of a form of communication, a language of hands and eyes only they could understand; something animals would do.

Catching me staring, Olivia tossed her Pantene Pro-V hair over her shoulder and gave a smile that no sane person should ever trust.

"Oh, hell no!" I yelled then turned to Mom. "We can hang out when I get off work or maybe even tomorrow, but there is no way—*no way*—she's coming with me to work!"

"That is so freaky. She looks just like her." Alicia stared in a trance while letting the blender whirl at high speed with no lid.

"I know. If you think that's bad, you should see her mom," I replied as I wiped up the mess she made on the counter. It was weird seeing the exact replica of a dead co-worker roaming around, but Alicia handled this poltergeist better than most.

Olivia had reached celebrity status in a matter of hours, which made for some hateful looks from female shoppers. She strolled the aisles, scared half the employees into the next life, and turned the heads of every male in the bookstore. Gunner hadn't even tried to be subtle while doing recon on the area. One high point was that none of the customers harassed me, except to ask for Olivia's number.

I was so not feeling the holiday cheer. The Colonial actors in their eighteenth century garb singing carols outside only solidified my bad mood. Between songs, a few would come in for hot drinks, and I became the Scrooge to their Dickens' story. To accent the shame to this misadventure, all the employees had to wear stupid Santa hats for the rest of the week.

Aside from the Colonial weirdoes, there wasn't much as far as entertainment in town, especially if you didn't have a car. So it came as no shock that half the kids I went to school with haunted the shopping center and movie theaters. It could have been the holiday sales or boredom, but it seemed that everyone decided to stop by the store today. It was like they could smell fresh meat.

Holding a stack of books in her hand, Olivia approached the counter. "I would like to buy these. And a latté and scone please," she said with a wicked smirk, knowing that I was obligated to do her bidding.

I rushed to make the drink, but Alicia was already on the job, leaving me to ring up Olivia's order and make small talk. "You know there are cashiers in the front of the store."

"Yes, but I can only purchase coffee here." She surveyed the busy atmosphere. "Cuppa-Joe. Interesting name. My sister really enjoyed working here. Not sure why she would make the choice to work, but she liked her independence."

Since no one else was in line, I snuck a peek at her reading selection, seeking some hint of humanity. I saw the familiar font of one of the books in the middle of the pile, and for the first time in recorded history, I was glad to see it. Making sure Alicia was out of earshot, I asked, "So, you like *Specter*?"

"Is this your attempt to relate to me?" she asked.

"Maybe. How's it working?"

"Not in your favor. Nice hat, by the way. Real politically correct," she commented. "If you must know, it's not for me. I'm buying the book for Mishka. She loves the series and she won't stop talking about it."

"What about you?" I asked.

"Lame. They portray ghosts wrong," she replied. "Ghosts are demons that impersonate the dead, not the lingering souls of the dead. Demons are imposters of the living."

"Interesting theory." Especially since she owned a demon and everyone around here thought she was Nadine's ghost. I examined the other books in her pile and stopped at a thick volume at the bottom. "*The Complete Works of William Shakespeare*. Wow." I took the book and thumbed through the pages. "I take it you're into Shakespeare?"

She shrugged. "Who isn't?"

"You'd be surprised. Some people only go as far as the high school requirement: *Romeo and Juliet*, *Macbeth*, *Hamlet*. They never get to the good stuff. Sometimes, I start talking Elizabethan for no reason." I chuckled to myself and scanned the bar code of the book.

"This sounds like a symptom of schizophrenia. If I'm not mistaken, there are psychology and mental illness books on the third aisle if you need a diagnosis."

Ignoring the dig, I asked, "What's your favorite play?"

"Titus Andromedus. Read it?"

I nodded in approval of her choice. I knew the play and it was by far one of the most eff'd up stories this side of Sweeney Todd—human meat pies and all. Evidently, Nadine's love for all things tragic and macabre ran in the family. Case in point: the book in Olivia's hand. I tilted my head sideways to read the title.

" '*I (Heart) You, Stab Stab*'. What's with you kids these days?"

"It's an interesting read. It's about this boy who's an outcast because his father is a serial killer who will soon be executed. The boy is teased at school, so he decides to take up the family trade. He's really good at it, very clever how he dispatches the popular kids that bullied him and not get caught. He meets a depressed girl who tries to kill herself and he saves her, which was strange since he followed her to kill her anyway."

"So, it's like, '*You're so pathetic, I don't have the heart to kill you now, so let's go out*,' " I summarized, then scanned the book.

Olivia nodded. "When she discovers his 'hobby,' she refuses to leave him. It's disgusting how she fawns over the killer just because he's cute and watches her. Even if she didn't know his crimes, his father's past should be enough to keep her away, don't you think, *Samara*?"

I had a feeling we weren't talking about the book anymore. The story line ran too close to Caleb and his family's past. I knew Olivia was bitter, and had every right to be, but she didn't know the whole truth. Her sister wasn't a saint and had some nasty skeletons in her closet, one by the name of Tobias.

Once the transaction was over, she collected her items then said, "I'll let you know how it ends; though I'm sure it won't be a happy ending." With a parting smirk, she drifted to a quiet corner of the café, completely oblivious of the father of three who tripped over his youngest child to check her out.

It was hard not to be paranoid with people watching you at every turn. If it wasn't Gunner patrolling around the cafe, it was Detective Ruiz prowling the aisles making sure Caleb was minding his p's and q's. Did anyone have a life in this town?

I couldn't wait for my break to come around, and when it did, the break room became my place of refuge. Caleb sat at the folding table with one earphone stuffed in his ear. His mandatory elf hat and a bag of Hershey's Kisses lay on the table next to him. He scrolled down the eight gigs of music on his phone with one hand while he jotted notes with the other. I assumed Robbie Ford had contacted him about the party and he was organizing a new playlist.

I hadn't expected him to be in the break room. In fact, I'd been avoiding him all day, trying not to imagine him naked, soaking wet, or covered in some dessert topping. I shook my head and concentrated on more constructive thoughts. I needed to focus and find a way to get Caleb to open up, just enough to get the ball rolling, because frankly, I had better communication with my toothbrush.

Caleb still refused to talk about any Cambion-related business, not the bonding, the inquisition, or the possibility of war being waged because of him.

"When the time comes, I'll do what I gotta do, even if that means siccing Capone on everyone in the room. I won't lose anyone else close to me, and no one will die because of me," was all he had to say on the matter. And that was three days ago.

It could be just me, but that sounded an awful lot like a suicide note, which did little for my sleep pattern for the past few nights. Though Caleb tried to be slick about it, I'd also noticed he was feeding more—three, sometimes four women a day—storing up reserves for the Battle Royale that I wanted to prevent. As much as I sympathized with his hurt, we needed to work this out together. Using brute force with him wasn't gonna cut it—I'd tried that already—so I needed a new tactic. Seduction.

The next fifteen minutes consisted of short answers and little to no eye contact from his end. I tried the "oops! I dropped something, so watch my butt while I pick it up" method. I tried the "I'm leaning over the table, so look down my shirt" approach. And my all-time favorite, the "watch me shake loose my hair and put on lip gloss really slowly" routine.

Alas, I'd picked the wrong time to flirt. Music was Caleb's grand passion and it was nearly impossible to pull him out of the creative zone. It was hard trying to act sexy with coffee and dried milk on my shirt anyway. Before I could think of my next move, he shot from his seat and gathered his stuff, including the candy.

"My break's over. Catch you later, Sam."

"I dreamt about you last night," I blurted out. I had no idea why I said that—I just panicked.

He held the door open and looked at me. With a smile that could melt butter, he said, "I dream about you *every* night."

There it was: that flutter in my stomach, the giddiness, and the reminder of where we stood. I wasn't clingy, I wasn't a bugaboo, and I believed in boundaries. I didn't want to be with Caleb every waking moment, but I needed to know that we were still okay. No matter how screwed up our situation was, our feelings for each other hadn't changed. Stability. Right now, in this moment, that was enough.

His smile deflated when he turned to leave and saw

Ruiz leaning against the wall in the hallway. The man clearly had too much time on his hands. He wasn't trying to hide it anymore—he was on Caleb's ass like a pair of drawers. Something had to be done, and done fast. I just wasn't sure what. Besides, I was too busy swooning over the lonely quarter that Caleb had set right in front of me when I wasn't looking.

Just when I thought my shift couldn't get any worse, I returned to the café and found Dougie sitting backward in a chair next to Olivia.

When he spotted me, he hiked his chin. "Sup, SNM. Just talking to Olivia here. I didn't know Nadine had a sister."

"Yeah, small world," I mumbled, holding on to my freak out until I was behind the counter.

I couldn't believe this. Of all the boys she could have in town, she found the one with the warning label appealing. Technically, since Mia and Dougie were on permanent hiatus, I had no right to say anything. And if I told Olivia to back off she would pursue him harder, because hateful harpies do that. I didn't like how they were staring at each other, like they were the only two people in the room. Dougie was instantly under her spell and I couldn't let him get sucked into my world.

Under the pretense of cleaning off the café tables, I passed the two every few minutes. Olivia sat with her legs crossed, her slender fingers picking at her half-eaten scone as she read her novel.

Dougie didn't seem at all deterred by her reading, or find her pet gorilla sitting behind them intimidating. Dude was just that thirsty. "Listen, how long are you gonna be in town?" he asked.

She tapped her lips with her finger, in coy contemplation. "Until the new year. Why?"

"Oh. Cool. You going to the New Year's party?" he asked.

"How'd you hear about the New Year's party?" I cut in, all attempt of pretending to work gone.

Not taking his eyes off his prey, Dougie reached in his pocket and pulled out his phone. In seconds, Jason Lao's blog appeared on the screen with the words in jumbo print: WIN A FREE INVITE TO NEW YEAR'S BASH. Retweet hashtag #RobbieFordVA

So much for being exclusive.

"So if you're still around, it'll be cool if you stop by. His parties are off the chain," he said to Olivia.

"Sounds fun." She smiled and bit her lip.

"Well now, don't let us keep you from your busy social life. Aren't you working on girlfriend number six?" I asked, totally messing up his game.

"I'm not dating anyone. I'm not trying to be tied down, though the pickings are easy these days."

"Really?" I asked.

He ripped his hungry stare from Olivia long enough to look at me. "Yeah, the girls around here are pretty hung up over Malik being gone. All a guy has to do is be a shoulder to cry on, tell a sob story about him, and bam, you're in there. Not that I need to stoop so low. That's just for those who can't get a girl, namsayin'?" He stroked the fuzz on his chin and winked at Olivia, who giggled at his antics.

"Smooth, Douglas, real smooth." I rolled my eyes then grabbed a stack of magazines that needed to be re-shelved. Why was Dougie even in the bookstore? I was still suspicious of whether the kid knew how to read, and the only reason he would ever drop by was when he was looking for . . .

"Mia! Hey! What are you doing here?" I said; really

loud and overly chipper as I blocked her path to Olivia's table. It did little good. I was too small and the café was too spacious.

"Same reason everybody else is here. I was looking for an outfit for the party before everything's gone and doing a little Christmas shopping," Mia explained, then leaned her head to look around me. "I texted you that I'd stop by for . . . some . . . coff . . . am I interrupting something?" Mia's stare bounced between Olivia and Dougie with suspicion.

"Yes," Dougie said and turned his chair so his back faced her. Of all the years I'd known Dougie he'd never been this rude to Mia, and I was sure that if Olivia weren't in the vicinity, he would have a different attitude.

But I never got to find out, because Mia rushed to the front of the store, taking any hope of reconciliation right along with her. I didn't ignore the look she gave me, like the whole scenario was my fault, because it *was* my fault.

These demon-Cambion whatevers were ruining my life and everything that made up that life was collapsing under the weight of secrecy. Whether by falsehood or omission, dishonesty was still in play. Dishonesty was the symptom of cowardice, and I was no punk. I was past sick and tired, I was beyond fed up, and I refused to go into the new year hauling all this baggage. I was going to sort my life out even if it killed me. Just not right now, not with so many of my own questions unanswered. Right now, I would stick to the lesson of the *Origin Tale*: when dealing with malevolent spirits, keep your mouth shut.

10

The Christmas holiday was pretty tame considering it was spent with my family.

Mom and I started early with the rounds, first Christmas mass with Grandpa Marshall, then breakfast at his house and the most boring conversation in the history of human language.

Grandpa was not the old fat guy with the white beard that I had in mind, and his evil lair was as far from the North Pole as you could get. In fact, since he had the heat cranked up pretty high, it felt more like hell than anywhere else. Though huge and surrounded by acres of land, Casa de Marshall was as personable as a mausoleum, and there was no television in sight. But Grandpa had insisted on seeing both of us regularly before he died. That was his tagline now, the fact that he was going to die . . . eventually.

He also wanted to get to know me, and perhaps persuade me to seek electroshock treatment for my "condition." Being a mulatto half breed wasn't bad enough in his estimation, but waking up one day suddenly having green eyes was simply unacceptable.

I couldn't see how a few random meals could make up for seventeen years of his bigotry and neglect, but Mom decided to give it a go for her own peace of mind. I wasn't so keen on the idea, so I kept to myself for most of the visit, only speaking when spoken to.

After that, we doubled back to our house where we opened gifts with Dad's family, the Watkins clan, all forty of them. The house was packed, there was more food than I could eat in a lifetime, and I had a blast. Mom was born for the role of hostess and took pictures of *everything*.

Dad rolled up late as usual with his wife and my two half siblings. Though a scrooge 364 days out of the year, Dad turned into the biggest child Christmas day; bouncing around and waiting for us to open our presents. Once the preliminaries were over, the twins dove into the pile and shredded the wrappings with their teeth. Kyle and Kenya were bad as hell, but Dad miraculously overlooked their streaks of mayhem and spoiled them rotten. Not that I was jealous or anything, of course.

My stepmother, Rhonda was going for the Michelle Obama look these days, with a knee-length dress and a tan cardigan, and she might've pulled it off if she weren't so tactless. I've ditched days from school and had seen more class. She approached me in the kitchen and handed me an envelope. "Your father and I are tired of guessing your measurements *of the week*, so we figured gift cards would be the safest bet instead of clothes. Enjoy."

"Thanks," I said through clenched teeth and took the card. She sauntered away, leaving me reeling from her attack.

"I can't stand that bougie heifer. For the life of me, I

don't know why my boy married her. You wanna borrow my switchblade, baby?" Nana leaned in and whispered in my ear.

I smiled down at the plump, tiny woman digging into her enormous bra for a concealed weapon. I swear, that woman had everything tucked in there: money, car keys, candy, jumper cables, you name it.

"No thanks, Nana." I hugged her for her offer.

I never believed in soul mates, not even now with Caleb as my Siamese twin, but Nana was definitely mine. We even had the same white streak in our hair. It was the wisdom streak, as she would say, but I preferred to cover that wisdom with red hair dye.

Hallucinations and mental breakdowns weren't good around family gatherings, so the living room was a no-fly zone for me. I watched the festivities from the safety of the dining room and held my sister in my lap, at Lilith's request.

She had a bit of a soft spot for children and she seemed to have taken a particular shine to Kenya. For once, I felt perfectly fine with playing dolls and braiding hair, no doubt a product of Lilith's ticking biological clock. I could feel a low rumbling in my back, similar to when a cat purrs in contentment. I sensed the longing burning inside her, not just to mate, but to nurture. Not one day goes by where my roommate doesn't fascinate or infuriate me, and we seemed to have reached a temporary truce.

Keeping with my new resolution for a stress-free year, I considered Dad's offer to seek therapy long and hard. I pulled him aside, out of earshot of his meddlesome wife, and asked, "You mentioned a while back a doctor who deals with grief counseling and trauma?"

"Yes," he said hopefully, as if he'd been waiting for this conversation all day.

The words were hard to get out. Saying them meant defeat, that I really had a problem that couldn't be fixed on my own. I didn't like feeling weak and sickly, but in order to handle Lilith I had to get my head right. My methods weren't working and this kind of thing was better left to a professional before I broke something. "I don't know what good it'll do, but I'd like to see what he has to say. I'm not promising anything."

Dad let out a sigh of relief and pulled me into his arms for a bear hug. "Thank you, baby girl. I'll set up an appointment the first of the year."

Our last stop for the evening was the Charlotte Hotel where we had tea with Angie and her family. The Ross brothers were there, each wearing a ridiculous holiday sweater. Haden wore a black turtle neck with a yellow zigzag across the stomach—Charlie Brown style. Caleb wore a maroon eyesore with white snowflake patterns. Underneath his gray trench coat, Michael sported a striking green number with a giant reindeer and a blinking red nose.

"That's a lot of holiday cheer." Mom stood beside me in the foyer with gifts and a chocolate cake in hand. Before she could get into the room good, the wolves descended and in seconds the Ross boys had Mom surrounded. Ruiz, who at the time appeared to be in a heavy conversation with Angie, stepped forward and reached for my mom's hand. Captivated, Mom abandoned her baked goods to the hounds and joined his side.

Laying on the Latin charm, Ruiz kissed her hand. "Feliz Navidad," he said, the words rolling off his tongue in a low purr.

I wanted to gag from all the syrup saturating the room, and Mom, of course, ate up the attention. She deserved it, but damn, I wasn't trying to see all that, plus there were children present. She was falling hard for this guy—

I could feel the energy inflating around her in a bubble—and to my utter disgust, Ruiz's mood-cloud was even bigger.

Caleb came forward and pulled me into his arms. Thankful for the distraction, I observed the fashion victim from head to toe.

"Wow! Is it hot in here or is it just you?" I teased and fanned myself with my hand.

"No fighting today, Sam. I've got on my best Cosby sweater and I just wanna open some gifts, eat until I pass out, and kiss my girl under that mistletoe over there." He tilted his head to the greenery hanging over the entryway. "Is that cool with you?"

"The coolest." I took his hand and led him to the living room.

I gave Caleb the lowdown on Angie's plan to fake our bonding, and he seemed gung ho to try it. He pulled me into a not so private corner, giving Ruiz a peep show. When we saw him enter the bathroom, we deliberately planted ourselves by the door and made out. But all Ruiz did was roll his eyes, told us to get a room, and threatened to tell my mother, which put our antics to a halt for the time being.

After coffee and what was left of Mom's cake, it was gift time. The brothers gave Caleb a pair of silver daggers to add to his weapon collection. Angie gave me a gold bracelet to replace my old one. Unfortunately, Lilith's name was not engraved on this one. Both Ruiz and Angie got Mom some bling along with a bunch of crystal knick-knacks to clutter our house even more.

As the evening wound down, Angie spent most of her time joking with Mom. Olivia read one of her new books in her room, Szymon and Mishka played video games, and Michael, who was roaring drunk by eight o'clock, played poker with Haden. With everyone preoccupied, it left Caleb and me plenty of time to have some privacy. We crept inside the study and closed the door.

I sat on the oak desk and dangled a gift bag with my fingers. "All right, gimme gimme."

He leaned against the door and placed a hand over his heart, feigning innocence. "Oh, whatever do you mean?"

"Don't even try it, Mr. Baker. This is our first Christmas as a couple. There's no way you'd come here empty handed if you intend us to *remain* a couple. You pulled me in here for a reason. Gimme gimme." I held out my hand.

"You first," he said in a challenge. I didn't expect anything less from him. We were always going toe-to-toe, even in our affections, and now we were in competition on outgiving each other.

I handed him the bag, and you would think I'd bought him a new town house from his reaction.

"Oh wow! The Blood Empire DVD box set! I have season one on my computer, but I missed the last two seasons. Thanks, Sam." He cheered, bouncing up and down like a giddy toddler.

"You're welcome." I enjoyed his enthusiasm. The hours of searching online and the bidding wars for his gift were worth it just to see him smile. "I can't believe that's all you wanted for Christmas, more weapons and a crappy TV show collection."

"Blood Empire is not a crappy show," he said indignantly. "It's badass and made of awesome. Vampires in Ancient Rome. Demons and gladiators. Zombies and chariot races . . ."

"Excessive gore and gratuitous nudity," I finished.

"Hey, what do you expect? It's cable."

Shaking my head, I conceded to the inescapable fact that Caleb Baker, Cambion and chick-magnet extraordinaire, was a complete nerd. I've known this for a while now, but I figured if I ignored it, it didn't exist. Watching him drool over the poster that came with the box set, I knew there was no keeping that secret under wraps.

Before he decided to run and find the nearest television, I dropped him back down to earth. "My turn. Hand it over."

"All right, all right." He moved behind the desk and pulled out a wide, rectangular object under the chair. It was lumpy, and I could tell by how carefully Caleb placed the package on the desk it had some weight to it.

I scooted next to him and admired the shiny wrapper and big bow. I wanted to shake it, but Caleb was firmly against that idea.

"What is it?" I asked.

"A vacuum cleaner, so open it and get to work. You can start with your room," he replied.

I poked him with my elbow then began tearing at the wrapping. The gift was heavy, but fragile according to Caleb, so I peeled away the paper without disturbing the box.

Once all the wrapping was off the top, I stopped moving. I stopped breathing. I stopped blinking. When I could function again, I covered my mouth to hold back the sob from breaking loose, but the tears flowed freely.

Caleb stepped behind me and his hand held my waist, probably to keep me from fainting. "I had it specially ordered," he whispered; his lips a playful ghost tickling the shell of my ear and the column of my neck. "It took forever to get here, but it arrived just in time. It even has your initials on the front of it. See?"

I looked to where he pointed. There, engraved in the gold plate on the front clasp, were the letters *SNM*. My trembling fingers dragged over the soft material of a legal style briefcase. It was made of custom leather with a flap

over the top, a shoulder strap, and multiple compartments.

"You need something professional for the courtroom,
Miss Marshall." I heard the smile in his tone. His hands
slid down either side of my arms in a gentle tickle.
"Aren't you gonna see what's inside?"

I swallowed hard then opened the clasp closure, exposing the mesh interior. I now understood why the thing
was so heavy. If I had to guess, there had to be over fifty
dollars' worth of quarters inside. Two hundred I love
you's that he meant, but wouldn't say out loud. I thought
I'd choke. Air was all around me and I couldn't breathe a
single bit of it. Myriad emotions came at me at once,
overtaking me in joy and girly gushiness. This was the
sweetest thing anyone had ever done for me and in that
moment, I was too through.

The polls had come in and the votes had been counted.
My future had played out in front of me in a vivid dream
sequence, complete with a soundtrack and celebrity
voice-over. I was going to marry this boy and have a mil-
lion biracial, sugar-addicted, Cambion mutant babies—
simple as that.

It wasn't because of the gift, or the money he chucked
out to get it, but his wordless support. He believed in my
dream to be a lawyer and this gift only made me want to
work harder to reach that goal. I would do whatever it
took to return the favor. Whether it be music or some
other field, his dream in life would be mine too.

"Sam? Are you okay?" he asked.

"No, I'm not okay!" I was straight up sobbing now.
My mascara was running and I didn't care. He'd earned
the privilege of seeing me do the nasty cry. "You give me
the best gift ever and I got you a lousy DVD box set!" I
wailed.

He looked genuinely confused, but held me anyway. He wasn't the emotional type, so I wasn't offended when he started timidly patting my head like I was a dog. "Um, okay. But I really wanted that DVD set. I couldn't find it anywhere in the store. I told you before, Sam, I'm pretty low maintenance. Doesn't take much to make me happy."

I just cried against his ugly sweater. "I love you, Caleb. I love you."

Since the beginning, those three words were difficult for us to say, but I didn't have that problem now. The words rolled off my tongue like a powerful incantation. Raw, honest truth poured into each syllable with enough conviction to crumble the walls around us. I had no regret or hesitation, just a need boiling in my stomach, channeling up my windpipe, and flying out of my mouth into blinding daylight. "I love you!"

"I know," he answered, all cocky and sure of himself. "I can taste it. It's hard to describe. It's sweeter than chocolate, stronger than liquor, better than any life I've tasted. Just because it's yours."

Everything was a blur of hands and lips after that. I didn't remember how Caleb wound up in the cushy desk chair or how I'd gotten on his lap, but there we were, trying our best to suck each other's faces off. Mouthwatering energy passed from his body to mine, and nothing else mattered but the wonders within our private universe. Through the haze, the only object left in focus was *him*, sharp and in high definition.

"Are you two done in here? I need to use the fax machine," a voice called from somewhere inside the room.

Once it occurred to us that we weren't alone anymore, Caleb and I looked up at the same time. I halted all movement—still parked on Caleb's lap with his bottom lip wedged between my teeth.

Detective Ruiz stood by the door, holding a manila folder in his hand. He didn't seem surprised at our compromising position, and a tiny smile tugged at the corner of his mouth. His presence was the cold shower we desperately needed, because if he hadn't come in, we wouldn't need to fake being bonded anymore.

11

New Year's Eve was under way.

Mom and Angie decided to have a girl's night in the Petrovsky suite, and Ruiz tagged along to play love-sick puppy. Haden and Michael stayed in their room to watch the ball drop on TV, while Caleb and I celebrated the only way we knew how.

"Sammy, my caramel candy goddess! I could simply eat you alive." Robbie Ford greeted me at his front door, dressed as the Monopoly guy, including the top hat and monocle over his eye. One could've mistaken him for a gentleman were it not for the string of mistletoe hanging from his crotch.

We pecked cheeks before I stepped inside.

"There's something different about you." Robbie squinted and adjusted his lens for a better look. "When did you get green contacts? They're hot."

I batted my lashes and placed a dainty hand over my heart. "Oh, these old things? I've had them a while now. Catch up, Robbie, you're behind on the times."

As usual, the house was packed with kids from all walks of life: jocks, stoners, townies, and a lot of scantily clad girls. By the sound of it, Caleb was already doing his thing. He had definitely found his element, and I was instantly swept away by the beat and the fast, flowing stream of energy. This spell caster, this pied piper controlled all who entered with hard bass and electronic refrain.

He stood at the deejay booth, rocking out under his headphones, but he almost scratched his album when he saw what I was wearing.

My smooth complexion was my only vanity, so I put as much of it as I could on display, with a glittery silver tank top and a mini skirt to cover up the naughty bits. And even in my most scandalous ensemble yet, I looked ready for Bible study compared to half the girls there. Heading the march to this burlesque show was Mia, who rushed to my side in her drawers and a sheer T-shirt posing as a dress.

I was happy to see her; however, I wasn't too thrilled with what she'd been doing before I showed up. "Okay, how much have you been drinking?"

"Just this. Robbie made it for me." She waved a Styrofoam cup in front of my face. The alcohol content that wafted off the cup burned the hairs in my nostrils. That was a red flag. Robbie's concoctions had people passed out by the second sip.

As to declare our grand arrival, deejay Cake Boy grabbed the mic and yelled, "Give it up for the hottest ladies in the building: my sexy girlfriend, Samara, and her BFF, Mia!"

Hoots and cheers followed as Mia and I stopped in the middle of the floor and struck a pose, letting everyone know the party could now begin with us on the scene. In school, I had to watch everything I said and did, but in a house full of drunk kids from six different school zones, I could be someone else for one night, and right now, I was diva!

After that warm welcome, we spent the next hour dancing badly and gossiping about people and their choice in outfits, as if we had room to talk. It was like old times.

"I've seen her before. Who is that?" Mia pointed across the room.

I groaned on sight of the tall blonde who had Dougie's undivided attention. Oh, that was no one, just the only reason I was even allowed to come to the party. Olivia was dying to experience the American teen nightlife, and having hired muscle as a chaperone granted us the green light. I saw Gunner's bulky frame lurking in the corner of the room. His icy blue eyes were steadily scanning the area for anything sketchy; though the only thing out of place around here was him.

"Mia, relax. You guys aren't together anymore. He's entitled to move on," I said.

"Do you think she's prettier than me?" she asked.

I said what any friend would say. "No! No way. She's all skinny and tall and she talks funny. She doesn't have a thing on you."

Mia tried to smile, but it withered before it could truly bloom. At the same time, a short guy with a curly red afro walked by us, holding a Dixie cup of something green and likely flammable. Mia snatched the cup from him and shoved him away. It could have been mouth-wash or antifreeze for all she knew, but she took it to the head like a pro.

Still dancing, I said, "You know drinking is not gonna solve your problem. It's just gonna be there when you sober up along with a headache. What's up with you? We used to talk about everything."

"Yeah, used to, but you seem to prefer secrets." She tossed the cup behind her then took my hand. "What happened to your bracelet? Did you get it fixed?"

Instinctively, I pulled my hand away and covered my wrist. "Yeah, I got a new one for Christmas."

"Oh. I always see you wearing that bracelet, so it must mean something to you. I don't understand why you had to cut it off instead of just unhooking the clasp."

It could've been the noise or the atmosphere, but I had to lean in to make sure I heard her correctly. "Excuse me?"

The music changed to a slow bump-and-grind, "I'm gonna get you pregnant on the dance floor" song, and howls filled the room.

"Oh, this's my jam!" Mia cheered and rubbed up on some fat kid in the corner who looked terrified. Maybe he was scared because a complete stranger had started humping his back or maybe it was because Mia had the dance moves of a mental patient.

Before she got low, I pulled her away from the traumatized boy. "You said something about my bracelet."

Already she seemed bored with the conversation and started searching for more liquor. "You left it in the parking lot when you left school."

I followed her to the dining room, past the keg and some half naked guy covered in mustard. "You found my bracelet?"

"Yeah, that's why I left it at your front door, duh," she said this as if it were common knowledge. "I knocked, but I guess you weren't home."

"Oh, I was home," I said in my head, as I recalled waking up on the ceiling.

"I didn't tell anybody. I might've been mad, but I didn't want you to get into trouble. And then when the police found Malik's truck, I didn't know what to think. Maybe he dropped you off at home before his crash or what."

I stared at her, not believing what I was hearing. "Can you tell me everything you saw that day? What time did we leave?"

Finding what she was looking for, she plucked another cup of green poison from the kitchen counter. "I don't wanna talk about this now. I wanna dance."

I blocked her path to the doorway. "In a second. What did you see?"

She rolled her eyes and scooted past me. "You don't re-member anything that happened? Did he drug you?" When I shook my head, she said, "Um, I don't know, around lunch sometime. I was cramping really bad so I went to the nurse. I got a note to go home early and I saw you walking to his truck when I was leaving. You dropped something on the ground and when you took off I went to pick it up."

I followed her through the party as the commotion went on around us without disturbance. "What? I cut my bracelet off?"

"Either you or Malik. Who's Lilith anyway? I saw the name on the bracelet. I've never heard you mention her before. I thought she was like a relative and that's why you wear the bracelet all the time. Did she die or some-thing?"

"Something like that," I mumbled. Anger boiled up in-side me so hot that I wanted to cry. The room began to grow small and the walls bent together in a colorless blob. Though my vision was impaired, my brain was still on duty.

"Sam, what's going on with you? Did Malik do something to you? I didn't say anything, but you need to tell the police what you know. Everyone's worried about him. Sam? Sam!"

"Huh? Yeah, I'm fine," I said. "Is this why you've been acting weird around me? You think I had something to do with his disappearance?"

"No. I don't think you kidnapped him, but I really don't know what to think these days. You've been acting weird all year, and I'd see you two together in the hall and it would just get under my skin. Malik is cute and all, but I've never been into him like that, you know? I just went crazy."

"You and half the school," I grumbled.

"I'm sorry for being so bitchy, but I couldn't help it. I . . . I thought you were cheating on Caleb and you know how I feel about that shit. I mean, if you don't want somebody; just leave. Don't stick around, come home at three A.M. with a lame excuse—just divorce her."

I didn't ignore the use in pronoun, and I suspected that her Freudian must've slipped. I knew Mia had some family issues that leaked into her own relationships. The Moralez family had more drama than all the daytime soaps combined, but with a better story line. They were their own reality show, ringing truth to that old adage, "More money; more problems." For that reason, Mia always dreaded going to her house and spent most of her time at mine.

She needed to find another way to cope or else she'd ruin any future with Dougie, but I couldn't play shrink tonight, not after she dropped this bomb on me.

"I gotta go get some air. I'll be back. I promise."

"Sam, I wish you would talk to me. Did Malik do something to you?" she whined and stomped her foot. "You're freaking me out! Stop it. I'm sick of these secrets. You can tell me anything, you know that, right?"

"I know. There's something I gotta straighten out right now, but I promise I'll tell you everything, okay?"

She nodded, satisfied for the moment, but the concern on her face was still there. "Honest promise?"

"Honest promise," I said and I meant it. I would tell her everything from beginning to end, back my U-Haul of drama right up to her front door, just as soon as I figured it out myself. I owed it to her.

The party was too loud and I couldn't hear myself think, but I did my best to tally up the facts. I was in Malik's truck during the blackout. Tobias was taking me somewhere that day, and Lilith went with him willingly. Was I the cause of the accident? Was that what Lilith was trying to keep from me? I let my imagination fill in the gaps. Jason Lao said Malik's truck was run off the road. Maybe Lilith freaked out and took control of the wheel. The car might've swerved and landed in the ditch. But if that was the case, how did I get home?

No. I would *not* obsess about this tonight. This was the last night of the year and I wouldn't ruin it by talking shop. Besides, I needed to find some place quiet to concentrate and this glorified saloon was not a proper think tank.

While waiting in line for the bathroom, I took down what Mia said and used my phone to e-mail myself with all the details. I needed to get all the clues down while they were still fresh—I couldn't afford to forget any of it.

With that done, I did a lap around the party, sucking in the energy around the room. The air was rich, potent, and teeming with virility. On my fourth round, I spotted Olivia doing some energy surfing as well. She stood in the middle of the dance floor swaying her hips to the beat with at least four boys surrounding her. She had some moves for someone so prim and proper; she could teach me a few things.

But what really shocked me was that she'd been watching me work the room. She seemed curious, wanting to see me feed. She pulled away from her partners and circled the floor, her eyes fixed on me with what I now knew was a challenge.

The current of energy rode the air in the room, moving faster as the music picked up tempo. I breathed it in through my mouth and held it, letting the light-headedness take over. Soon there were hands and shoulders rubbing against me on the dance floor. Bodies ground together and I no longer cared who I was dancing with. The beat picked up, loud and hard against my chest, my heart a speaker trembling from the bass.

"I swear, I'm gonna marry Caleb! Or he's gonna deejay my wedding—not sure yet!" Mia screamed as she flung her arms around me. "Em gonna tell you a secret," she said in a sneaky tone. The smell of pineapples and jet fuel shot from her mouth like dragon fire. "Okay, don't get mad, but I have a little, teeny, tiny crush on Caleb. Not like dat tho. Wait, hold on. Listen, I'm try'na tell you somefin'. Em not gonna go after him or anyfing. Thaz breakin' da buddy code—bros before hoes 'n all dat," she slurred. "I mean, he's a kick-ass deejay and . . . I dunno, he has dis thing, ya know?"

"Yeah, he has a thing all right." I gently pulled away and shook off the drink she splashed on my top.

"Right? I dunno know why, he's not even hot. Wait, don't get mad—hey, juz listen." She kept petting my hair, trying to make sure I was paying attention, yet she was the one swinging in and out of the conversation. "He's cute, but come on, Sam, we both know Dougie's way hotter."

We do? I thought.

"But he has doze eyes, ya know?" she continued. "Hiz eyes are like magicians. Wait . . . no that's not it. Hippo—

hypnotist—hypnotic. Yeah, dat's it. I can't describe it. It's like lookin' into—"

"Oblivion," I supplied.

"Yeah. Ovulation. Dat's da word."

I took the cup from her hand and set it on the coffee table. "Okay, Mia, no more drinks for you tonight. Let's sit down before you break your neck in those heels."

The moment of truth was fast approaching. Holding a beer in his hand, Robbie jumped onto the coffee table and announced, "Two minutes 'til midnight!" followed by an eruption of cheers. At this point of the evening, all he wore was the top hat, jacket and boxers, his pasty torso bare to anyone with the stomach to look. Three giggling girls tackled him to the floor and smothered him with kisses.

The clock was ticking and people scrambled around for a partner. Mia was the odd one out. I looked to Dougie who leaned in as Olivia whispered in his ear. I couldn't leave Mia alone like this. This was the worst night of the year to be dateless. I'd never realized that until now.

"Go find Caleb," she said over the noise.

"No, it's cool. I'll stay here."

"Uh, Sam, you cute. You really are. But I ain't gonna kiss you at midnight. No point in both us with no man, so go. I'll be fine." She patted my head again. I was really getting sick of people petting me.

I searched the deejay booth for Caleb and found it empty. He must have left to look for me. There were too many people, so I jumped to see over the heads on the dance floor as the partygoers began to chant. "Thirty-nine . . . thirty-eight . . . thirty-seven . . ."

I shouldered through the crowd, but all my efforts were wasted. I began to panic.

"Thirteen . . . twelve . . . eleven . . ."

I doubled back and headed toward the couch. Mia was still sitting there, looking sad and abandoned, holding her cup in her lap. Out of nowhere, Dougie appeared in front of her, took her drink, and set it aside. He pulled her up and trapped her face in his hands.

"Three . . . two . . . one! Happy New Year!" Just as he leaned in and kissed her, soft fingers touched my chin and turned my head. A pair of lips met mine and I didn't need to see who they belonged to.

I knew those lips, knew that touch and scent. I simply closed my eyes and wrapped my arms around his neck. Noise-makers and horns honked, glitter fell from the ceiling, and elation rained over us in a gentle downpour. I was trapped in a snow globe of confetti and I wanted this moment to last forever. Everything was as it should be, though I knew it wouldn't last. In this time in this place, drunk with the joy of it all, I wanted to believe that it could.

After the party, everyone exchanged hugs and left. Cabs were called and keys were passed off to the DD's. Mia was drunk off her ass and there was no way she was driving home, a fact that Dougie made a point to enforce. Caleb stayed behind to pack his equipment and promised to meet up with me at the hotel. Since I arrived at the party with Olivia, I swallowed my pride and caught a ride with her.

The journey back to the hotel was tense and nothing but the roar of the engine broke the silence. Gunner sat behind the wheel while Olivia and I kept to our appointed sides of the back seat. I kept sneaking glances at her, while copying her posture and how she crossed her legs. She made grace look effortless whereas I nearly broke into a sweat in my attempt to be ladylike.

Growing sick of the hostility, I said, "I saw what you did with Dougie tonight. I appreciate it. Thanks."

She fumbled with the beaded clutch bag on her lap. "Sure."

"No really, thanks. You had him wrapped around your finger and you let him go. You can have any guy you want."

"I know." She stared out of her window and watched the lights and trees speed by in a blur. Her hair swooped to one side and a black teardrop earring dangled against her neck. "But I don't want someone who is in love with someone else. It's sickening to watch, and even worse to taste. I'm not that heartless."

"I never said you were heartless," I argued. "I know you have some issues with me, and I don't blame you for hating me."

"I don't hate you. I think you're stupid, but I don't hate you."

I adjusted in my seat to look at her fully. "Excuse me?"

"What else would you call someone who continues to date a boy who feeds off women without shame? The son of a killer? The same boy who let my sister die instead of helping her?"

"Helping her? Caleb did everything he could to save Nadine. Her neck was broken; there was nothing either of us could do," I said in his defense.

"He could have given her his life," she muttered.

I paused mid outburst. "What? How?"

"It appears that you haven't been reading the journals as you were instructed."

"I've been kinda busy," I mumbled.

With a loud sigh, she returned her gaze back to the window. "There was a story about a Cambion female in Greece whose son was dying from a war wound. The physician lived too far away. She couldn't bear the thought of living without her son, so she gave him her energy while he was on the brink of death. His life was gone, but his soul had yet to leave the body. It was enough to revive him in time for the physician to arrive and treat the wound. This is rare for our kind to do this since we are designed to take life, not give it away. But it is not impossible if enough human will is put behind it."

I settled back in my seat, drinking all this in. Though a new revelation, the story seemed to line up with my own experience with donating life. When Caleb was in a coma, I had to give a good amount of my energy to sustain him, but he needed more than I could supply. Not even his brothers' energy was enough to bring him out. The deadly cost of giving too much energy had sparked my next question. "What happened to the mother, the Cambion?"

"Her heart gave out and she died," she replied.

And there was the catch. "Great story, Olivia. Four out of five stars. And you wanted Caleb to do that for Nadine? That might not have even worked. He might've died."

"Death is always a possibility, but it's a noble risk. It would be the least he could have done after what he allowed his father to become. Nathan Ross murdered many women and the brothers stood by and watched. His sacrifice would've been penance for his cowardice. But we will never know. And he will probably die anyway when the Santiago family sees him for what he is."

Wow, I'd never seen a cold-blooded creature walk upright. At least now I knew her position on the matter, and right now she was two seconds away from getting snatched bald. "You do know that Cambions can't kill those in the same line, right? They can't harm their source. For example, I can't stab you in the neck with my car key—Lilith won't let me." I smiled nastily.

Olivia rolled her eyes. "Which is why the rogue Cambion must be reported to those who can do what his family could not. The brothers' disobedience will not go unpunished. The Santiagos are ruthless."

"So am I. Ask Nathan Ross."

She scoffed, but all her snark fell away when she saw I wasn't kidding. In that moment, I didn't feel the need to emulate her anymore. I had something that she couldn't have, something that years of pampering and Swiss tutors couldn't teach her. So I uncrossed my legs and stared out of my window, forgoing any further attempts to be anyone else but Samara Nicole Marshall.

Not much was said after that and I was perfectly fine with the arrangement. The car pulled up to the Charlotte Hotel and not a moment too soon. When the valet opened the door, Olivia flew out of the car and raced through the revolving doors. I strolled behind and by the time I made it to the lobby, she was already gone. Probably to her room to cry, but I wasn't sure. I was too distracted by the sound of drowning kittens coming from the lounge.

I entered the dimly lit room and saw Michael on the tiny stage near the piano. Drink in hand, Michael sang his heart out in a pitch high enough to torment every dog in the area. Haden sat by the bar, waving a lighter in the air.

I moved over to him and grabbed a seat. "Hey. What's going on?"

"I dared Michael to serenade the brunette in the first row and he lost. The boy needs to get laid. He won't be so crazy all the time."

I looked up at the stage to Michael slow dancing with the microphone stand. His shades were off and he was using his powers of seduction to win over the crowd, which was primarily female. The ladies giggled and squealed at his lighthearted solo.

I leaned in to Haden and asked, "How drunk is he?"

"Very. That's the only way I can get him to do anything. He's painfully shy. It's crippling."

"Why is he like that? Not the shy thing, but the whole twitch, talking-to-himself, klepto-schizo thing."

He pondered the question for a moment then asked, "You ever wanted to be a super hero?"

Not sure where this was going, I shrugged and said, "Sure. I wanna be Catwoman when I grow up. I'd look good in leather."

"Well, Michael thought he could be a super hero, fighting the forces of darkness, using his ability to take down evildoers. There was a time in his life when he would feed only on the wicked: murderers, rapists, child abusers, and all that. Thought he was doing the world a service." Haden's face went hard. "That's the last thing our kind should ever do."

"He was feeding off males?" I asked. "There are evil women in the world too, you know: gold-diggers, black widows, child pageant moms. Will his spirit even accept male energy? I thought it preys on its opposite."

"It does, which was another reason why it didn't work. But what every Cambion must know is to never feed off the insane, or else the insanity might latch on to you," he explained. "Imagine feeding off a killer, seeing all his victims, experiencing the thrill of each murder. The remorse that the killer should've had is now yours to bear."

I nodded my understanding. "Imagine knowing not

only the killer's entire life history, but the history of every victim. Yeah, I know the feeling."

Haden looked to me, conveying sympathy that I didn't want. "I'm sorry, Samara."

"Me too. We should probably get Michael to bed." I pointed to the stage where he was now stretched out across the top of the piano, hitting a high note that could make glass shatter.

Caleb soon joined us and winced at the display. Together, the brothers finally pulled Michael off the stage. The audience booed them and demanded one more song.

"Sorry, ladies. Maybe tomorrow night," Caleb yelled back at them.

I helped the brothers drag Michael to the elevator. Michael leaned his head against Caleb's shoulder and stroked his cheek lovingly. "I don't mean to be forward, but I dink you're a v-very beautiful woman, and I'd be . . . honored to buy you a drink," Michael slurred then puckered his lips, ready to kiss him.

Disgusted, Caleb looked to me for aid, but got nothing but laughter. "Go ahead, don't play hard to get," I teased, then made kissing noises.

Caleb gave thanks to the ceiling when we reached his floor. The elevator door slid open and Haden was the first to step out. From what little I could see, someone was standing in the hallway waiting to step in. I peeked around Haden's broad shoulder and saw Olivia's bodyguard standing there looking more intimidating than ever before.

His skin glistened with sweat, and his chest rose and fell from heavy breathing. There was something threatening about his posture, the way his shoulders hunched, the way his head bowed, and the promise of murder in his eyes.

I didn't need extrasensory powers to detect immediate danger. It was as apparent and straightforward as the weapon in his hand, the one that now pointed directly at us.

"Hey look, guys! Gunner's got a gun. That's funny." Michael giggled.

12

"Get back in the elevator!" Haden yelled and took a step back and in the same moment, a gunshot cracked in the air.

I hit the floor and Caleb followed suit, managing to pull Michael with him. In the sea of moving limbs and flashes of darkness, I lifted my head to get a better look and saw Haden tumble back into the elevator. Still on the floor, Caleb reached for the up button on the wall and the doors began to close. Another shot fired into the car and punched a hole into the back wall. Then another fired into the top right corner.

There were bodies all around me, blocking my view, but I could see the gap of the sliding doors grow smaller. Gunner charged forward, one hand stretched out to wedge between the doors. His face twisted in a fierce mask of anger, while his eyes glowed bright gold.

Michael's weight was on my legs, crushing my shins. There was a jingling sound at my right and I turned as best as I could. Caleb got to his feet, holding his key chain and a tiny Swiss army knife attached to the link. With one of the blades raised, Caleb sliced the meaty fingers peeking between the doors. A howl came from outside of the door, but Gunner kept to his mission to pry his way in. Blood dripped down the metal panel and over the fingers, making it too slippery to keep his grip.

The doors were trying to open again. I reached over and pushed the close button repeatedly until finally the bloody fingers disappeared. Only when I felt the car begin to lift did I stop.

Don't freak out, don't trip, just be cool, I chanted to myself. This wasn't happening. I was just having a good time and talking to my boyfriend, not being held at gunpoint in an elevator. Of all people, why Gunner? Did Olivia hate Caleb so much that she put a hit out on him? Did she even have that kind of pull?

I dismissed that idea before it could settle. I saw Gunner's eyes, small and spaced too close together, but instead of their usual piercing blue shade, they were like fire. Only one person had eyes like that, and he had the means and the motive to dispatch an enemy; he was the only one right now with a good reason to want to kill any of us.

"Is everyone okay?" Haden groaned from the opposite side of the car. I couldn't see him—Michael's shoulder was in the way—but I could hear evident pain in his voice.

"Yeah. What the hell was that?" Caleb asked and helped pull me to my feet.

"I think that was Tobias. In fact, I'm sure of it," I said.

He looked at me with impatience. "Sam, don't start—"

"You saw it yourself. Gunner has blue eyes, now he's walking around with glowing yellow ones. And he's a hired guard who just tried to kill us. Do the math, Caleb."

"Gunner's possessed? We need to tell Evangeline. He was hired to protect Olivia. Where's Olivia?" Haden asked, crouched on the floor holding the left side of his chest.

I looked at the dark red spot growing on his white T-shirt. "Oh my God! Haden, you've been shot!"

"Just a scratch. Don't worry about it," he said, but his scrunched up face told me it was much worse than that.

The elevator doors opened and the familiar design of Angie's hallway came into view. Caleb poked his head out and searched both ends of the small corridor. Satisfied, he helped Haden up and draped his arm around his waist. I did the same with Michael who teetered in and out of consciousness.

No sign of any crazy gunmen appeared in the short hall and the glass door leading to Angie's suite was in plain view. I could see Olivia inside, her shoes dangling in her hand as she neared the stairs. Any hope of turning in for the night was ruined when she heard our knock.

"What happened?" Olivia cried and rushed to the door.

When she opened the door, we all spilled into the foyer. Both Caleb and I held a body in our arms. "Call the police!" I ordered then dragged Michael to the living room and dropped him on the couch like old luggage.

Caleb didn't make it as far—Haden collapsed in the middle of the foyer floor. "We need to get you to the hospital." Caleb lifted Haden's shirt to assess the damage. "No exit wound. Looks nasty. I need something to stop the bleeding."

Olivia's head bounced back and forth as she looked in horror at the living room and the foyer, and being completely useless. "Will someone tell me what's going on?"

"Gunner's got a gun!" Michael sang, shooting finger guns at the ceiling.

"Gunner?" Olivia stepped back, shaking her head frantically. "Impossible."

"Believe it. Your guard's gone trigger happy," I looked around the sitting area and spotted champagne, an ice bucket, and some folded dinner cloths. A little fancy, but they would serve the purpose. I snatched the cloths, brushed passed Olivia and joined Caleb back on the floor.

Caleb took a cloth and placed it over the dark gash on Haden's chest. Then and only then did I notice the thick trail of blood on the floor. Against the white of the marble it looked like barbecue sauce. "That's a lot of blood. He needs help now. Olivia, would you stop staring and call the police?" I yelled at her.

"I've got you. You're gonna be fine. You'll be fine," Caleb chanted over and over, more to comfort himself than Haden. I could see the tension in his arms as he pressed down, I saw the strain in his face, but worst of all I could feel every twist of pain coursing through his body. This was his brother, biologically and spiritually, and another family member he could lose.

"Here, hold this. Press down as hard as you can." Caleb and I switched positions, while he pulled out his cell.

His hands, slippery with blood, were shaking so bad he almost dropped the phone, but now was not the time to go into shock. He seemed to agree and worked up enough strength to dial. Meanwhile, I placed my full weight over the wound. The muscles in my arms burned as Haden's heartbeat thumped against my hand. Blood soaked through the cloth and I quickly replaced it with another.

"Operator says the police are on their way now. Some-one must've heard the shots downstairs and called already. Might take longer for the ambulance to come," Caleb reported quickly then continued his call. "Yeah, I'm still here."

Haden was turning pale. His lips were almost white and dark circles were shadowing his eyes. I kept pressing down, not really seeing him anymore, not paying attention to Caleb's panicky voice on the phone, but focusing on the task at hand. This wasn't the first, second, or the third time I stood over a person who was dying. But if this one had a chance at a better ending, I had to pull myself together, fast. If Caleb couldn't wig out right now, neither could I.

"What on earth is going on?" Angie raced downstairs in a silk nightgown, gawking at the entire scene. Szymon and Mishka tumbled behind in their pajamas and rubbed the sleep from their eyes. Just looking at them reminded me of enchanted forests, breadcrumbs and gingerbread houses. My first instinct was to shield their eyes from all the blood, but Angie beat me to it and ordered them back upstairs.

More questions flew at us as the panic grew, and I had no idea which one to answer first. Olivia was dead weight, Caleb was screaming to the operator, and Haden was bleeding all over the marble floor.

From the couch, Michael had felt the situation needed a jazzy soundtrack. Snapping his fingers, he sang into his fist Sinatra style. "Gunner's got a gun, pow, pow, pow. Gunner's got a gun."

"Gunner did this? Why?" Angie shook her head, dislodging the confusion from her brain. "He's been our loyal guard since Olivia was a child. Why would he do such a thing?"

"They did something to him." Olivia accused as Angie held her.

Caleb ended the call and looked up at Olivia, rage blazing in his eyes. "Yes, because that would explain why *Haden* is bleeding all over the place. We didn't do anything."

Olivia ripped from her mother's hold and rounded on Caleb. "You *always* do something. Everything you touch, you destroy. I'll kill you before you hurt my friend." Her eyes lifted to something over Caleb's shoulder. "Gunner!" She leapt over Haden's body and raced to the door.

"*Nooo!*" was the unified cry in the room.

I snatched my bag off the floor and dug inside for the tiny spray bottle of olive oil. I wasn't sure what good it would do, but it was the only weapon I could find. Maybe if we tackled Gunner, I could force him to drink it. A long shot, but it was worth a try.

Everything seemed to be suspended in time, making it impossible to move fast enough. Olivia slipped through the door, her hair a long tangled mess trailing behind her as she dashed out into the hallway. Through the glass doors, I saw Gunner step out of the elevator. With pistol still in hand, he spotted Olivia.

I couldn't see her face, but I could almost feel the transition in her moods: relief, confusion, and as she planted her feet to stop, fear.

I was at the door and Caleb was right behind me. Gunner studied the girl in front of him. Through his new demon eyes, his reaction was no different than others who looked at Olivia. He stood in the presence of a ghost, one that had come back to haunt him. For a brief second, his expression softened and as if enchanted by the vision, he reached out to touch her.

"Olivia, run!" Caleb warned.

Gunner saw our advance, then yanked Olivia by the arm. When he spun her around, I could now see her face, and the terror there was just as I imagined. Gunner pointed the pistol at us with one hand while holding Olivia's fighting body by the throat with the other. And thus began the hostage negotiations.

"What do you want?" I asked, choosing my words carefully. I couldn't say Tobias's name in front of Olivia. That would only compound the problem.

"I already told you and you're going to help me." He held tight to Olivia's throat. She gasped and choked while her bare feet dangled in the air.

I hid the bottle of oil in my bra, then stepped from behind Caleb and held out my hand in surrender. Maybe he would agree to a swap—me for Olivia. If I could get close enough, I could hose him down. "Fine, whatever you want—just don't hurt her," I said.

"Let my daughter go!" Angie cried from the doorway.

"Mama!" Olivia croaked.

"Ah, the great queen of the demon hunters. You sure have beautiful daughters." Gunner looked down at Olivia's tear stained face. "It's remarkable. She looks just like her." Thick, bloody fingers reached out and brushed the hair off her face. "Only there's one little difference." His eyes lifted to meet mine. "Isn't there, Lilith?"

He was toying with me, and I hated it. I also hated how close his mouth was to Olivia's. I recalled the black cloud in my room, that swirling storm system with the gold light in its center, and the voices that came out of it. I wouldn't let Olivia join that chorus, and judging from the light green filter over my vision, I knew Lilith had my back.

"Fine, you've made your point. Let her go and I'll go with you. Anywhere you want." I stepped forward, but the steel bar of Caleb's arm blocked me.

Gunner snickered. "It's a little late for that. I want my body. Those demon mutts stole it."

"What?" I turned my head to Caleb who looked just as confused as I was.

Caleb shook his head slowly. "I don't know what you're talking about."

"Think real long and hard. I'm sure it'll come to you what you did to me and Lilith."

"Again, what are you talking about?" Caleb yelled.

"I swear if you hurt my child, I will rip your heart out!" Angie cried.

"I'm sorry, what was that?" His hand squeezed Olivia's neck. She yelped in pain, still wiggling in the air.

"Let her go!" I demanded.

With the gun pointed at us, he took a step back and then another toward the elevator. "I want what's mine, and you get what's yours."

"No, no! Olivia!" Angie rushed to the elevator doors. "I'll find you. No matter where you go, I'll find you," Angie promised as the elevator doors began to close. "And when I do, I'll kill you. You hear me, demon!"

"Mama!" Olivia shook her head wildly, terrified that we would leave her, but we had to do what he said for her sake. The elevator door slid closed and her screams could be heard from several floors down.

"Olivia!" Angie desperately pushed at the button on the wall.

"Come on." Caleb tugged my arm, leading me to the twin elevator to our right. The doors wouldn't open and the number at the top had gone black, indicating it was out of service.

"Stay here and watch Haden! Stop the bleeding until the medics arrive," he ordered Angie as we dashed to the service stairs.

The twelve-story descent was a slow and dizzying spiral to the lobby where complete pandemonium met us at the bottom. Guests stood by the main doors as security raced toward the elevator.

"Everyone stay calm. Everything is under control. The elevators are currently out of service. If you need to get to your rooms, the emergency stairs are down the hall. We appreciate your patience. Please remain calm," the security officer ordered. He then alerted the front desk over his radio that he needed backup for crowd control.

I shouldered through the masses, my eyes glued to the revolving doors. Guests in the lounge filled into the lobby inquiring about the commotion. Walkie-talkies crackled static. Cell phones were out and in use. Fingers pointed at the entrance. Witnesses watched in horror, demanding police assistance but offering no help themselves. Voices mingled in a steady rumble of noise.

"Oh my God, look at them! Why is he covered in blood?"

"Ladies and gentlemen, the police are on their way. *Please* remain calm—"

"There were shots heard on the eighth floor—"

". . . blood all over the floor. Bullet holes in the wall and—"

"Dammit! I can't get a signal. Let me use your phone—"

"He had a gun, so I couldn't do anything. I feel bad—someone needs to help that poor girl—"

"Did you get a good look at the guy? Big son-of-a-bitch too—"

". . . thin, blond girl, maybe eighteen—didn't get a good look—"

"Yes, a girl's just been abducted at the Charlotte Hotel. Charlotte. C-H-A-R—"

". . . stole my car! Someone call the police! God, I think my nose is broken!"

We finally made it outside then raced to the grassy patch in the middle of the driveway. We stopped by the fountain and allowed the helplessness to seep into our skin with the cold. My nerves were fried. Old phantoms stared me square in the face. Images flashed in my head, featuring a blond girl lying dead on the floor, broken and cast aside as collateral damage in a senseless war.

Olivia would not join her sister, not on my watch. But there was too much commotion, too much confusion, and not enough time. The odds were against us especially since Olivia and Gunner had completely vanished from sight in a matter of seconds.

We could go after them, patrol the streets all night, but what would that accomplish? We had no weapons to stop him and we didn't even know what kind of car Gunner took. No, we would need help with the search, and I could only pray that Tobias would keep her alive until then.

Plus the rough hands on our shoulders made it clear that we weren't going anywhere.

We turned around to find Detective Ruiz standing behind us wearing a black suit and tie. He appeared to have been enjoying the New Year's celebration like we had before the world came to an end. "I think it's best that you come back inside before you make a scene," he said and tipped his head toward the crowd.

We soon noticed we had an audience. Guests kept their distance as they looked directly at us, noting our attire, which was comprised of sweat and a lot of blood. I stared out to the black night and the spinning flash of the police lights. Five squad cars charged up the paved strip toward the hotel. One thing about Williamsburg, when wealthy people are in trouble, the cops come a runnin'.

Not knowing what else to do, I looked to Caleb. His eyes had cooled to their normal shade. Despite the tremor of rage coursing through his body, he managed to have enough sense to understand that we were in for a long night.

13

What a way to bring in the new year, but then why would this be different from any other celebration?

It seems no holiday could go by without some mishap that had to be explained to the authorities. Seriously, why did we keep going out? The very definition of crazy was to repeat the same pattern in hopes of a different result. But if I was crazy, I wasn't the only lunatic in the Petrovsky suite.

The past three hours had been absolute madness. The police took statements from everyone, and it was only by Evangeline's "powers of persuasion" that they didn't call my parents. Ruiz had escorted Mom home only moments before we arrived to the hotel, which was inconvenient because we carpooled to the hotel earlier tonight and she was my ride. I called and informed her that I was spending the night with Angie, and covered the phone to block out the three-ring circus performing in the background. With that done, I tucked my phone in my bra, shook my limbs loose and dove back into the fray.

The paramedics took Haden to the hospital. He'd lost a lot of blood and he was going into shock. It took three police officers to restrain Caleb, insisting that he had to stay until he finished the interview. It required twice as many men to keep Angie from destroying the room.

I'd never seen her so distraught and rightfully so. Her hair was flying everywhere, her makeup was smudged, and she couldn't care less who saw her sleepwear or the otherworldly glow in her eyes. She was putting out some serious homicidal vibes and making eye contact was not conducive to one's survival.

For the most part Caleb and I just sat on the couch eating chocolate after-dinner mints while Angie and Ruiz discussed arcane Cambion politics. Michael was passed out on the couch across from us and people walked by like he was part of the décor.

I could tell by the reddened faces in the room that somebody was going to swing, and I had my money riding on Angie. I figured it was best to stay out of grown folks' business. We were already in enough hot water for not telling Ruiz that there was a body-snatching demon parading around Williamsburg. Again I adhered to the policy of keeping my mouth shut when dealing with otherworldly creatures. It was just safer.

Between the failed attempts to get to the door, Angie sought the comfort of her cancer sticks and parked in front of her laptop, monitoring Olivia's location from her bracelet. According to the tiny dot on the digital map, Olivia hadn't changed locations in twenty minutes. Since Tobias knew well about the bracelet's tracking device, I hoped he hadn't had time to remove it like he had done with mine.

Equipped with this information along with extra photographs of Olivia, the police left vowing to exhaust all their resources to begin the search. Considering Angie's affluence and Cambion allure, I believed them, but this kind of missing persons case was well out of their jurisdiction. In any case, we needed supernatural backup posthaste.

During Angie's fifth effort to get to the door, Ruiz blocked her path. "No. Let us handle this. We can't afford to have you hurt."

"He has my daughter!" she screamed.

"I understand that but you'll create an incident—" Ruiz barely got the words out before a white hand wrapped around his throat.

The movement was too fast for sight. The flow of black silk that trailed behind her was the only evidence to prove that she hadn't teleported five feet to get to the detective. She might as well have, because in a blink she held the man who was twice her weight by the neck and a good foot off the ground. Caleb broke from his thoughts to watch the scene while I moved in to intercede. I wasn't sure what Angie was capable of in her current state, but things didn't look good. In fact, it was downright fugly.

"I lost one daughter and you allow another to be taken from me on behalf of protocol?" She hissed and if she had fangs, they would've been on full display and planted in Ruiz's jugular. It amazed me how someone could look graceful and gruesome at the same time.

"Evangeline." I placed a hand on her very tense shoulder. "Don't kill him. Please."

"I say have at him," Caleb muttered.

My head whipped in his direction. "Caleb, so not helping."

"You forget your place, David. I told you what would happen if any of my progeny were harmed. I warned you," she growled.

The look on Ruiz's face was priceless. I had to hand it

to him, he didn't seem scared and didn't back down, and I was sure that was one of the reasons he was called the Cuban Necktie. But he couldn't look directly into Angie's eyes, and he winced whenever he tried. The piercing green light bounced off his olive skin like a laser pointer on a sniper rifle, and was just as deadly a weapon.

She must not have been holding him too tight because he was able to speak. "If you kill me, you will wage war against every Cambion this side of the world. Do you really want that? I'm not in the habit of striking women, so don't make me start now. Put. Me. Down."

A notable pause engulfed the room. Finally, Angie released Ruiz's neck one finger at a time. He slipped from her fingers and plummeted to the floor.

Towering over him, she said, "Alert your people and call for reinforcements. Cambions, none who can be persuaded or possessed. If the family objects, I will declare war, if they interfere in any way, I will declare war. I will burn this city to the ground before another demon hurts my child. In the meantime, make yourself useful and take Samara home and guard her house. She and her mother are in danger."

I stepped between the two of them. "No. I wanna stay. I can help you."

"You will not get involved with this, little one. You will stay safe," Angie said.

"Then let me at least stay here. I already told Mom I was spending the night anyway. I don't want to be left in the dark."

"Fine." Angie turned away and drifted to the security of her laptop. "You are free to leave, David. Return at noon to take Samara home."

Ruiz got to his feet and straightened his suit. "I'll have men here in five hours. No one—and I mean no one— leaves this building until I return. You want to declare war? Refuse to comply." He swept a glance to all of us before leaving the suite with his tail between his legs.

"That was pretty badass, Angie," I said once we were alone.

She lifted her head to the ceiling and sighed. "No. That was foolish. I should not have threatened him. We can't afford a war among the family. I need their support and I may have made things worse."

I shrugged. "So what? Ruiz isn't one of us. He doesn't have pull like that. You're afraid the Santiagos will show up?"

Angie laughed and lit another cigarette. "Samara, they have already arrived. They have been here for months. Do you really believe that the family would allow an outsider to know so many Cambion secrets? Have you ever wondered why Ruiz knows so much about our kind?"

"Yeah, it did cross my mind a few times." I looked to Caleb and then back to Angie. "Wait, are you saying he's a Santiago?"

"Nephew of the eldest leader. He would have been second in line to lead if things were . . . different," Angie explained. "He has influence inside and outside of our circle. That is why he's so valuable."

Caleb drew closer, intrigued by this new discovery. "But the Santiago spirit is male. How did it skip over him like that? Was he adopted?"

"That, I'm afraid, is a story he alone should share." Angie stared at the computer screen again. "I'll need to fly the children back home tomorrow. It's not safe here. I need to call their father to pick them up," Angie muttered, thinking out loud, I figured. She went on for a few more minutes reciting her to-do list.

I looked up at the bottom right corner of the screen and noticed it was four A.M. Looking at the time sent a signal to my brain, telling me that I was tired. All the energy I took tonight had burned off and I was running on fumes.

"If it's any help, I don't think he'll kill her. She's a good bargaining chip. He needs her alive," Caleb said, wearing down the floor with his pacing.

"He doesn't seem to feel the same about your brother," Angie replied. "Do you know where his vessel is?"

Caleb shrugged. "I have no idea, but once Michael sobers up, I'll be sure to ask him."

"That would explain why they keep disappearing. I'm pretty sure they have it hidden somewhere," I added.

Angie crossed the room and placed her hands on my shoulders. "Samara, you do realize what must be done, don't you? He must be destroyed and I will not leave until he is found."

"I'm all for that plan, Angie, but how would we kill him if his soul is out of his body? How can he die?"

"We must first make sure he is back inside his own body. The vessel would have to be consecrated and burned. If it is destroyed before he is reunited with it, he will be trapped in whatever body he currently resides. He will be a Cambion with Gunner as his host."

"He won't be one for long, if he consumes enough human energy," Caleb jumped in. "Tobias wants immortality more than anything else. Knowing him, he'll be back to full demon status in a week and this merry-go-round will start all over again, like some screwed up reincarnation."

Damn, these demons were like cockroaches—they just wouldn't die. But Caleb presented a valid point. Tobias's longevity was the root of all his actions, including his obsession with me. "So if he's trapped inside Gunner, what happens to Gunner's humanity? Could he fight the transition like we do?" I asked.

"It depends on his human will," Angie said. "It is a

balancing act that takes years to master. You should know from experience how difficult control can be. Gunner knows nothing about our world or how to combat it. But that will not matter; he would have to be destroyed as well if Tobias is inside him."

Her flippant attitude toward murder took me aback. "There has to be another way. Is there a chance that Tobias can leave Gunner's body after his vessel is destroyed?"

"I'm afraid that is highly improbable if he wants to survive. The body keeps us anchored to this world. The soul alone cannot exist on this plane. It needs a body and life or else it will fade—it cannot simply float on the wind. If Tobias is as fearful of death as you say, naturally he will latch on to any human rather than face the beyond."

I recognized the ugly truth in what she was saying. I was a living example of what a soul would do to dwell among the land of the living. If there hadn't been a human body nearby, Lilith would've faded to God-knew-where.

" 'Who would fardels bear, to grunt and sweat under a weary life, but that the dread of something after death: the undiscovered country, from whose bourn no traveler returns? Puzzles the will,' " I recited to no one in particular.

" 'And makes us rather bear those ills we have than fly to others that we know not of. Thus conscience does make cowards of us all,' " Caleb finished the next line.

I stared in quiet amazement, and not because he knew Hamlet's monologue. He didn't; he'd never even seen the movies, but he knew me and that was equally impressive.

"We cannot risk Tobias resurfacing," Angie spoke up, effectively killing the moment. "The demon must be destroyed completely, both body and spirit. If Gunner isn't dead already, I'll see to it that he is dispatched. In the meantime, you two will figure out where Tobias's vessel is held."

"If you kill him, you know what will happen to us," Caleb warned.

"I'm afraid the rules had changed the moment he touched my daughter. I will not lose another child on account of him. I suggest you handle your affairs quickly. I trust that you will make the right decision when the time comes," Angie answered solemnly, the edict of a queen facing the detriments of war.

In that moment, I saw why males feared Cambion females. They were some bad bitches.

I looked to Caleb for suggestions, and a small shake of the head was his only answer. Even now with death so close to our front door, he wouldn't bend under the pressure. We would bond on our own terms and for our own reasons. End of discussion.

Caleb turned to his brother still snoring on the couch. Actually, the sound coming from Michael's mouth went beyond the basic snore, but more like two grizzlies fighting over a salmon.

"I should get him to bed. He's drooling all over the upholstery," Caleb said.

"I'll help you." I took one of Michael's arms and helped pull him to his feet.

"Sam, you need to stay here," he warned.

"No I don't. Ruiz said not to leave the building. Last time I checked your room was still in the building. You really wanna fight about this? Tell me you don't want me around and I'll stay here." I waited. In the corner of my eye, I saw Angie look up from her laptop, anticipating his reply.

He didn't answer and his face gave nothing away as he

draped his brother's limp arm over his shoulder. We each took a side and dragged Michael out of the room.

Since the elevators were out of service, the four flights of stairs were a workout that I would've been happy to have worked without. I saw the police caution tape stretched across the elevator doors as we towed Michael down the hall.

Once inside Caleb's suite, we lugged Michael into his bedroom and dropped him on the bed. He looked half dead, lying face down with his mouth wide open. His hair fell loose and draped over the side of the bed. I always wondered why he didn't cut his hair, but it was a pretty walnut brown and felt cool to the touch. I removed his shoes and put a blanket over him, and by the time I looked up, I noticed that I was the only conscious person in the room.

It didn't surprise me that the door to Caleb's bedroom was open. I poked my head inside, following the negative energy thickening the air. Caleb had a large room with a king size bed, an adjoined bathroom, and sitting area. It was dimly lit with neutral, unisex beige carpet, walls, and matching curtains that danced in the cold air from the opened window. Caleb sat on the edge of the bed, holding his head in his hands. He knew I was here, but he was too deep into his dark world to care.

"Are you okay?" I asked, still standing at the door.

"No. I'm as far from okay as one can get. I am in complete and direct opposition to okay. I am the antithesis of okay. I am un-okay."

"Um . . . okay. Sorry I asked," was all I could say after that reply.

When I stepped into the room and closed the door, he sprang off the bed and went to the window. "Just one holiday, one night, could I just have a good time and not have someone die, end up in the hospital, or kidnapped? One fucking night!" he yelled out to the black sky.

His fists slammed against the window sill and the impact cracked the glass and plaster. The air shifted around his body, so strong and violent that I could see it travel across the room in a wave of turbulence. Pictures fell from the walls, chairs and lamps tipped and clattered to the floor; pillows flew off the bed, and anything that wasn't nailed down had been struck by the gale.

It reached my side of the room with enough force to push me back a step. As it passed through me, I gathered that it wasn't just the momentum that took my breath away, but the energy itself. It was rage, pain, frustration; all the things that summed up Caleb's current mood.

I surveyed the disaster area, happy that I didn't have to clean it up. I'd never seen anything like it, not from Caleb, not even on his worst day. This left no doubt that there were some shady dealings afoot.

"Capone?" I called out.

"No, it's still me, Sam. I'm just really pissed off." He hunched over the window, his hands gripping the sill for balance.

I let out a deep breath in gratitude. The last thing we needed was Capone showing up. That was a whole other can of BS that I didn't want opened. I took a seat on his bed. Caleb's mood wasn't going to get any better, so I decided to tackle an issue that's been simmering on the back burner for weeks. "While we're on the topic of Capone, I'll be honest; this X-Men thing you've got going on has me a little concerned. I know you're upset and all, but how much have you fed tonight?"

He turned to me wearily. "Sam I—"

"How much?"

"Five," he mumbled.

"Five girls? Directly?" I took his silence as a yes. "That

is way over the daily limit, dude. Do we need to have an intervention?"

"I'm just trying to hold on to my mind right now. I just saw my brother get shot and Angie's daughter get kidnapped. And all the while I hear Olivia's words. She's right, you know? Everything I touch I destroy. Even you. You were normal before you met me."

"Uh-huh, that's nice. Back to the feeding," I began, refusing to join his pity party. "This has been going on long before tonight. That inferiority complex of yours is making you a power whore, and that power comes at a price. Do you wanna be an incubus? Is that your target goal? Because I already have one of those hunting me down and I don't need another."

"What I want," he began through gritted teeth, "is for no one else to die!" He inhaled deeply, paused, and pushed the air out in a long, shuddering breath.

Correction: It wasn't a breath. That was a sonic shock wave of anger. The air thickened into invisible water rippling from one wall to another then bounced back to its source. This happened twice before the wrinkles smoothed out and the room came into clear focus again.

"All right, that's it. Forget it. You're a grown ass man and I'm not your momma. Do whatever the hell you want. Just do me a favor, don't wreck my new car or shape-shift into any of my classmates when you turn into a demon, okay?" I turned to leave the room.

"Sam, wait, please. I'm sorry."

"Well, you can go and be sorry by yourself. I've got enough blood on my hands." I showed him both of my stained hands to show that I meant it literally. I stepped inside the bathroom and slammed the door for good measure.

I took in the décor, which only reminded me that I was

far from home. The bathroom was spacious and modern, with earth toned tiles in the shower and on the floor, chocolate cabinets, and circular bulbs lining the top of the sink mirror. A stack of plush towels rested on the counter against a raised porcelain sink in the shape of a bowl.

Watching the water turn pink around the drain, I thought about the angry Cambion pacing behind the door, trying his best not to destroy more furniture. But if this was how he coped, who was I to judge him? Emotions were running pretty high tonight and we wouldn't accomplish anything by turning on each other. The body count was climbing and his family was in shambles, all because of obsession and power, power that he was gambling his soul to acquire.

While drying my hands, I recalled what Tobias said tonight. He mentioned something that was done to him and Lilith, something we should remember. Was he talking about the blackout? Then I remembered what Mia told me at the party. I looked around the space for my phone and then cursed at myself for leaving my bag upstairs in Angie's suite. My hand was on the door, ready to go get it, when instinct told me to check inside my top. Just like Nana, I had a habit of storing items inside my bra, including my cell and the body spray bottle of oil I'd taken earlier. I scrolled down the display and searched for the notes I took at the party, but the self-e-mail was gone. I checked my history of sent mail, which was wiped clean of any evidence that the message was sent.

This couldn't have been chalked up to drunk-texting; I was stone sober and coherent enough to operate my phone blindfolded. But then I wasn't the only intelligent being in the room. I didn't ask Lilith if she deleted the e-mail. It could've been a simple error on my part, but the slim possibility of underhanded deeds had my back up. I just knew for certain that I was sick of her hiding info from me.

Everything kept coming back to that day, back to her. I was tired of waiting for the pieces to fall into my lap. People were dying and I needed answers, and there was only one person who could give them to me.

I gripped the counter and screamed in my head, "What is wrong with you? Don't you care about anyone but yourself?"

No response.

My eyes fell on the bottle on the counter. It was less than half empty, maybe two teaspoons at best, but it was enough for me to do what I had to do. I twisted off the spray cap, and without a second thought, I threw my head back and chugged. I pursed my lips tight and held the oil in my mouth and breathed through my nose. I leaned on the counter and focused my attention on the enemy in the mirror. I knew she would hear me.

You have one shot, demon. Come clean or we're both going down. Tell me everything, and I mean everything.

Maybe this was a fatal flaw on my part, but spite was my preferred weapon. She knew I wasn't bluffing, which was why I couldn't feel her moving. I had her where I wanted her, where she should've been all along. If she tried to take over, I would swallow. If she made any sudden movement, if she gave me a report that I didn't like, I would swallow.

I waited for what felt like years for a revelation as saliva collected in my mouth. Then the corner of my vision began to soften and I felt a slight pressure on the back of my head. The room began to move in a swinging motion as music and the sound of a truck engine roared in my ears . . .

14

I've never heard the song on the radio before, but I can tell Tobias likes the tune by the way he sways about as he drives.

The windshield wipers part the downpour and dance in the exact rhythm. Nothing is chasing behind us but the sun and nothing lays ahead but empty road and opportunity. There are no yellow and white lines on this road, but miles of cobblestone and brick bridges rich with history. It's so romantic—our great escape.

I have no idea where we're going, or what we'll do for food and shelter, and I don't care. He mentioned something about "friends in low places," but I can't be bothered with the specifics. A bit of me hopes that we can camp outside under the stars where I can feel the cold against my skin. I can scarcely recall what cold feels like, but I know how it makes Samara uncomfortable, how she prefers dry heat over frost. I have to see what all the fuss is about and experience life without a biased opinion.

Brutal as it seems, I have no regret about taking over. If anything, I feel gratitude. I rejoice in this cramped vessel that she takes for granted, and I covet the treasures that she considers flaws. Underneath all her strength, Samara's just a child, ignorant of her gifts and frightened of her power. Such a waste of potential.

"I like your hair better when it's down," Tobias comments from behind the wheel. I can feel him watching me again, each glance heavier and more heated than the one before. Whenever he stares too long, the truck drifts to the shoulder of the road before righting itself again. After all this time, I still get under his skin.

"I like it too," I say and comb the springy curls through my fingers. Samara's hair smells sweet like something edible, another sign of her innocence.

"How long do you think you can hold on?" he asks.

I turn to look at his perfect profile. His exotic features never fail to take my breath away and the supernatural energy traveling under his skin only enhances it. His tan complexion, the dark fall of waves that touched his shoulders speaks of a life before his fall from grace.

I place my hand on his knee. The touch makes him smile and his gaze settles on the wet road ahead of us. "I'm not sure, but I'll hold on for as long as I can," I promise, and though I mean it, I know it won't be long enough.

His smile fades. "This can't go on, Lilith. Something's gotta give here. You need to make a choice."

"I've made my choice," I assure him.

"Then why is that demon mutt still alive?" he asks. "You said you'd take care of it, but then you turn around and feed him my energy. Whose side are you on?"

"I'm on mine," I reply. "I have to play this right. Samara is more spiteful than Nadine could ever be. Do you really want to be shut out for another three years? She's my vessel and I will protect her, even from herself. She loves Caleb and I won't have her deteriorate like Nadine did."

He chuckles. "She's a fiery one, isn't she? It drives me crazy. It's all I can do to show restraint." He licks his lips and his eyes grow heavy at the thought of her.

"I know. She's perfect." I smile with genuine pride. From the first time Nadine saw her, I knew Samara had spirit. She lifted some of the sadness from Nadine and leaked little cracks of light through the dark. She's so alive; sometimes it's too much to take at once.

Tobias sneaks a glimpse at me. "You love her, don't you?"

I look to the window. "Succubae don't love, Tobias. We consume, and on those rare occasions, become consumed," I reply. "Which is why you can't kill Caleb. I underestimated her feelings for him; she nearly went insane when he was in a coma."

"All the more reason Samara and I should mate," he argues. "I could give her anything she wanted. Money isn't a factor. We could be immortal, be together again, and you wouldn't want for anything."

"Except a daughter," I say.

"Except a daughter," he repeats in a flat, exhausted tone. He rubs his eyes wearily, knowing this argument all too well. Time hadn't changed my feelings on the matter and nothing ever will.

"You always had a zeal for children." He chuckles again, but this time the humor is gone.

"And you don't? You don't want to replenish our race, ensure the lineage carries on? Your kind is an endangered species—maybe fifty left in the world. We need to rebuild, but we can only reproduce through a human body. I told you before; I won't convert until I have at least one offspring. For that to happen I need Samara's consent and the only male she desires is Caleb. He is useful to us." I reach over and run my fingers through his hair.

He quivers at my touch. His frustration flows in ripples around the small space in the truck.

None of this is fair. I was attached to two beings and I can have neither, not yet. Not completely. What is a marriage without a honeymoon? What is a meal without dessert? What is a succubus without her freedom, her feminine power?

"You're right; we need to cover all of our bases. A child would ensure that we carried on, an exit strategy," he agrees just as something large slams behind us.

Tobias's arm braces across my chest before my head hits the dashboard. The impact whips me back against my seat.

"You okay?" Tobias asks, his focus divided between me and the road ahead.

I nod and rub my throbbing forehead. That collision must've shaken something loose, because Samara is gaining consciousness. I can feel her rousing and swimming to the surface again. How much of our conversation did she hear?

I don't have long to consider it as the other vehicle rams into us again. Over and over, it hits the truck then veers into the opposite lane. Tobias steps on the gas, but we can't lose them. We ride side by side on the lane, past the speed limit and at the risk of killing ourselves. I recognize the black Jeep. Oh no! How did he find us so fast?

The Jeep swerves and barrels into Tobias's door in an attempt to push us off the road. Tobias clutches the steering wheel as the tires slip against the wet pavement. When he gains control again, he strikes back by charging the Jeep. The truck crosses the unmarked line to get to the other lane. Before Tobias has time to stop, the Jeep jerks to a halt. The tires screech, fighting for traction against the slick pavement. It soon comes to a complete stop behind us.

Meanwhile, we drift farther and farther into the left lane, coasting its shoulder, then fall into a shallow ditch.

Tobias presses on the gas, but the wheels spin and slip against the mud. No gear can get us out of this mess. "Dammit! We're stuck. We have to go on foot." He glances at the rear view then to his window. "We can hide in the woods."

"I can't. Samara's coming back. I don't have much time."

He holds my face in his hands, his eyes wide and frantic as he says, "I'm not leaving you, you hear me? I'm not losing you again." A door slams, and our attention moves to the rear window. The Jeep is parked a few yards behind us and two men leap out with Caleb. It has to be Haden and Michael.

Tobias takes my hand. "Come on, they're coming."

"I can't." I pull away and try to concentrate on Capone. I need to center on his emotions and know his motives. What little I discover makes me jump. "I have to go with them!"

Tobias's body shakes at my words. "No!"

"We knew this was a longshot. Just go," I plead. "Caleb's brothers are with him and they're armed. They won't hurt me, but they're here to kill you."

"They'll have to catch me first," Tobias says as his body begins to dissolve before my eyes. I reach out and touch the translucent shape of his face, which passes through my fingers like smoke. I can't lose him, not like this. He's right; if this is how it will end, they would have to catch him first. Maybe I can distract them.

"Samara!" I hear Caleb's voice and approaching foot-steps.

I open my door and dash in the direction of the woods.

"Samara!" Caleb yells. "Stop!"

I race deeper into the forest. Rain and wet leaves slap my face, but I have no time to enjoy its texture. Trees and branches cross my vision until an overcast of foliage hides the sunlight. I can't find Tobias, but I can still feel him nearby.

"Samara! Where are you?" someone yells, but I can't tell who it is.

A moving swatch of black appears to my left, then another appears to my right. Twigs snap. Leaves rustle. Tiny specks of color blink in the forest. They're gaining on me fast, cutting through the brush, trying to cage me in. They move as I do, and they bound over bushes and fallen logs.

I run faster, harder, pushing this human body to its limits. It can't fly like I want it to and it can't dissolve into specks of matter and mingle with the ether. Tobias told me what it was like to ascend, and maybe one day I will know the experience for myself, but for now, I have to keep moving. I can't let them find me, no matter how futile it might be. Caleb will always know where I am and he would comb the earth to find his mate. He's as much a part of me as Samara, and in this moment, I hate him.

The trees begin to thin out and I can see the sun again. Further on, the forest gives way to a small field swept clean of trees, leaving a graveyard of stumps and stacked logs as ruined tombs.

A sharp pain hits my spine and I stumble and lose my speed. Samara's will digs into me, pulling herself out of her shallow grave. She's fighting hard to weigh me down, to stall me, but I have to keep moving. Just a little bit farther, just a little bit longer. I need more time, but she isn't in a generous mood.

"Lilith!" Caleb's voice echoes in the forest.

I search the trees, but my vision begins to swell again. Dizziness overtakes me and the world pulls away as it always does.

"Oh no. Not yet, Samara, not yet."

I'm not strong enough, but I'll fight for one more second, needing more than anything to stay here. I have to keep going, even if I have to crawl. Just a little farther. Just one . . . more . . .

"Lilith, stop, or I swear I'll shoot you in the leg!" he threatens.

I obey, but I keep my back to him. I don't want to look into his eyes. I know what I'll see if I do. "Why do you always ruin everything?" I ask.

"It's a gift." He moves closer. Leaves and grass shuffle under his feet. "Where is Tobias?"

"He's gone."

"You're lying," he says from somewhere to my left. "I'm too close to you and he can't stand it. He would never leave you alone any more than I would." He drifts around me slowly, carefully and I sense a change in his demeanor, something raw and primal that I didn't recognize until now. The darkness inside him did not originate from Caleb, but something living in Caleb's nature that should never be exposed to light. Capone.

I look in his direction as he emerges from behind a tree. His damp hair sticks to his face; his wild gaze shoots through the wet strands. The hostile vibe in the air suddenly thickens. But what concerns me more is the weapon in his hand, a sharp, treacherous tool I've seen many times before, specifically on Halloween night. I have no doubt that he knows how to use it. Capone knows what Caleb knows, they've been together since birth.

I stare at Capone, noting the difference between him and his master. There isn't any, only the bright glow to his eyes that hurts to look directly into.

"You expect me to stand by while you hurt my mate? Haven't you and your family taken enough from me?" I ask.

He stops. "You blame me for Nadine's death. You want revenge, I get it. Is that why you poisoned me?"

I flinch at his words. "How do you know about that?"

"The energy Samara fed me in the hospital had a lot of interesting memories with it. Like the one with anointing oil and a cup of hot chocolate. I thought it was Samara's doing at first, but when she mentioned her blackouts and Tobias, well, things added up. I took the memory from Caleb. He can never know you betrayed us."

He circles around me, slow and methodical in his attempt to lure me in. His glare pins me in place. The anger lights his eyes in a radiant swirl of lilac, the brightest I've ever seen them. And yet his eyes give the false impression of heat, because the emotion rolling off his body is ice cold. I deserve this hostility, but he needs to see my side of things. I've been robbed of something I can never get back again.

"You don't understand. Tobias is . . . he was my mate. I want that feeling again, to belong to someone. It's different with you and me; we don't have that connection."

"And where does this leave Caleb? Where does this leave me?"

I've never cried before, not in a human way. It prickles the eyes a little and contracts the lungs a bit, but it doesn't quite express pain as we know it. Worst of all, Capone can feel all of it right now. Not even this can I keep from him.

"How do you think Samara will handle knowing what you made her do? You forget who your master is and you underestimate me. Both are very stupid moves, Lilith. Now where is Tobias!" he demands.

Before I can respond, the wind picks up, drawing our attention to the sky. With Capone distracted, I turn and rush toward the field. The wind grows stronger, pushing back the tree limbs and flattening the grass in the forest bed. It moves closer in a dark miasma cloaking around me.

"Lilith!" Capone calls behind me, but I ignore him.

The storm condenses and solidifies as it settles to the ground. Tobias steps forward, his body still taking shape, the black mist swirling in a moving galaxy in human form.

I race into his arms, seeking refuge, an escape. This is my last chance, but our window is brief. Instantly, we're surrounded on all sides in the field. Purple lights float in the air, watching us.

Haden speaks first, closing in at our right. He points a pistol at Tobias's head. "Give us a reason to shoot you. Please do."

"You messed with the wrong family, demon!" Michael moves to our left, tossing a long, jagged blade from hand to hand.

Tobias steps In front of me. "You can't have her, and you can't kill me. What can you do?"

"Improvise." Capone answers and lifts the longbow.

Tobias spins around and faces Capone. "An arrow? It's gonna take more than that to get rid of me. I'm immortal."

"Not . . . quite." Capone pulls back the string of the bow. One eye levels with the arrow head, which points directly to my heart.

Tobias jumps. "Are you crazy? Stop!"

"Caleb, what are you doing?" Michael yells.

I looked to the man on the left. He called him Caleb. He doesn't know what's happening.

Tobias chuckles nervously. "You're bluffing. You wouldn't kill your mate."

"Unlike you, I'm not afraid of dying. And I'd rather have her die than to be with you."

A scream cradles in my throat as I watch Capone's posture straighten. His bent arm lines perfectly with his shoulder. He isn't bluffing.

"I'll make it quick. Don't move. Don't even breathe," Capone warns.

His words, this entire situation is all too familiar. The events on Halloween night return to me: the smell of wet grass, the oil in the hot cocoa, glittery fairy wings catching on the breeze, and the candy apple resting on Samara's head. And the arrow. Samara trusted Caleb's aim, trusted him to never hurt her. But this wasn't Caleb.

With a pluck of his finger, he lets the arrow fly and I close my eyes and await my fate.

"No!" A voice yells just as a hand shoves me to the right. I stumble and something whizzes past my ear. Then the woods are quiet. My eyes fly open and the first thing I see is Capone lowering his bow. He smirks wickedly as the target in front of him stumbles.

Tobias kneels a foot away from me, gaping at the arrow lodged in his chest. For a millisecond, I see the proud look on his face. Human weapons can't kill him, and he finds Capone's feeble attempt insulting. But that look vanishes the second the burning begins. It rushes in like a ball of fire, dropping all three of us to our knees simultaneously.

I've felt this torture before, and in this instant, everything comes to light with startling clarity. The arrow. It was laced, a poison dart covered in olive oil. Not even

Capone had anticipated the crippling pain that came with that one strike.

I keep my focus on Tobias. He's curled on his side, clutching his throat. His free hand pounds into the ground, his fingers pull clumps of soil out of the earth. He uses what strength he has left to drag himself toward me, but that soon gives way and he collapses. Wide, glassy eyes stare out into somewhere none of us can see, a place we will soon follow. His face contorts and twists as blood trickles from his mouth.

Fire eats through my bones and pokes holes in my lungs. There is air all around me, it passes through my hair, it dances across my cheeks, it carries the smell of rain and burning flesh to my nostrils, but I can't inhale a single draft. My chest caves in and my heart feels as though it is about to explode.

"Caleb, get Sam out of here now!" A rough voice calls in the distance. The English accent tells me that it's Haden, but it's thicker than usual, the words running into each other in frenzy.

"He's weak, but still alive. We have to finish this now!" Capone yells. He's close, somewhere next to me. I try to reach out to him, but I can't move my hands.

"Not until we find a way to kill him for good. He's disabled right now and we'll make sure he stays that way. The oil will buy us more time. Get Sam home. Call her mum and tell her she's safe," Michael says. More footsteps crunch the grass.

"I'm not leaving—"

"You can't know where we take his body, Caleb! You and Sam are still connected to him. We'll take care of this. Now go!" Haden's voice thunders through the trees, carrying his command deeper into the forest.

A hand tucks under me and lifts me off the ground and solid arms cradle me like a child, a dying bride. I open my eyes and behold the gentle face of my groom, my murderer. He smells so sweet and the lilac shade has cooled to a deep royal purple.

"Lilith," he rasps. "You have to feed from me now, or Tobias will drag you down with him. You need my energy. I have enough for the both of us."

I turn my head away from his mouth. "You knew, didn't you? You knew he would jump in the path of the arrow."

"It's what I would've done if the tables were turned, so yeah. It was a risk, but it was worth it."

"What do you want, Capone?" I ask.

"What I've always wanted. Even after all the shit you put us through, I still want you. You're my mate and Caleb loves Samara, which only compounds what I feel. That hold you say Tobias has on you, you have on me." He turns my head to look him in the eyes. "But I won't have you compromise my vessel again. I've been miserable for too long and Samara's the only thing that brings him joy. Whether you want to admit it or not, Sam's love for him overrides anything you might feel. Nadine is gone and her hold on you is gone with it, including Tobias's. Sam is safe with Caleb. No other male will claim her but him, and I will kill anyone who tries, you understand?"

I know he means every word, and that truth hurts worse than the poison eating through my bones. I'm being torn in two and I have to choose quickly. Life with Capone or death with Tobias. To thrive or to burn.

"If I agree, I want something in return." I look over to Tobias who lay still on the grass. Haden and Michael tower over him in triumph, weapons at the ready. "Never tell Samara what happened here today or what happened on Halloween. She won't remember anything when she revives and she can never know."

He closes his eyes and nods. "You protect Samara, I

protect Caleb. Once they are bonded, she might not be so quick to put herself in danger."

He doesn't wait for me to nod; he knows my answer, knows I have nowhere else to go. He's all I have now and I'm at his mercy.

"You're not so different from me. Our lives depend on Samara. Yours more than mine. Remember that." His fingers brush the hair away from my face and his lips press against mine.

Electricity passes into my mouth and the familiar flavor of life crackles on my wet tongue, a sweetness I almost forgot. It slides down smooth and coats over my body like a salve, and the sensation of falling overtakes me. I can still see the violet glow of his eyes as I close mine.

So bright, so peaceful . . .

15

How did I let this happen?

I asked that question twenty times while this horror show played to its conclusion, and got no decent answer. The credits rolled, the theater was empty, the ushers swept up the fallen popcorn, and I was still seated in a state of petrification.

Hot tears flooded my vision and burned my skin as they ran down my cheeks. Gut-churning nausea was kicking in and I just wanted to die. No, scratch that, I wanted this psychotic demon bitch living inside me to die. I couldn't remember being so mad in my life. All the weeks of grieving over Caleb; the nights I prayed for his recovery came back to scorn me. Worst of all, I'd known what Lilith was capable of.

You tried to kill my boyfriend. Are you crazy? I took care of you and you do this to me?

Lilith jittered and crawled under my skin like a worm, but I closed it out. She'd lost all her special privileges, explicitly my compassion. This betrayal in all its potency spiked my system with poison, killing any ounce of kindness or respect for her life. To be fair, what's to stop her from trying again? She'd always be there, biding her time until I lowered my guard, and I couldn't lock myself in a sealed bunker of depression for the rest of my life like Nadine had. This would never end, and Lilith would only play me again if I let her. A rush of relief washed over me and I felt light with the soothing knowledge that in one gulp it would be all over.

"Sam! Are you all right?" Caleb said through the door.

I froze. I completely forgot that he was still there, but then this *was* his hotel room. I didn't know what to do. I couldn't speak and if I kept quiet, he'd think there was something wrong. Knowing him, he would try to stop me, save me from myself or some other nonsense. I didn't want to be saved right now. I wanted blood; I wanted the head of my enemy on my dashboard. Since I couldn't have that, this was as close as I would get.

Murder was on the agenda this evening, but my throat, that stubborn accomplice, refused to cooperate. My cheeks puffed out, spit pooled in my mouth, making me drool, but my throat wouldn't open or flex. As a devout eater and drinker, I never had to consciously will food to go down, not even that nasty medicine I had to take as a kid that tasted like bubble gum. The pounding on the door startled me, but not even the element of surprise loosened my throat.

"What are you doing in there?" he demanded, his energy leaking under the door, through the fibers of the wood to touch me. Though jumbled, those violent pulses conveyed anger, fear, and named me as the source.

Suddenly, in a type of electric jolt, realization struck and presented a sobering account of what I was doing, what I was *about* to do and what was still in my mouth. I couldn't do this, not to him and certainly not to myself, whoever she was anymore.

I bent over the sink and spat out all the oil, then dipped my mouth under the nozzle and rinsed repeatedly. I used one of the tiny sample packets of tooth paste to help wash away any evidence of oil.

The knocking grew more persistent—police drug raid style—making the wood of the door wobble from the impact. "Sam, can you hear me?"

"Yeah, I'll be out in a second." I washed my hands and face before going out to meet him.

I opened the door and found Caleb outside watching me carefully, looking for blood, some self-inflicted wound, or an alien probe. "What's wrong?" he asked.

"Lilith poisoned you on Halloween and Capone tried to kill me with an arrow," I answered in one breath.

It took a few times of repeating it for him to finally get it. "I would remember something like that, Sam."

"Not if Capone doesn't want you to remember." I told him the vision from beginning to end. I watched his expression morph into confusion, then surprise and rage; it was like watching a rare flower come into bloom then quickly shrivel. It was as remarkable as much as it was tragic.

When I finished, he leaned against the wall and stared straight ahead, his face wiped clean of emotion. Caleb may bug me at times—okay, ninety percent of the time—but the one thing I couldn't stand, what I absolutely loathed was his silence. It was a slow, agonizing death that I couldn't bear.

"Say something," I begged.

"What were you doing in the bathroom just now?" The question made me wish he'd kept silent. When I didn't answer, he said, "Capone was going crazy. I was a second away from busting the door down."

"I had a bottle of olive oil in my bra."

He didn't need a calculator to add things up, and the result made his eyes blaze with fury. With frightening speed, he crowded my personal space, forcing me to retreat to the bathroom. He kept coming then caught my cheeks in his hand and studied me carefully. "Did you swallow any of it?"

It was hard to talk with him holding my face like that, so I shook my head.

"Are you lying?" he asked, his voice thick with fear.

I shook my head again then he dragged his trembling hands around my neck. He looked like he wanted to choke me, but he just traced my jawline with his thumbs. "Get undressed and take a shower."

The randomness of the command threw me off. "What—"

"Shower, wash your hair, brush your teeth, scrub every trace of oil off you. I'll wait outside." Caleb left the bathroom with a slam that almost broke the door.

I didn't know what else to do, so I removed my clothes then climbed into the shower. I followed his instructions to the letter, lathering, rinsing, and scrubbing until my skin was red and raw. To say Caleb was livid did him a disfavor and I deserved every ounce of his wrath. Under the hot, needling spray, I felt too weak to do anything but absorb the current of rage aimed at me.

Once I dried off, I wrapped up in a fluffy white towel, then opened the door. Caleb stood against the wall by the bedroom door, staring at the ceiling with his hands behind his back.

Before I could speak or even step into the room, he said, "Memories are weird. It's hard to tell which ones are yours; what's food and what's real experience. Michael has trouble sorting out the two, so he blocks it out with alcohol and whatever he can get his hands on. I've seen what it does to him—that's why I don't drink, but I can really use one right now."

"You remember what happened?" I clicked off the bathroom light and stepped into the bedroom.

He nodded. "I guess Capone figured there was no point in holding back now. Let me see if I've got this right. Lilith takes over your body and Tobias snatches you out of school in that Malik guy's truck. Capone rams the truck off the road, shoots Tobias with a poisoned arrow, and then my brothers hide his body. You and I go back to normal, having no clue of what happened. Now Tobias's soul is possessing innocent men, shooting people, and kidnapping young girls because he wants his body back. Just a typical holiday in Williamsburg, huh?" He rubbed his eyes in a circular motion. "I really could've done without knowing this, Sam, I really could've." After a deep breath, he asked, "You feeling better?"

"No. Having a hard time getting this knife out of my back," I replied. "Lilith should have her own slogan. Sentient beings: we put the 'suck' in succubus."

Caleb looked up at me, and in that moment he looked old and tired. "You're really that shocked? Demons and Cambions prey on vulnerable victims. You've seen what the draw can do; perfectly sane people turn into mindless slaves, risking death for just one taste of what we offer. Everyone has their weaknesses. Tobias happens to be hers."

"That weakness almost got us killed and she took my memories away to cover her tracks!"

"Lilith knows you pretty well. She knew what you would try to do if you found out. You have a bad temper and you shoot first and ask questions later," he replied.

I couldn't believe what I was hearing. Was he actually defending her? "You don't know that."

"You just proved her right! Just now in the bathroom!" His face was turning red; his eyes brimmed with tears too stubborn to fall. "How could you do something like that? How could you hurt yourself and not give a shit about how it would affect the people around you, including me? *Especially* me."

He sure knew how to put a negative slant on things. "I had to get rid of Lilith. I figured you would understand, seeing as you're the one that she almost killed! She took over and was ready to skip town, and who knows what would've happened if you didn't stop her."

There was something very unsettling about his laugh. It was a low, deep rumble in his chest, ripe with derision. "Every decision you make affects me, more than anyone else. I'd figured you would've gotten that by now, but obviously you haven't." He pushed off the wall and stalked forward. "You really think you're helping anyone by taking your own life? What do you think my reaction would be? 'Cause you know I've never had to mourn over a woman I cared about, so that would be a new and exciting experience for me."

"I didn't go through with it, okay? So calm down. It wasn't about you."

"That's the point!" he snapped. "You weren't thinking about me, or your parents, or anyone else that might care about you."

"Why should I?" I yelled. "I'm the victim here—no one else is going through this shit but me! No one else is being hijacked and used as a hand puppet. Everyone has their petty lives and their petty dramas while I'm fighting for my soul. You say you don't like being manipulated, well guess what, neither do I. I've been dropped into a freaky ass world full of death and half explanations. I've lied to every single person I know, including myself. I don't know who I am anymore!" I squatted on the floor and screamed into my palms.

The need for retribution was still raging. I wanted my pound of flesh and I felt cheated. I screamed and screamed until my throat burned, until I was empty of the poison in my veins, empty of sound, empty of thought. I wanted to claim and make a new home in that white noise that came with nothing. But Caleb, my *sweet, worrisome* Caleb, wouldn't let me.

I felt his hands scoop under my arms to pull me up, and then he wrapped his arms around me. My head rested against his chest and I listened to the quick flutter of his heartbeat. We twisted from side to side in a gentle rocking motion that made me drowsy.

Resting his chin on the top of my head, he said, "You're Samara Nicole Marshall, esquire, barista, bookworm, and Shakespearean Tae Bo master. Fellow sugar junkie and perpetual smartass. My main squeeze. My best friend."

This was the second time in a week I'd cried in front of him, and it wasn't pretty.

He must've noticed that too, because he asked, "Aw hell, are you crying, again? Please don't cry. The 'fighting and cussing' Sam I can handle, but the 'sad and weepy' Sam is beyond my capability."

"I can't help it." I sniffled and wiped my tears on his shirt.

"No seriously, try. We're linked. If you start crying, then I'm gonna cry, and then it's just gonna get weird."

I gripped the lapel of his shirt and laughed. He held my face and wiped my tears with his thumbs. His expression changed to a more serious one. "Don't ever do that to me again, Sam. Promise me."

"I promise," I answered. "I know it was stupid, I just

had a weak moment. I was overdue for a meltdown, don't you think? You had yours; why can't I have mine?"

"Yeah. It's been a really screwed up year and you've taken all of it like a champ. But you don't have to go through it alone. I know everything you're going through—I can feel it. We need to trust each other completely now, no matter what. I'll make a deal with you. I'll cut back on the feeding if you let this go. Just let this one thing slide."

I shook my head. "It's not that easy."

"It's not that easy for me to cut my diet, but I'll do it for you. Capone needs his mate as much as I need mine." He pulled away and held my shoulders at arm's length. Stooping down with watery eyes leveled to mine, he said, "Listen to me. I'm not trying to be sweet or romantic or feed you some line to get into your pants. I'm not some kid with a crush and I'm not whipped. This is a physical and literal fact. I. Can't. Live. Without. You."

I wasn't sure how to take those words, unclear if they were a form of endearment or condemnation. Both meanings made my pulse skip and the look he offered me, stripped bare of pretense and sarcasm, managed to steal my air supply.

We stared at each other, silently debating what would happen next. Warmth spread over my shoulders and wrapped me in a cozy blanket of his power. I gave in to the intoxicating feeling and allowed my knees to go weak with the complete understanding of what it meant. I didn't want to fight anymore, not with him and not over something so easy to fix. I just wanted him to hold me. I wanted to kiss him and fall asleep next to him.

We had reached that agreement at the same time and sealed our contract with a kiss that could've gone on for hours, days, eons, if our bodies hadn't plotted mutiny. My lips parted and slanted over his, finding that perfect, familiar fit. His tongue plunged inside and on contact, my stomach dropped.

His fingers sank into my hair and combed loose the wet curls. Not wanting to be idle, I let my fingers do some loosening too, starting with the buttons of his shirt. Each free button exposed more of his creamy white skin and strengthened my resolve to continue. His body tensed, his breathing sped up, straining to keep still as he studied my reaction.

I admired our color contrast of porcelain and copper, and enjoyed the texture and the pulsating energy under my hand. I kissed everywhere my mouth could reach and my lips burned from the salty heat of his skin. He smelled sweet, a heady musk of vanilla and sugar and other confections that seemed to seep out of his pores. He must have had enough because he gripped my hair and kissed me again. The kiss was a devouring of the sweetest and highest order where breathing was no longer a top priority.

I didn't notice we were moving until I felt the soft padding of the mattress. He crawled over me, leaving nips on my neck and shoulder and lower still. His hair spilled over his face and slid over my skin in satin ribbons.

"Tell me to stop," he demanded softly, his breath hot and sweet against my neck. "Hit me. Push me away, scream out; anything to make me stop." He began to move against me, the rough texture of his jeans creating a delicious friction.

My hands threaded through his hair, then held a chunk of it in a fist as his hands slipped under my towel. His tongue invaded my mouth and stroked in the same maddening rhythm as his fingers. Just before I went cross-eyed, he broke the kiss long enough for me to catch my breath.

"It's not too late to stop," he pleaded then licked the seam of my mouth in a slow, languorous glide.

"Yes it is," I said just below a whisper, which was as loud as my lung capacity would allow. It was true; it was too late—months too late—and I needed to feel something other than anguish right now. There was that conscious part of me that screamed for me to hit the brakes and consider the consequences of going farther, but all I could focus on was his hands and the fire quickly spreading in my belly.

He stopped touching me and I whimpered at the loss and reached blindly for his warmth.

I opened my eyes and found him kneeling over me, peeling off his shirt one shoulder at a time. He made a show of it, and if I had cash on hand I would've slipped it into his jeans. In that moment I would've emptied my bank account, broken into my college fund to see more. The look he gave me implied that this was a private performance, free of charge.

He tossed the shirt behind his head to the floor and I did the same with my towel without a second thought. Caleb unbuttoned his jeans then stopped to watch me. The cool air latched to my skin, but it was the feral glow in his eyes that caused the goose bumps.

I relaxed and laid back on the pillow while his hands squeezed the inside of my leg, my hip, and the doughy curve of my belly. "You have the softest skin, Samara. I'll never get over it. Never."

He began a slow crawl up the length of my body then wrapped my legs around his waist. Not wanting to separate again, he rocked from side to side and wiggled his jeans down his hips while I helped push them off his legs with my feet.

Soft lips outlined my jaw and neck as he whispered, "I

don't wanna hurt you, but you're kinda, um, new to this." He propped his weight on his elbows and searched my face for any hesitation, any change of heart. I gave him my answer by pulling him closer.

He pinned my hands over my head, laced his fingers between mine then began to move, and only he heard the sharp gasp that followed. Caleb had covered my mouth with his own, capturing the sound, keeping my momentary pain all to himself. Trembling, he waited for me to relax, kissed the tears from my face and whispered sweet talk that made it impossible for me to keep still.

My hands traced the smooth muscles in his back and he took that as a signal to continue. The groove of his spine tightened and relaxed under each motion. The weight of his body was a foreign but welcomed discovery, the contact of bare skin against skin; the kiss of our belly buttons. I clutched on to his shoulder blade for leverage and rode out the wave that threatened to drown us both.

Our spirits met in a clash of color, the impact rattling every knot in my spine, making me arch off the bed. Emerald and amethyst melded and swirled behind my eyelids in a trippy screensaver. The past, fragmented and disjointed, filled my memory bank, inviting me to partake in his life as I assumed he was doing with mine. It took all my strength to breathe and the humidity made the air too thick to take in.

His heartbeat thrummed within my own chest, uneven at first but slowly ebbing into a strange harmony. Our energies mingled in a captivating dance before returning to its owner. Back and forth it went, heightening its pitch, building intensity until an outpour of energy left me paralyzed, speechless, and without sight.

"I love you, Samara. I . . . love . . ." The broken utterance tore from his lips and it was the last sound I heard before the world faded to black. My final thought was one of pure joy for being able to give him the perfect gift, the one thing he always wanted: for me to be his and his alone.

The sun was rising outside when I forced myself awake. Caleb was somewhere behind me—I could feel his warmth on my back—and I tried my best not to wake him as I got up. Even in lethargy, I couldn't block out what had happened between us. It was too surreal and it would be branded in my brain forever.

I studied the walls around the room with embarrassment. The things these walls had seen. Cold air filled the room, likely due to the opened window, and I immediately wanted to crawl back under the covers. The pillows called me to come back and I teetered toward them, but snapped back up, remembering my mission. With one eye open, I padded to the bathroom, which was a challenge as my brain was in what I call astral-potty.

> *astral-potty [as-tral-pä-tē] ~noun*
> *The half-conscious state where the need to urinate is incorporated in one's dream due to the refusal to disrupt sleep. The individual falls under a false belief of wakefulness and performs bathroom functions while still in bed. The dreamer is known to awake at the last minute, but results may vary. Side effects include: bedwetting, disorientation, humiliation, soiling of clothing, and falling asleep while still on the toilet.*

Whether it was sleep, or the lack thereof, I felt a little out of sorts. I felt taller, heavier, with a deep craving for pancakes. I clicked on the light and was instantly blinded by the hot bulb burning my sockets. I waded blindly to the toilet, and out of habit, lifted the seat and . . . wait, why did I do that?

My eyes still tried to adjust to the lights when I looked down to find nothing but white skin, long hairy legs, a flat chest, a toned stomach and a thin line of hair beneath the navel leading to . . . *whoa!*

I was pretty sure everyone in the hotel could hear my scream. It was a good thing I was standing over the toilet, because panic didn't really help a heavy bladder.

"Omigod, omigod, omigod!" I had no other response, nothing articulate anyway. I was still partially asleep and my brain was pretty much oatmeal right now, so this could very well be a dream. I could still be in the astral-potty phase; because there was no way on God's green earth that I was standing half a foot taller over a toilet while sporting guy junk.

"Sam?" I knew that voice, and it sounded foreign coming through the door. It was mine.

"Sam, you all right?" The door opened and there I was, standing in the doorway, naked as the day I was born. Arms, legs, belly, hair, eyes—all of it stood across the room. I screamed again, which made the other me follow suit.

"What the hell?" the other me asked, all wide-eyed and hysterical.

"I don't know!" I answered, jumping up and down.

"Aim in the bowl!" The other me pointed to where I was spraying.

I held my hands up in the air. I didn't want to touch anything. Freaking out was not the right term for what I was going through, and in all honesty, I didn't know what to freak out about. All the events rammed into each other, fighting for top billing.

"Stop screaming!" the other me said.

"Then why are *you* screaming?" I asked.

"I don't know!" the doppelganger said before lowering her voice. "It's me, it's Caleb. Sam, just—"

"Get out!"

"Why? That's my body." She pointed at me or rather to the fire hose still going off on its own.

"Get out!" I pointed to the door.

"Fine." The other me, or, Caleb, closed the door.

Alone, I took a breath to calm down, then I saw that I was still peeing. What was he, a camel? Before I marked my territory on everything in the bathroom, I managed to angle directly into the bowl.

I'd had strange moments as a Cambion, I've had demons impersonate me, but I've never had a full body swap before. I *was* Caleb. I was inside him. His arms and legs were mine, his hair and teeth were mine, and after I flushed the toilet and went to the mirror, I realized that his eyes were also mine.

This sort of thing was written nowhere in Angie's Cambion handbook for dummies. But as my vision began to clear and I could register the cold tiles under my feet, I knew that it was a journal entry in the making.

I tried to concentrate, sensing Capone wiggling around inside. It was a strange fit. Instead of zings up my back, there was a sensation more like rolling surf beginning at the pit of my stomach and rising all the way to the base of my skull. A funny tickle traced my torso and I knew it was him. He seemed friendly, frisky even, like an eager puppy wanting to be petted.

Feeling adventurous, I took my time examining these new body parts. From a scientific standpoint; it fascinated me to see how the other half lived. His skin was so smooth.

"Samara! Cut that out!" Caleb yelled from outside.

I jumped, startled to have been caught with my hands in the cookie jar. "What?"

"I can feel that," he said in my voice.

"You can?"

"Yup, just like you can feel this," he said and I felt a sharp pinch on my butt.

I yelped then stared at the door and the unseen horrors that stood behind it.

"Can you come out here now? I'll explain what happened."

There was no way to prolong this, but I gave it my best shot. I took a towel and wiped up the mess I made, washed my hands, then grabbed another towel to wrap around my waist. It was distracting having his guy parts waving in the breeze.

I stepped out of the bathroom and found him—me—sitting on the bed wearing Caleb's buttoned shirt.

I stood there for a minute, staring at myself, not a mirror image or demonic duplicate, but my real body. But the posture and sly curl to the lips was all Caleb.

"Uh, hey," was all I could say.

"Hey. You all right?"

"Well, I don't know. Let's see, I go to sleep for a few hours and wake up a tall white dude. You tell me."

"How do you think I feel? I'm a short black chick with perky breasts now." He pulled open his collar and peeked inside his shirt. Licking his lips, he crooned, "Hmm. *Hello* ladies!"

"Stop that!" I slapped his hand. "How do we go back to normal? I can't go to school like this."

"The same way we got into this mess. This is part of the Cambion bonding. This is why a mated pair can't live without each other, because we *are* each other. We're one."

"So, you're saying the only way to go back is . . ."

He patted the bed. "Ready for round two?"

"Oh, hell no!" I leaped back. "Okay, Caleb, there is

weird, there's really weird, and then there's this. I'm looking at myself right now."

He slipped off the bed and stepped forward. As he did so, he let the hem of the button down shirt fall to the knees. My hair was a wild tumbleweed of curls, my lips were swollen and I had to admit, I had a charming, child-like appeal. However, the look Caleb was giving me was far from innocent. Those jade green eyes looked at me like I was prime rib. What was worse, I was having a re-action to this sight, on account of the heavy, delightful ache that was creating a tent in my towel. My heart was racing and I was growing dizzy from a sudden blood rush. I couldn't believe it. I was actually getting turned on by looking at my own body.

Did this mean I was a lesbian? Was this narcissism on a whole other level? It was a good thing I was getting therapy soon, because I knew I would need it after this. This was enough to traumatize anyone for life.

"It's the only way to get back to normal. They don't call it the mating *process* for no reason."

I shook my head dumbly. "Are we going to go through this every time?"

"I don't think so." When I didn't move, he said, "It's me, Sam. It's just us. For now on, it'll always be just us."

His words, though comforting, did nothing to diminish the freak factor of this entire experience. But I took the hand offered and with my eyes closed, allowed him to lead me back to the bed. Let it go on record that the first of this year was the craziest day of my life, one that I would never forget. And it was only seven A.M.

16

I woke up to the sound of loud breathing next to my ear. At first, the presence alarmed me, but the white sheets, the jumbo pillows, and the heavy arm slung over my waist refreshed my memory. The sun poured through the blowing curtains, warming the room in a buttery yellow filter.

I rolled over to face my noisy sleep mate, thankful that he was back in his own body. Caleb lay on his stomach, his damp hair spilling over his face and into his eyes. Dark lashes fanned over his flushed cheeks, and his jaw was shadowed with stubble. He looked so peaceful when he slept, but even the most troublesome child had an angelic bed manner. Though his eyes remained closed, a faint smile touched his lips, lips that were still red and swollen from kissing.

My hands circled the curve of his shoulder and down to his arm, squeezing the distension of muscle. Feeling wicked, I traced his spine with my fingers and then slid them under the sheet. Cake Boy may be pale and thin, but he had the cutest butt.

"You done molesting me, woman?" he mumbled against the pillow.

"Nope," I said and continued my exploration.

"You need to stop doing that, or else you're asking for trouble," Caleb warned. "Guys tend to have issues in the morning."

"I noticed." I smiled. "I also noticed you snore."

"So what? You drool." He opened one eye, and a prismatic whirl of color peeked through his lashes. "How long have you been awake?"

I brushed the fallen strands from his face. "A couple minutes. I'm just watching you sleep."

He cringed. "Oh, God! Why? That's so creepy."

"Can't help it. You give me plenty to think about."

His one opened eye narrowed at me. "Right. You hungry?"

I nodded. "Starving."

"I thought so. I'll order room service."

"With actual food or the server?"

"Food. We need to build our strength; we've worked up an appetite." He wagged his eyebrows. Still lying on his belly, he leaned over the side of the bed to the phone that had fallen from the nightstand.

"You seem peppy today. The world is falling apart and you're cooler than a fan. Why?" I asked.

"Well, I just woke up, Sam, and spazzing out is counterproductive. Waking up with you helps."

As he ordered our meal, Caleb watched me stretch across the bed, bound like a mummy in the sheets. We were both grinning fools today, and I wasn't sure if last night was something to cheese about.

When he hung up, he crawled over to me, pulled me

closer to him, and looked at me with such warmth, I felt myself blush. "How are you feeling?"

"I'm a little sore, but I'm good. In fact I got a nice little buzz going on." I giggled. My eyes were closed, basking in my high, when I felt something cold and flat over my eyelids. I could tell by the size and weight of these two small objects to know that they were quarters.

"This is a good look for you," he said.

"What? Wearing your change?" I kept still so the quarters wouldn't fall.

"No. Lying in my bed. It's the perfect fit and flatters your figure. Very becoming." I could feel him lean in, felt his lips hovering over mine when a knock on the door killed the moment.

Caleb and I stopped moving. My eyes flew open and the coins slid from my face to each side of my temples. We knew it had to be Michael and we weren't ready to face the world just yet. Maybe if we were quiet he would go away, but the voice through the door spoiled that plan.

"I know you're in there. Wake up, I need to talk to you," Michael called.

Caleb looked to me for suggestions but there was nothing I could do. Our time had run out and reality and all the crazy it entailed would have caught up with us eventually. With reluctance, Caleb crawled out of bed, slid on his boxers, then went to the door. I pulled the covers around me and enjoyed the noon sun bouncing off his naked torso. His back muscles flexed and rolled under his skin. The things that body could do had me giggling like a total idiot.

Caleb opened the door and stared up at his brother in the hall. Michael looked grave and disheveled, a clear side effect of his drinking binge.

"Any word about Haden?" Caleb asked before Michael could open his mouth.

"He's still in ICU. Ruiz needs to see us," he replied.

"That's funny, because I need to see you. We need you to help us get Tobias's body and destroy it. We know you and Haden hid it somewhere."

Michael shot a quick glimpse over his shoulder, then stepped forward. "You know we can't. You're still connected. We can't kill him until you and Sam . . ." He paused as Caleb flung the door wider. Michael's gaze fell on me, curled on the bed covered neck deep in a sheet. I shrieked and burrowed deeper under the covers, exposing only my eyes. After Michael got his eyeful, Caleb narrowed the door so his body stood in the crack.

"Tell Ruiz we'll be out in five minutes. I have an idea, one that will solve all of our problems." Caleb slammed the door in his brother's face.

Five minutes was more like fifteen. Caleb let me borrow a pair of sweats and we dressed in silence. I tried not to think about what would happen after today. Being a bound pair would make our lives durable as well as fragile. We would be stronger together and we could survive where other Cambions couldn't. It was a small comfort, enough to get me through the day, at least.

The room was a sight, clothes and objects lay everywhere, and the rumpled bed sheets had their own story to tell, but it had been our world for a few strange and glorious hours. I wanted to stay here. Was I being clingy?

Caleb looked at me as if he could hear my thoughts exclusively. I knew he couldn't, but he could feel the desperation behind them. He covered his own reaction with a smile, but the somber emotion behind the grin betrayed him. Without a word, he took my hand and led me to the living room.

Michael hovered over the dining cart and devoured the breakfast that Caleb ordered. Ruiz paced the sitting area, holding my shoulder bag in his hand. He must've brought it from Angie's suite. He turned and saw us enter the room and immediately, his stare fell on our locked hands.

"Your mother asked me to bring you home," he announced.

"My mom?" Oh lord, did she know I spent the night here?

"She's under the impression that you stayed with Evangeline after your celebration," Ruiz explained as if he could read my mind. "It's best that she remains under that impression. Wouldn't you agree?" His keen eyes assessed the shapeless drape of my clothes, which were obviously not mine. He only needed to look at the balled-up material I tucked behind my back to learn where my evening clothes went, but he'd seen enough.

Michael stopped chewing long enough to look at us. He gave us a thumbs-up then plopped on the couch with a handful of cinnamon rolls. It then dawned on me that all in company knew what Caleb and I did last night. I was completely mortified while Caleb all but did a victory dance in the living room.

"Let's go." Ruiz gestured toward the door.

I turned to Caleb, silently pleading for a rescue, but he placed his hands on my shoulders and kissed me.

"Go on. Don't want her worrying about you. I'll call you with updates," he said.

I wrapped my arms around his neck and squeezed him tight, as if by doing so would keep me here with him. "What's going to happen?" I whispered.

"I don't know, but we'll be fine. I promise." He kissed my ear and the side of my neck.

"Samara." Ruiz's voice crashed down on us with the threat of doom.

Why was this so hard? One would think we were headed to the gallows the way we clung to each other, dragging out this tearful good-bye, recording the touch and scent of each other to memory. I stepped out of Caleb's hold, my arms slipping away from his to where only our fingers connected. The word "heartbreak" was inaccurate to describe what we were feeling. It was a tearing, the pulling apart of muscle tissue like Velcro.

We started out as two romance-aphobes learning the rules of dating, and now we were trapped in our own Shakespearean tragedy. I recalled laughing at how Juliet went emo when Romeo left her bedroom to go into exile. Looking back at Caleb who trailed behind us down the hall, that farewell scene wasn't so funny.

The elevator to the right was now in service, while the one on the left—with the bullet holes—still had yellow caution tape across it. I stepped inside the elevator then turned to Caleb standing in the hall watching me with haunted grief in his eyes. His shirt was wrinkled, the button of his jeans was undone, and his hair was in complete disarray. He looked a hot, smoldering mess and I never saw anything more beautiful. Because he was mine and mine alone. That last image stayed long after the elevator doors closed.

The drive back home was quiet for the first five minutes. I stared out of my window when Ruiz took it upon himself to fill the silence with inappropriate chatter.

"I take it that you and Caleb are a bound pair now," he said.

"That's none of your business," I snapped.

"It's all right, Samara. I'm only congratulating you. I understand the rarity of finding a mate who is your equal." Ruiz spoke with a low, jaded voice of experience, but then he said a lot of things that a non-Cambion shouldn't know from experience.

"In any case," he continued. "I'll have to inform the family of your union. Hopefully, they will reconsider their punishment."

"What do you mean *hopefully*? They can't kill Caleb without killing me."

"They may not see that as a problem given your recent behavior, Samara. The two of you have caused nothing but grief and controversy in the Cambion community. It would be simpler just to dispatch you both."

Was that a threat? I quickly grew aware of my surroundings. I was trapped inside a moving car with a man that I couldn't trust. I could kick myself for not calling Mom before I left the hotel.

"However, doing so would anger Evangeline and she's made it clear that harming you would be a declaration of war." He rubbed the plum-colored bruises on his neck as exhibit A. "Don't worry, Samara. This is not a hit. I'm just taking you home. As hard as it is to believe, I don't enjoy the idea of you or Caleb dying. I would like to avoid that if possible, but the family is under pressure and their reputation is at stake. This incubus situation is another matter altogether."

I stayed quiet, but kept my hand on the door handle, just in case I needed to jump out.

"This demon presents a very beneficial opportunity for all of us. As you probably know, incubi are rare. The Cambion families have made a point of keeping it that way. There hasn't been one reported in over a century, and to have one come to light and captured, well, it would restore the faith in the Santiago name."

"So you want to catch the demon so the family can regain their street cred? What's in it for us?"

"Life," he answered simply. "If the demon is captured

with your help, it would be a sign of good faith and devotion to the cause. They're all about loyalty. They eat that up."

I'd seen enough crime shows to know what this was. The cops would make a deal with the small time street dealer in exchange for info to get to the big cartel guy. Ruiz wanted me to sell out Tobias to save my own neck. Everything in my body screamed "take the deal," but something wasn't right.

"Angie told me you're a Santiago." I waited for him to flinch or have any reaction to my words, but mannequins had more emotion. "You're not a Cambion, so how did you get involved in all this?"

"It wasn't always that way." He nestled in his seat, as if knowing it would be a long discussion. "My birth name is Ruiz-Santiago. Ruiz is my mother's name. It's a Cuban tradition to have both last names of your parents. It helps when I want to go unnoticed during investigations. Like Petrovsky, the Santiago name goes a long way in our world, and I don't want that following me while on a case."

"I'm curious, how many siblings do you have?"

"Five brothers, three sisters, and a whole lot of cousins," he answered. "That's one thing about Cambions; they're a horny bunch and they believe in large families. The Petrovskys are the smallest family on record, if I'm not mistaken, which might also explain why you're so valuable to Evangeline. Children are important to Cambions."

I'd figured as much, and I thanked my lucky stars that I was on the pill. "Were you adopted? How did you dodge that bullet?"

"A very interesting turn of phrase, because that's exactly how it happened." At the stop light, he undid three buttons on his shirt, and revealed a raised white scar over his heart. "I was off duty on my way home and a kid was robbing a convenience store. Pulled the trigger without thinking twice. Next thing I remembered was waking up in the hospital and there was nothing. No humming, no pressure on my spine, no spirit." His gaze drifted past my shoulder to another point in time.

Before he traveled too far, I tipped my head to the street. "The light's green."

Ruiz let the car cruise along and stared out to the road ahead, but his thoughts were elsewhere. "I don't know what's worse, almost dying or having your spirit snatched from you. It's part of you; it's fused into every cell, every molecule. It grows up with you, feels everything with you. I fell into a depression and had to leave my position on the force when I couldn't feel him anymore, and it took years to function in normal society. I never felt so relieved and empty at once."

"So it just left the body?" I leaned closer. "I thought they only left when their host dies."

"I *did* die," he clarified with a note of dread. "For three minutes and forty-six seconds. The doctors brought me back and they were amazed that I didn't suffer brain damage."

"You *can* get rid of it?" I whispered, excitement charging through me. If there was a procedure to remove the spirit from the body without killing us, then I could go back to normal. I could revert to the original canon where I operated under my own decree. No more hungry stares from strangers, no more weird cravings, no more memories to store. No more Tobias. "There is a cure."

"The risks are high, Samara. I know that this is new to you, but you have people around you who care about you and can offer support—Caleb most of all."

"Yeah," I mumbled, not allowing that little snag to ruin this new development.

I felt Ruiz watching me carefully, trying to follow the

path of my thoughts. Not liking where they led, he cut the conversation short. "You should get some rest when you get home. We'll have a lot to deal with in the next few days."

"Can you guarantee that Caleb and I won't get hurt if we help you find him?" I asked.

I could tell he was choosing his words carefully as he said, "The odds are higher than they are now." And that was as close to a promise as I was going to get.

He pulled up to my house but kept the engine running. I opened the door then stopped to look at him. "You're not coming in?"

"I gotta get back. I know if I go in there I won't want to leave," he replied.

I wasn't sure if he meant for me to see the raw rush of emotion, but I did and I couldn't despise him entirely, so I settled for mild contempt. He treated my mom pretty well, but there were still things that needed to be resolved, namely my mortality. And on a completely serious note, the idea of the Cuban Necktie as a future stepdad didn't sit well with me. I doubted it ever would.

"Do what you gotta do, man. I'll tell her you say hi," I said as I got out of the car, but he called me back.

"Actually, tell her *'Estoy pensando en ti.'*" He pronounced the words slowly enough for me to remember. "She'll know what it means."

Three years of remedial Spanish taught me what the words meant, but I kept that fun fact to myself. I couldn't take handling someone else's mush—I had my own to stomach. So I nodded, closed the door, and trudged across the grass to my porch.

The house was quiet and blessedly free of chaos. I dropped my bag at the door and moved to the kitchen. I found Mom at the table, drinking her customary mug of tea.

"Hey, Mom." I went to the fridge and went straight for the orange juice. Michael ate my breakfast and I needed a vitamin fix somethin' terrible.

"Hey sweetie. How was the party?"

I stopped. With everything going on, I'd completely forgotten about the party. I mean, come on, that was *so* last year. "It was cool. Mia got drunk and Dougie kissed her at midnight."

"Aww, that's sweet. Do you think they made up?" she asked.

"Here's hopin'." I saluted her, then drank the orange juice straight from the carton.

"Use a glass, Samara." Mom sniggered in distaste then searched the entryway. "Where's David? Thought he would come inside with you."

"Naw, he had to run back to the hotel. Cambion business." I relayed his message, which made her blush and twirl her hair. "You really like him, don't you?"

She leaned back in the chair to ponder her answer. "Yeah. I think I do. He's sweet and so charming—a true gentleman. I just feel funny whenever he looks at me. You told me that the Cambion allure is through eye contact, right? Well, he's got it too, but without the 'I wanna suck the life force out of you' part. So intense."

"Yeah." I didn't want to tell her about Ruiz's excommunication, so to speak. That was his story to tell and it was better if she heard it from him. But that wouldn't stop me from dishing the dirt to Caleb. I took the carton with me to my room, plopped on my bed, then called Caleb and did just that. He was rightfully surprised and threatened to tell Mom about the olive oil incident if I ever decided to get any bright ideas.

He filled me in on the latest news since I was gone. Michael told him that Tobias was hidden in a storage unit across town. Caleb didn't go into details, but he explained that no one could destroy it just yet, not until they knew Tobias was in his own vessel. Plus, the storage place was closed until tomorrow. There was only one problem: the unit was in Haden's name. We needed his security code, which was why Caleb's end of the call took place in the hospital waiting room.

Haden was still in bad shape and had to have a blood transfusion, but he was able to breathe on his own. The bullet was removed and it was a miracle it missed his lung. He was drugged up pretty heavy, so he kept going in and out of consciousness.

The call lasted for several hours while I caught up on work, recounted the love quarters in my coin jar, and discussed everything with him except our night together. That peculiar tension hung in the air, thick and solid enough to reach through the line and slap us both. Minutes would go by with neither of us saying a word and that was great. Sappy, but great. Corny as hell, but great. Caleb's rapidly dying cell phone battery was the only reason we hung up. After taking a long bath, Mom called me to come downstairs.

She was sitting in the kitchen exactly where I left her. She hadn't moved in five hours and the only difference was she had the phone in her hand and tears in her eyes. This was a bad sign. Either Dad was on the phone, or it was . . .

"Evangeline called," Mom spoke before I could complete the thought.

Yep, that was my second guess. Knowing this would be a long, heavy talk, I stepped into the room and took a seat on the bar stool. "I take it you heard about Olivia."

"Angie told me. My question is why you didn't."

"I don't want you worrying."

"I'm a parent. I'm supposed to worry," she snapped and pushed away from the table. "That's it. I'm done!

This whole thing with demons and energy feeding—all of it. I'm done! And you're grounded!"

I jumped back and almost fell off the stool. And she wondered why I didn't tell her anything. "What? What did I do?"

"Do you need a list? I don't want you involved in this. If that means I have to lock you in your room, so be it."

"That's gonna be pretty hard since all this involves me. Not to sound full of myself, but I'm kind of a big deal. If you do put me on lockdown, Caleb could still get hurt and it'll affect me. You can't exactly ground him too."

"I can sure as hell try, even if I have to call the police on him. You're too young for all this responsibility. You both are." Her anger made it hard to tell whether or not she was bluffing, but I knew she was grasping at whatever control and reason that she could hold.

I kept my face blank, my nerve iron clad, but inwardly, panic gnawed at my flesh.

Going into lawyer mode, I said, "You could. Maybe the police can actually find a charge that will stick this time and lock Caleb up. But where would that leave us? Caleb would be surrounded by criminals that could hurt him, and I'll feel his pain and loneliness. I'll go through withdrawal and possibly hurt innocent people to get the energy only he can provide. I know you're scared and want to protect me, but that's not a good way to go about it. As angry as you are, you care about Caleb, too."

Mom leaned back in her chair, crumbling into herself and weighing her options. She looked so wounded and forlorn, like all hope in the world was lost. "What about you and Tobias? Can he be killed now that he's, well, disembodied? Will it still hurt you if he dies?"

"We're working on that," I dismissed, not wanting to lie more than I had to. The truth was I still didn't know how my bond with Caleb would affect Tobias, and I wasn't going to tell Mom about that part. There were some things you just didn't do and discussing your sex life with the folks was on top of the list. "We need to focus on finding Olivia first. Angie is going crazy."

"Yeah. She said that they found her bracelet but she's still missing. Tobias must've removed it."

I shut my eyes and held back a curse. "I knew it. But Cambions have a connection with all of their children. Angie will be able to find her. Might take longer, but there's no need to give up hope now," I assured, but the doubt crept in anyway.

"I don't want the same thing to happen to you, baby."

"I don't want that either, but that's my life now. And there are some things that are gonna suck real hard, but I gotta be a big girl and handle it."

The bad part was that that policy went for Lilith as well. I thought of Ruiz's story, and as tempting as it was, it wasn't worth risking my life again. I had Caleb to think about now and he mattered more to me than revenge.

Speaking of Lilith, she seemed agitated all of a sudden. She had been lying low all day, virtually purring in the afterglow of the bonding, but now she had perked up in alarm. There was a presence nearby, someone she knew, someone she was connected to. Whoever it was, they were scared.

Before I could concentrate on the sensation, there was a knock on the door. It was a soft, weak tap, but I heard it all the same. I looked at Mom and she slowly rose and moved to the counter. She gave me a curt nod then pulled a knife from the rack. With Mom right behind me, I went to the door and pressed my back against the wood. "Who's there?"

"Olivia," a small voice answered from outside, then broke into a sob.

Mom and I looked at each other with wide eyes. I touched the knob but Mom stopped me.

"Are you alone?" Mom asked.

"Yes. Please help me."

"Where's Gunner?" I asked.

More crying came from outside and then, "*Prosze, wpuść mnie.*"

Okay, so Mom was paranoid on a good day and more so due to recent events, so I didn't find it odd at all that she greeted our guest at the door with a butcher knife pointed in her face. When Mom saw that it really was Olivia, she pulled her by the arm and dragged her inside and closed the door behind her.

Olivia stumbled into the foyer, and I got a good look at her. She was still wearing her black party dress. Dirt and scratches tracked her bare feet, legs and arms. Leaves and dirt tangled in her ratty hair. She trembled in the middle of the foyer, hugging her waist. She must've been freezing and I wondered how long she'd been walking in the cold.

Once Mom locked the door, she led Olivia to the living room. The girl sat on the couch and curled into herself, her eyes planted to the floor.

"Do you want some tea?" Mom asked and draped a blanket over Olivia's shoulders.

She shook her head keenly.

I knelt in front of her and rubbed her icy feet. "Do you wanna tell us what happened?"

Olivia shook her head again and leaves fell from her hair. "I didn't know where else to go. I was walking for hours and I felt you. I remembered your house and . . ." she started sobbing again.

"Hey, it's okay. You're safe here," I said then noticed the dirt on her dress. "You wanna clean up? You can used the bathroom—"

"She shouldn't take a shower right now. Not until she

gets looked at," Mom said with the phone in her hand. "Olivia, honey, did Gunner hurt you?"

Olivia rocked back and forth and kept mumbling, "*Przykro mi. Przykro mi, proszę mi wybaczyć. Przykro mi.*"

Mom covered the phone with her hand and asked, "What is she saying?"

I ignored her and focused on the quivering mass on the couch. "What are you sorry about, Olivia?"

"*On nie żyje*," she muttered.

I blinked, not sure if I heard what I thought I did. "Who's dead? Gunner?"

She nodded. "I . . . killed him."

"Oh," was all I could say. There was really no proper response to that.

No doubt calling Angie, Mom drifted to the dining room while I continued to break Olivia out of her shock. But if I stayed in this room any longer, Olivia wouldn't be the only one traumatized.

From where I was kneeling, I caught a pale hand poking from behind the couch. I didn't need to see the rest. I knew Nadine hadn't moved or changed clothes or tried to repair the broken bone in her neck. That would defeat its purpose and lose its intended effect. This was a preserved image, where time and the wane of human memory couldn't dull its clarity.

Pressure built in my ears. The walls narrowed, the furniture slanted and melted in thick, waxy globs, but I wouldn't budge. I always left the room at this point, running scared, but I needed to be strong for Olivia's sake. I could do this.

I channeled all my energy, all my will on the shipwrecked girl in front of me and pushed back the shadows that framed my vision. This wasn't about me or Nadine, and if Lilith had any compassion in her cold, rancid heart, she would do me this one solid and make the sway-ing stop.

I released a long, measured breath and opened my eyes again. To my relief, everything was still. The furniture was situated in their proper places, whole and firm. The pressure decreased and the cloud of motion sickness dis-persed, letting light in again. Nadine's body remained on the floor and I had a feeling it was there to stay. I could at least handle that much. I heard Mom talking on the phone. Olivia watched me curiously, as if I were a new concept for her. Maybe I was.

I placed my hand on Olivia's arm and she flinched, but slowly melted into my touch. "Can you tell me anything else?" I asked.

After a huge gulp of air, she whimpered, "He fright-ened me. I didn't know what he would do. He cut off my bracelet. I didn't know where he was taking me. So I . . . fed from him. I could feel his life—so much light and strength. He was strong, he fought back, but I kept going until . . ." She took a hard swallow. "His heart was skip-ping. He fell on the ground and he couldn't breathe. Then something came out of his mouth. Not energy . . . something else."

I didn't need to know any more, but Mom said from the entryway, "A black mist with a gold light in the cen-ter?"

Olivia looked up at Mom, her wide eyes shot through the curtain of dirty strands. "How did you know?"

"Gunner was possessed by a demon named Tobias, an incubus," I supplied. "It wasn't Gunner."

"No. No, it was him. His eyes were blue. I saw it, Gunner was there . . . They were blue."

"Maybe he was fighting it. He's loyal and would do anything to protect you. Maybe that was his way, so you could escape." I tried to be comforting, but it sounded lame to my own ears. There was no cushioning, no padding for this particular blow.

She didn't seem to be listening anyway; she was too engrossed with the thread fibers in the carpet. "I ate my friend's life. I killed him. But I had to. I had . . ."

I didn't get much out of her after that because she totally zoned out. Whatever she went through had rocked her to the core. Worst of all, she had to resort to basic Cambion instinct to survive, the very thing she resented Caleb for.

Mom hung up the phone and reentered the room with a wet towel. She knelt down in front of Olivia and brushed the hair out of the girl's eyes. "Olivia, sweetheart, your mother is on her way. She's coming for you, okay? You're safe now." Mom wiped Olivia's face clean and sat next to her on the couch.

Olivia's eyes fell on Mom's with such naked, earnest trust; it made my heart constrict. Olivia barely knew this woman, but she unpacked her torment without saying a word. The hurt and despair oozed out of her and slid over my skin like trickling water. And even from what I could feel, I knew it was overflow, just a taste of what was roiling inside of her. We were almost the same age, but death had a way of making people grow faster than necessary.

Mom held Olivia and rocked her and in moments, the crying had stopped. How did this woman do it? There was something about her that unnatural beings seemed to gravitate toward. She might not like Cambions or their lifestyle, but they sure liked her.

Angie arrived twenty minutes later, and had even less luck getting info out of Olivia. She didn't tell us where Gunner's body could be found or where he had taken her or whether she needed medical attention, but I figured Angie would take it from here. None of that seemed to matter as long as Olivia was all right, but "all right" was a relative term. No one was really all right after killing someone. The Cambion motto was to celebrate life, because death was a regular visitor who always came unannounced.

Wrapped in her mother's coat, Olivia stopped at the door and glanced at me from over her shoulder. Albeit brief, a small smile tugged at her mouth. I had no idea what that look meant, but I had a feeling our beef was at a stalemate until further notice. The odds of us being pen pals were slim to none, but we were Cambion siblings and that counted for something. What, I had no idea.

Mom and I watched as the car pulled away from our street. With the house quiet again, it then occurred to me that I was extremely tired; not just physically, but emotionally, mentally, and cosmically tired. I wanted to crawl into bed and die. A warm blanket and fluffy pillows were only a few feet away, but given the extra weight of sleep deprivation and stress, it could have been five miles.

What a way to bring in the new year.

"Something has to be done about this," Mom grumbled, staring out at the street.

I stepped inside and punched the security code in the alarm by the door. "I know, but we need some sleep first." I turned around and noticed that Mom wasn't behind me.

By the time I reached the porch, she had wandered across the street to the neighbors' lawn. She stared at the display, taking in the divine splendor of the nativity scene. As if this made perfect sense, she stooped down and plucked the baby from inside the manger.

I watched, slack jawed, as she walked back toward the house, cradling the ceramic child in her arms. It was official, the utter collapse of my mother's mental health was now complete, and though done indirectly, it was still my fault. I brought this plague upon us and there was no remedy in sight.

When she stepped onto the porch, I asked, "Mom, what are you doing?"

"It's high time someone knocked the Cunninghams down a peg or two." Mom tucked the ornament under her arm and stepped inside the house.

"There're other ways to do that, you know. Are you nuts? I can't believe you stole baby Jesus!" I cried.

"No, I'm not nuts, just tired. Considering what happened tonight, we're gonna need him a lot more than they do right now." Mom ascended the stairs to her room. When she reached the top of the stairs, she called out, "And you're still grounded!" which was followed by the slam of her bedroom door.

17

"Come on, Sam. Are you at least gonna tell me a little bit?" Mia whined, swinging from side to side in her swivel chair.

"Nope. It's personal," I answered, then spun my own chair back to my computer. We weren't supposed to be talking during lab, but that rule, along with most of our school's policies didn't apply to Mia.

I had no idea how she knew that Caleb and I got together, but as soon as she saw me this morning she called me out—no hello or anything. She gawked at me all through first period. I kept looking for the neon sign saying I GAVE CALEB THE BUSINESS that hung over my head, because according to her, it was *that* obvious.

"Oh please, I told you about me and Dougie this summer," she whispered, though loud enough for everyone in the lab to hear. Students turned heads, sized up Mia, then continued to type. Mr. Carver, the assistant teacher with sweat gland issues, sat behind his desk, sniffing his Wite-Out pen thinking no one was looking.

I turned my focus to my monitor. "Yeah, against my will. And you didn't just tell me, you put the event into interpretative dance."

Underneath the tapping of keys in the room, I heard the wheels of Mia's chair rolling closer. From the corner of my left eye, I saw her crawl into view, and I could almost hear the *Jaws* theme in my head. "Come on, you can tell me. Was it weird?" she asked.

"Yeah, it was awkward, painful, messy, and then kinda amazing." Adjectives were all she was getting out of me. For one thing, it was too weird to even explain to someone non-demon affiliated, and for another, I wanted to keep something to myself. Those few hours in Caleb's room were mine, and by nature, I was pretty stingy with my stuff. It was bad enough that every Cambion in Virginia knew that Caleb and I did the nasty, but Mia wanted a play-by-play with a sound bite.

"Yeah, it was the same for me and Dougie, but I'm glad it was him. Someone I cared about, not some random guy at a party, you know?" She had a far-off look in her eyes as she recalled some event that I could die happy not knowing about.

But she was smiling again, her eyes twinkled, and that was worth any headache. Hell, she was talking to me again, which was a miracle in itself.

"So are you and Dougie back together?" I asked, trying to change topics.

A smile split her face, no doubt prompted by the thought of the boy in question. "Yeah, kinda. You should've seen him on New Year's. He was really sweet, Sam. He took me home, right, but I was really out of it and I got sick on the way, and you know what he did? He pulled over to the side of the road and held back my hair. You know that's love when a guy helps you while you puke."

Trust Mia to swoon over the most disgusting situations. I couldn't blame her. Caleb had some really gross habits that had my heart fluttering. "Yeah, that's true devotion." I grabbed my book bag from the floor and dug into the front pocket for my cell.

"We're taking things slow, you know. Trust is a serious problem for us and we need to work that out."

"I think we can all learn a little trust around here." I looked at my phone, checking my messages.

The entire day consisted of digital correspondence from Caleb and Angie. She left me a message during first period telling me that Olivia, Szymon, and Mishka had left for Poland this morning and assuring that their next visit in the States would be more "congenial." That was one way of putting it. Though she insisted that I stay out of harm's way, I managed to wiggle a few details out of her.

It appeared that Ruiz pulled some strings and commissioned a group of local Cambions to help retrieve Gunner's body and destroy Tobias's. Since this whole situation was under Santiago territory, it was only fair, not to mention faster, to gather fellow Cambions in the region. From what Angie had told me, there were Cambions in Florida and D.C. as well as New York, though small and with little influence. The fact that there were more of us out there, living seminormal everyday lives both comforted and disturbed me.

To add on to the agitation, demon Armageddon was taking place, and I was stuck playing spider solitaire in my computer lab and missing all the action. The wait was eating me alive. It wasn't like I wanted to be on the front lines—far from it—but the "not knowing" part was the killer.

But Caleb's recent text indicated that little action was taking place:

CALEB: still at the hospital. Haden's awake. Explain more later.

No one knew if Tobias's spirit had returned to his vessel. Olivia had seen him leave Gunner's body, so he could be anywhere. Everything was up in the air until we could get inside that storage unit and see Tobias's remains.

And that's where Haden came in. It seemed that he and his morphine drip were holding up progress. Caleb tried for hours to get him to talk, but Haden could barely keep his eyes open. He was in a lot of pain and it would be inhumane to deny him relief, but we needed answers before someone else was killed.

School was the only place where things seemed normal. I managed to catch up all my assignments and had two major tests before report cards came out. Fourth period was canceled for an assembly to commemorate Malik Davis, which doubled as a talent competition. If the guilt didn't beat me down before, the slide show and the choir version of *My Heart Will Go On* finished the job.

"... and I was like, 'sure, I'd love some gum,' and that's when I knew we were just meant to be together. It's fate. So anyway, I'm gonna watch Dougie practice today. You wanna come?" Mia's voice broke me out of my thoughts.

"Uh, no thanks. I'll pass on the male erotica for today," I teased.

"Wrestling is a competitive sport." Mia pouted.

I slid my phone into my back pocket. "Maybe, but I'm not trying to see all his goodies in that stank outfit he wears. I see how he gets during a match: rolling on the floor, sweaty limbs intertwining, locking in a passionate embrace—"

"It's called a choke hold, Sam," Mia disputed, rolling her neck. "Joke all you want, but my baby is *all man*."

I had a good comeback, but the words never formed, because Mia's face started to bend and smear in swells of color. My head swam, causing me to rock in my chair. I didn't remember hitting the floor, but there were kids circled around me from above.

Mr. Carver stood over me, his sagging gut eclipsing the rest of his body. A large sweaty hand shot out and helped me to my feet. "Are you all right, Samara?" he asked.

"Yeah, I'm just a little light-headed."

He pulled a pad out of his damp shirt pocket and straightened his glasses. "Do you need to go to the nurse?"

"No, I'm . . ." I paused as another dizzy rush kicked in again. "Maybe that's a good idea."

"I'll help her." Mia took hold of my arm to keep me balanced as she guided me out of the door.

I had to stop and rest against the wall and took a series of deep breaths before heading down the corridor. The world moved slower than I did; voices droned from behind class room doors, while conversations garbled around my ears as if spoken underwater. My focus remained on the last room on the right with the big red cross on the door. My eyes stayed glued to that shape even as I turned the knob.

I surveyed the modest clinic, with the cartoon characters, hygiene reminders, and corny motivational slogans on the wall. The medicine cabinet in the back was a junkie's wet dream and sealed off tighter than Fort Knox, which was pointless. The only reason anyone came to the nurses' office was if they ran out of tampons or to use the private bathroom when they had to do more than just pee. What freaked me out the most was the kitten paraphernalia that Mrs. Lafaye had on the desk and walls.

The small, ancient woman came to my side and helped me to the cot by the door. I fell on the paper-covered pillow and closed my eyes, mainly to avoid the lolcats poster on the ceiling. After some water, a box of animal crackers, and convincing Mia that I didn't need an ambulance, the see-sawing motion began to die down. I could hear chatter and squeaking sneakers outside of the door, and I pulled the curtain partition for some privacy.

"Do you need me to call a parent to pick you up?" Mrs. Lafaye asked, her voice a melodic tinkle of something that should own a wand and fairy dust.

"I think I can stick it out. School's out in less than half an hour."

"Well, just stay here for a few more minutes, then you can go." She moved back to her desk and feline fan club, her white pants swishing with each movement.

I grinned and reached for my now vibrating phone. I put it to my ear, knowing who it was. "Hey."

"Hey, where are you?" Caleb asked, sounding a bit breathy and tired.

"I'm at the nurse's office now. I got dizzy in class. I forgot to feed at lunch today and I'm paying for it now."

"Uh, yeah, about that . . ." he began hesitantly. "That might be my fault. I gave Haden some of my energy. You might be feeling the drain. Sorry about that."

Mia poked her head in. "I'm gonna go. I'll drop off your bag after the bell. Call me if you need me."

I waved her on then returned my focus to my call. "You might wanna give me a heads up before you do that from now on. How much did you give him?"

"Maybe too much apparently, but he's in a lot of pain. I didn't mean for you to be affected. You're so sensitive to me now; I'll have to be more careful. That's interesting." It got quiet on the line and I felt movement over my skin, trailing up the side of my waist. I knew it was his fingers.

"Stop, that tickles," I protested, fighting a smile.

"It's supposed to. I'm figuring out how this works. It

seems you can feel me when we're both thinking about each other. I think the only exception is pain and sickness. That will come involuntarily. Other than that, concentration makes me feel what you feel. Everything."

"Everything? Like if I have some bad chili or drink too much coffee, or get drunk at a party, you'll get sick too?" I asked.

"Yup."

Rubbing my forehead, I asked, "So, what if I get plastic surgery or get a new kidney, will you feel the knife? Will you bleed all over the place?"

"Probably. I may have to check into the hospital too, but I won't feel pain if you don't."

"Okay, but what if we have babies someday? Will you feel it kick or have morning sickness? Ooh, what about labor pains?"

"Uh, Sam? I don't wanna talk about that now. Can we make it to your prom first?" he derided, clearly disturbed by the idea of us being fruitful and multiplying. "We have time to learn as we go. It's not going to be easy, but nothing about us ever is."

"True dat." I smiled again. This was a new dimension to our relationship that we needed to explore. And there was a part of me that regretted not waiting, that we weren't ready to handle what came with this connection. But the feeling of belonging to someone so completely helped alleviate the doubt.

Memories of our time in his room had replayed in my head throughout the day, and now was no different. Just thinking about him and all his two thousand parts made me light-headed again, so I tried to change the subject. "How's Haden?"

"He's pretty delirious. Keeps talking about Mom a lot."

I winced. "Ooh, that's not good. He might not be any

use to us right now. Are you sure Michael doesn't know the combination?"

"No. Haden was in charge of all that. He's the more responsible of the two." He snickered. "All he said was it was a six digit code. It could mean anything."

Through the crack in the curtain, I saw a dark-haired boy standing in front of Mrs. Lafaye's desk. His back faced me so I couldn't see who it was. He mumbled something to her and she stood up. There was more pants swooshing, followed by the clinic door shutting with a decisive click.

"Sam, are you still there?" Caleb asked.

I shook my head, trying to stay focused. "Yeah, I'm still here. What were you saying?"

"Ruiz stationed a couple of guards outside Haden's room. At least we don't have to worry about Tobias sneaking up on us."

"Good. Listen, I'm gonna stop by my house then come over . . ."

A heavy, dark green object flew through the curtain. Only when it slid across the floor and hit the far wall did I recognize it as my book bag. Someone must have gotten it out of class for me, but they didn't have to be rude about it. The curtain flew back in a whirl and I looked up to meet the angry deliverer.

I drew back and stared up at the boy in front of me. "Dougie? What are you doing here?"

He smiled brightly, the way he would when he had juicy gossip to share. But the latest rumor wasn't what he came here to reveal. Dougie's hazel green eyes had disappeared and in their place was an eerie orange-yellow glow. "Sup, Flower. We should talk."

My breath caught and I almost dropped the phone. The ground gave under me and my stomach went into a free fall. Terror crept across my skin, its icy fingers crawling inside and gripping my heart in a vise. I scooted to the top of the bed until my back hit the wall.

"Sam? Did you hear me? Sam?" Caleb asked, his voice rising as the seconds stretched.

This couldn't be happening. Maybe I was hallucinating. I was energy deprived and I could be seeing and hearing things. Maybe he'd overheard Malik call me that name in the hallway. Maybe he was wearing contacts. Maybe he was a friggin' warlock—something! I would believe anything but what I knew deep down in my bones to be the most logical answer.

"Sam! What's wrong? Why are you scared? It's making my heart race."

I snapped my eyes shut, fighting the tears beginning to gather. I breathed deep and put the phone back to my ear. "I—I . . . I'll call you back."

18

I ended the call, turned off the phone, then put it back into my pocket.

This was going to be a royally screwed-up conversation and I thought it better to have it without distraction. Lilith applied her own method of preparation by clawing at the interior lining of my body, either to escape or make room. Both reasons were painful and I had to regulate my breathing to keep her calm. I had to keep *myself* calm.

"Tobias?" I whispered.

The smile he gave me was sly and devious as he took a seat at the foot of the bed. "Relax. I won't bite you. Yet."

I studied every line and bend of his face, searching for some trace, some lost remnant of my friend. Everything looked the same: short, spiky black hair slathered in gel, thin lips, a straight nose with wide nostrils, and a square jaw with a thin patch of hair at the chin.

His eyes were brighter, a shiny penny with flecks of gold, but they lacked the playful gleam that came with

Dougie's personality. Looking at him reminded me how the body was not the sum of our parts, but just a shell. "Is Dougie in there?" I asked.

"Yes. He's a tough one, too, a fighter. But he's not getting out anytime soon, so don't get too happy. He's my insurance policy. Just in case you go crazy with the olive oil or your mom comes out of nowhere and starts swinging again. What the hell was that anyway?"

"It's called breaking and entering," I replied. "Is Dougie hurt?"

"No. He's unconscious, but he's trying to surface. Like when people fight to wake up from a bad dream, but this dream can last forever." He stretched out, taking more than two-thirds of the bed.

I stayed to my little corner, curled up until my knees touched my chin. "What about Gunner? Is he gonna wake up from that dream?"

He chuckled, but his expression softened to something close to remorse. "Olivia has a lot of her sister in her. I was impressed. She'll do well in the world once she embraces everything she is, even the bad."

At the mention of Olivia, my hackles rose. "You used her as a hostage. You're telling me you wouldn't have killed her once you'd gotten what you wanted?"

His head teetered from side to side as he weighed the issue. "Maybe. We'll never know because she struck first."

"Where's Gunner?" I asked.

"Where most people disappear around here. The parkway. You're familiar with that place, aren't you, Flower?" His stare bored into me, forcing his point with bitter intensity.

I couldn't put my finger on it, but there was something about Tobias that just screamed "jump me". It didn't matter who he disguised himself as, or what "bodysuit" he wore, he worked with what he had and rocked it better than the original owner. True to his nature, he was an incubus, an instrument of pure lust sent from below to torment women on sight. That was the only reason that could justify the sudden heat on my skin, my shallow breathing, and my aching need to touch him. I shouldn't be looking at Dougie this way. It was borderline incest and all shades of wrong.

Tobias reclined on the bed and rested his weight on his arms. "Here's the thing, I need my body back and I need you to help me."

I shook my head slowly. "Why me?"

"It's the least you can do after what you've done." His voice was low and rolled down my arm and neck with a touch of silk, making it hard for me to concentrate.

"What I've done? Do you need me to go down the list of shit that you've done to me and my family?"

"Aww, poor thing. Careful, don't want to upset Douglas with your sad tale. He might become distraught and try to hang himself in his garage tonight. But before he does, he might visit Mia and give her a long kiss good-bye."

With a deep breath, I uncurled my fist. The joints ached as the fingers extended, revealing indentations where my nails bit the palm. "You bastard."

"I play to win, Flower. I told you I had a plan. Several. And you try my patience. Now here's what you're going to do. You're going to help me retrieve my body. They've been dousing it with oil, so I'm too weak to move. It's in a storage facility at the end of town. Century Storage, unit 521."

"Well, go get it yourself."

"If it were that easy, I would, but I can't," he replied. "It's a state-of-the-art storage facility. Instead of pad-locks, there's a security code on each unit. I could go in past the gate and maybe even get into the facility itself, but the unit is locked. Guess who has the key code." He smiled nastily.

"Why don't you just 'mystify' or whatever you do and creep under the door?"

He had the nerve to look at me like I was stupid. "I tried that. The entryway leading to that unit is covered with oil. I can't cross the threshold. And even if I could, how would I get my body? It's immobile. So I need another person—a human—to carry it."

"So why can't you use someone else's body?"

"Because that still leaves me without the combination. I need you to get it for me. That's the very least you could do."

"This would be a whole lot easier if you hadn't shot the one guy who knows the code to get you out."

He shrugged, uninterested. "I let the other two live."

"Yeah, but the one who knows the code to the unit is the one you busted a cap in. Good job, genius. Why is the body so important to you? Why don't you just find a good-looking guy and possess him?" I shot a quick glance up his body. "Oh wait, you already did."

"I don't know, Flower, how would you like giving up your body?" he replied bitterly. "It's mine. It's how I shape-shift, it's how I compel the elements, it's how I'm able to breathe and touch. It's a part of me, it anchors me to this world and it's still alive. I was born with it and I want it back."

I shook my head, finding it hard to believe that something this evil had a mother. "Were you ever truly human?"

He hadn't expected that question and his features slackened. His brows knit together and his eyes wandered as he sifted through the junk pile of memories. "Once. Many, many centuries ago. I don't remember much about my old life, one of the costs of taking lives and adapting to cultures." With another shrug, he dismissed the issue altogether.

"This isn't a deal, but a warning. You will help me get my body back and I will kill the demon mutts who did this to me. Business as usual."

He got to his feet in a move too graceful to be masculine, or even human. "I'll expect the delivery tonight. If not, I'll have to take matters into my own hands, and those hands will be bloody by the time I'm done. In the meantime, I have a date with a Filipino hottie who hates waiting."

"Don't you hurt Mia." I leaned forward, but the object in his hand made me stop. I didn't even see him move, but then I wasn't looking at his hands.

Right under Dougie's jaw was a rugged and very nasty butterfly knife, the kind you'd see a guy doing cool juggling tricks with in a gang movie. I saw where it dug into the skin, not quite drawing blood, but that could change at any second. We really needed metal detectors in this school.

He made a tsk-ing sound and pouted. "Don't do that. Someone might get hurt. Then I'll have to shop around for a new body, and that's a headache."

"If you hurt him, you hurt yourself," I warned.

He blinked and gave me a look which seemed to say, "Is she kidding?" "Samara, my body has been sponge bathed in the demon equivalent of battery acid; you think a slit throat will hurt me? You don't know what pain is. But you will if you keep fucking with me."

I started to tremble uncontrollably, a type of cracked-out tremor born from pure hate. Tears began to break, but I opened my eyes wider for the air to dry them. In that moment, I wondered if Tobias could still hear my tears in Dougie's body as he did with his own. It was one of his many supernatural talents and he could always tell from miles away if I was upset.

He must have at least seen them now, because he reached out and touched my face. I didn't move, and for a moment I wanted to lean into his hand and taste the energy vibrating underneath his skin. I seemed sensitive to it now, drawn to it.

His eyes were so pretty and his lips looked so soft. I absently licked my own to soothe the burning. I vaguely remembered the last time he kissed me. We stood outside in the rain near the back entrance of the cafeteria. He had asked me to run away with him and I would've shot to the moon with him if he asked. Then I remembered him disguised as Malik Davis and that bruising kiss under the bleachers. The simple contact of his lips was enough to break down any barrier Lilith might've built against him. Her mental block was useless against his touch, but where she was weak, I was strong.

"You are so innocent, Flower. It's all over your face. It is your face actually, like a delicate doll's. Yet you have this temper that even us demons fear. Lilith has met her match with you." His face grew dark as if he was struck by a revelation. He leaned in, barely inches away from my face and inhaled deeply. "I can't call you Flower anymore, can I? Doesn't seem appropriate now."

"It wasn't appropriate *then*." I snatched away from him before our lips touched. "I told you I've made my choice."

"And I told you, it doesn't matter. The result will be the same. He will still die and you will come to me." His mouth hovered inches from mine and I couldn't move back any farther. I turned my head, but his eyes wouldn't let me look away.

"Bonding with that demon mutt won't change anything. We're still connected; we will always be connected in some way. A part of me is inside you and a part of Lilith is inside me. That doesn't just disappear. And when he dies, we can try again," he whispered.

Was he serious? This guy just would not take a hint. "Tell me you're not doing this for love, or whatever it is you think you feel. Let's not cover this up with romance and call it what it is."

"I'm beyond love now. I'm all about survival and vengeance. I need you to survive." The deadened look in his eyes told me he wasn't kidding. Whatever warm and fuzzies he had for Lilith had gone cold and prickly. That ship had sailed as soon as she chose Capone, which meant I too was on his hit list.

I wasn't worried about myself. There were other people caught in the crossfire who needed cover. "There's no way Dougie is going to survive this, is there?" I asked.

"That, Samara, is entirely up to you." He backed away from me and disappeared behind the curtain. I wasn't sure if he expected me to follow, so I didn't. It would do no good and I needed to catch my breath anyway. He'd said his piece, the rules of the games had been explained and the clock was ticking.

At the final bell, I searched the halls for Mia. I covered her usual haunts: her locker, the bathroom, and the commons area before hitting the student parking lot. I wouldn't let the traffic of students slow me down and I threw bows at anyone in my way. I tried her on my cell, but all my calls went straight to voice mail. By the time I made it to the parking lot, her car was still there, but Dougie's Range Rover was gone.

Walking to my car, I tried dialing Mia one last time and I was actually surprised that she picked up.

"Hey, can I call you back? I'm a little busy," she said, her voice thick with laughter.

"Mia, where are you?" I yelled. Obviously she hadn't gotten my text to meet me and stay away from Dougie, though a text wouldn't stop Tobias's influence.

"Chill, Sam. I'm okay. Dougie decided to skip practice today, and we're gonna grab something to eat," she answered, still laughing.

I could hear Dougie's voice over the engine. "I'm starving and I could eat just about anything," he said. "You should join us, Sam. How about you meet us at the rec park late tonight, around ten?"

"It's closed for the season," Mia said, sounding confused.

"I know. More fun for us." There was shuffling and I could hear his voice more clearly. He must have taken the phone. "Ten o'clock. See you then," he said before the line went dead.

I stood in the middle of the parking lot staring at my phone as cars honked and rolled past me. The dizziness hit me again and I needed somewhere soft to land, so I stumbled to my car. Plopping inside, I put the key into the ignition, but I couldn't turn on the engine. I rested my head on the steering wheel and allowed the weight of decision and fear to crush me.

I thought of Dougie. For the first time in forever I actually thought of Douglas Emerson III. He was always just there in the background, blending into the scenery. Now the landscape felt naked without him.

We met in day camp when we were nine and he had that spoiled brat quality, like most boys at that age. But he was one of the only kids who didn't poke fun of my hair or call me zebra, or talk shit about my mother. He was a bit of a prep then, short and chubby like me, but in the eighth grade, he rolled up to school all "yo,yo, whazup" and that was the end of it. I figured someone had to be the token black in our group of friends, so why not him?

And then there was Mia. They couldn't stand each other for years, but somehow he got under her skin. I've been the witness to their roller-coaster romance since day one and now I would to be the one to end it. I had to hand it to Tobias—he was a true strategist. God, if anything happened to Dougie, she would die. Not the way a mated Cambion would, but slower and that would probably kill me, and then send a domino effect through everyone I knew.

But what choice did I have? If I delivered Tobias's body, he would only go after Caleb and his brothers again, and then probably kill Dougie anyway just to spite me.

I felt tired again, which reminded me that I hadn't fed. My weight grew heavy as my head pressed against the steering wheel. A warm sensation rushed over me like a breath and I knew what it meant. I heard footsteps approaching, rubber crunching against gravelly concrete, then a tapping on the glass.

"Sam! Sam, are you all right?" Caleb asked.

I shook my head. I didn't know what to tell him, didn't know how to even comprehend it myself.

"Open the door," he demanded.

I shook my head again.

"Sam, please, talk to me."

With my head still on the steering wheel, I reached over and clicked the lock. Immediately, the cold from outside rushed in and a hand pulled me back against the seat. I opened my eyes and saw two glowing orbs staring back at me. "What happened? Are you all right?"

He unhooked my seat belt and pulled me out of the car. After setting me down, I leaned against the car while he cupped my face with his chilly hands. "You hungry?"

I nodded.

"Feed from me." He drew closer, ready to kiss me.

"Tobias has Dougie." I pushed out the words in one breath.

He stopped, his eyes wide with surprise. "He has him or he *is* him?"

I let the sob answer that question.

"Did you look in his eyes?" he asked. His voice was controlled and soothing, as if he was coaxing a jumper off a ledge. "Did he kiss you?"

I didn't know what that had to do with anything, but I shook my head. "I had a reaction to him. It's stronger than it was before. I'm not immune to him anymore, but that's not the reason I feel weak. I'm more afraid of what he'll do with Dougie."

He pulled me into his arms and squeezed. "I'm so sorry, Sam."

What was he apologizing for? It was too early for that. I pushed away and almost fell over, but he caught my arms. "You make it sound like he's dead. He's not dead. We can still help him if we give Tobias his body."

He offered me a neutral half smile. I knew he was trying to be careful with me, trying not to say the wrong thing, but he must have forgotten that I could feel his pity. "You know we can't do that. And you know once Angie finds out where Tobias's soul is, Doug is as good as dead."

I stepped back and used the car for support to stand. "Not if we can get him out first, not if he's back in his own body. She said that was the only way for Tobias to be destroyed for good," I replied. "He wants his body back by tonight or he's gonna kill both Mia and Dougie."

Letting out a breath, he spun around the parking lot then stopped on sight of Mia's BMW in the lane ahead. "Where's Mia now?"

"She's with him and he won't hesitate to kill her."

Caleb tilted his head, still looking at Mia's car. "Oh, I think he'll hesitate, seeing the body he's using. That might buy us some time."

I had to think about that for a minute. It was possible. Gunner had resisted and was able to gain control for a few seconds, but it wasn't enough.

He looked down at me and touched my face. "You're not driving like this and you need energy—you're about to faint. Let's go to my Jeep where it's warm. I'll take care of you."

Did everything he said lately sound suggestive, or was it just me? Either way, I couldn't say no and I didn't own the strength to bitch at him for gorging on hospital staff. He didn't need to tell me, I knew that he had fed before he got here, gaining back what he donated. But he was full to the brim with energy, so much whirling, living power that if it were dark, he would glow from radiation. Just standing next to him was drugging, a contact high that gave me the munchies and he was the food.

I buried my nose into his collar and breathed him in. "We need to get to that storage unit. Did Haden say anything?" I asked.

He held the small of my back as he helped me to the side door of his Jeep. "No. I told you, he just kept going on about Mom . . ." He stopped moving and his eyes widened as if an idea struck him. "But I think I might have a clue of what the code is."

19

After Caleb's dirty version of a "reboot," I was able to function within a world that didn't spin.

Rich, potent life regenerated each cell and had me trembling in its aftershocks. I sat back against the headrest inside his Jeep, savoring the kinetic activity and wondering how much Caleb fed today. He promised that he would cut back, but he was able to revive me and still have enough extra pep to carry out this mission. I would've confronted him about it, but he was busy doing God knew what in the rental office.

Century Storage looked like any other self-storage facility. U-Haul-style trucks and pickups were parked in the back. Portable pods and minitrailers were lined in a row on the grass. Across the lot was a plain white brick building with a big sign advertising Century's deal on moving trucks for twenty dollars.

I expected a maze of outdoor units with metal roll-up doors, but they were indoor compartments trapped in a concrete warehouse at the side of the property. That was our target, but for some reason Caleb went inside the office to talk to the owner and waste precious daylight hours. He'd been in there for forty minutes, and I wasn't trying to be here after dark.

To kill time, I called Mia and got her voicemail again. I texted Angie with the location of Gunner's body, but left out how I came about that information. Hopefully, the search for Gunner would keep the Cambion militia distracted for a few hours. Mom called me twice to check on me, but I left her a vague text telling her I was with Caleb and turned off my phone. I figured if I was going to be grounded, I might as well be legit about it. It was for a good cause.

With that accomplished, I looked in the back seat to double check the inventory in the duffel bag. Before arriving here, we'd made a quick stop at the hardware store for supplies: a hand saw, some rope, gloves, bolt cutters, a lighter, a can of kerosene, and a bag of Starburst. This was a sketchy combination to have rolling down the conveyer belt, but the tattoo-clad girl ringing up our items couldn't have cared less if we were setting a church on fire.

"Have you ever done something like this before?" I had asked Caleb once we were back in his Jeep.

His eyes were on the road and with a slick, dimpled grin, he said, "Search my memories for the answer later."

Thinking now of what we were about to do and what was at stake, I realized that we were still unprepared. All we had was half a plan and a whole lot of nerve, but countries had gone to war with less.

The sun was falling behind the trees, pulling away its warm coat to reveal an early glimpse of stars. With darkness approaching we had maybe four hours to hit the rendezvous point. There was no telling how long it would take to get Tobias's body, and Caleb was operating on his own directive.

Just when I was about to fall asleep, Caleb approached the Jeep with keys in his hand.

I rolled down his window and asked, "What was that about?"

He leaned inside the window, chewing on a cherry Starburst and looking all kinds of hotness. "Rented a moving truck. Whatever they've got in that unit is gonna be big and won't fit in my Jeep. We need to be mobile. Got a good deal too. The dealer's a nice old guy, but can't see for shit. He'd seen my brother around here a few times and he thought I was him."

"Are you really that surprised? You guys are like really messed-up triplets. I have perfect vision and still get confused."

"Yeah, but I'm the cute one." His smile fell as quickly as it appeared. "I'm gonna pull the truck back here, then we'll go into the building. I checked out the area—we should be fine. There're only men around so in case anyone approaches us, I'll need you to work your magic." He winked at me then leaned farther in the window for a quick peck on my lips.

I couldn't argue with that. At least Cake Boy was on point, and though I might not know all the details of his plan, I trusted him. I had to.

He left for a few minutes, spoke to the owner, then returned inside a white industrial pickup. Caleb parked the truck then climbed out. I joined his side with the duffel bag of supplies. We walked toward the doors, staying cool and keeping an eye out for any overly helpful workers.

No, we didn't look obvious at all rolling up in A-Team posse formation. All we needed was to walk in super slow motion with hard techno music in the background. Adrenaline pumped in my system, excitement, fear, and raw badassery.

Since it was business hours, the automatic glass doors

slid open without a key. The air sucked through the vents in a vacuum and as we stepped in, the doors sealed closed again with a Tupperware burp.

"It's climate controlled; keeps moisture out," Caleb explained.

The place was an oversized cinder block with metal stairs, a giant freight elevator on the bottom level, and very active security cameras in the black ball in the corner. I felt like a spy on a secret mission with all the covert ducking and dodging.

Caleb spotted a cart with wheels and pulled it into the elevator with us.

Before I could ask, he dropped the duffel bag inside and said, "We need some way to get it out, just in case."

The doors opened and we stepped into the wide hallway of cell block five. Gray walls with glass doors lined either side of us. Just as Tobias said, the floor was covered in oil. It glistened inside the cracks in the concrete, though black with dirt and tread. We followed the letters on each unit—odds on the left, even on the right.

Stopping in front of our desired unit, I understood why it was hard for Tobias to just crawl under the door. The doors were airtight with thick tinted glass; hiding whatever was inside from view. The key pad was imbedded into the wall so it couldn't be pulled out or broken.

"Are you sure it's this one?" Caleb asked.

I nodded. "That's what he said, 521."

Caleb stood in front of the key pad and punched in a series of numbers too quick for me to see. Nothing happened. Swearing, he tried another set of numbers and failed. He pressed his back against the wall and stared up at the ceiling, consulting the overhead bulbs for insight. I kept eyeing the elevator, getting anxious as the risk of being caught grew severe.

Caleb used five more codes with no success. He placed

his head against the glass and took a deep breath. He must've had a eureka moment, because his head shot up and he rushed to the security box again. This next code elicited a beeping noise then a metallic clank. I looked down and saw the door part from the wall an inch.

"Awesome! What was the code?" I pulled the handle and almost dislocated my shoulder. The glass was at least four inches thick.

Caleb grabbed hold and pulled it the rest of the way. "At first I thought it was Mom's birthday. Then I thought it was the day she died. I even tried all of our birthdays. But turns out it was our parents' wedding day."

"Aww. That's so sweet." My smile withered when I caught the strong whiff of spring flowers and something sour just underneath it.

"Yeah, Haden's a softy like that." Caleb scrunched up his face, no doubt smelling the odor, too, then stepped inside.

He clicked on the switch by the door and glaring fluorescent lights flooded the empty room from above. Two sets of air fresheners were taped to opposite walls, the kind with those battery-operated spritzers with a timer. I half expected a coffin or some sort of time capsule, so it came as a disappointment when we found a large deep-freezer on top of a wooden pallet in the center of the room. The front of the white box was sealed with a metal latch and reinforced with a padlock.

"Now what?" I touched the lock and found greasy residue on the metal. I wiped my hands on my jeans.

"It's a simple padlock; a bolt cutter should do it." He went for the cart in the hall and returned with the cutters. Once the lock was off, he lifted the latch and went no further. We stepped back, expecting an explosion or some glow to fill the room like an angry genie, but nothing happened. That meant we had to open it manually. Great.

"We shouldn't look in there," I muttered, the full weight of what we were doing now coming to a head.

"It could be pork chops in there for all we know. We need to make sure it's Tobias's body." He said a whole lot for someone who didn't move a muscle.

I tipped my head toward the box. "Fine, you look in there."

He shook his head keenly. "No, you look."

"You're the man with the plan. You go see. Didn't you want to be the hero here to save the day? Well, here you go." I gestured to the ice box with a sweep of my hand.

"Where's all that feminist rhetoric now? You wanted empowerment; have at it."

"Feminism has nothing to do with crusty dead things. Unless Tobias's corpse is being sexually harassed on the job, or not getting equal pay, then it's not my department. Now hop to it."

We just stared at the freezer, terrified at whatever curse came with opening Pandora's Box. Whether it was from superstition, watching too many movies, or good ole common sense, we completely froze, but we'd come too far to turn back now.

"Fine, we'll open it together," he decided, his voice thick with uncertainty.

Side by side, we snuck toward the box. We stretched our arms out as far as they could go until our fingers tucked under the lid.

Eyes glued to mine, he said, "Ready? On the count of three. One, two, three!"

The lid flipped open and we backed away and almost fell to the floor from the odor that shot out of the freezer. Rotting meat, sewage, and decay rolled up in a mixture of eye-watering funk. I'd never smelled a dead body before, but it was an odor I would never forget. I covered my nose in the collar of my shirt and inched closer.

Sure enough, Tobias's body—what was left of it—lay at the bottom of the freezer. I recognized his inky black hair, muscular frame, and the angelic, ambiguous features. He lay on his back with his knees bent so he could fit inside. His eyes were shut and his mouth was closed, giving the impression of peaceful sleep. But the illusion fell flat due to the broken arrow poking out of his chest and the dark circle of blood around the piercing. This sad image had all the makings of a slain vampire in his coffin, except a vampire should've turned to dust, whereas Tobias looked, well . . . soupy.

Half his body was submerged in a dark green liquid, which I guessed was olive oil. It had mixed with something else, parts of Tobias too disgusting to name. Everything below the shallow surface had dissolved into a thick sludge of grease. Only his face, his hands, which rested on his stomach, and his bent knees were intact, but hollow and as thin as a plastic mask floating in water. Sustaining its familiar, human form, the skin looked delicate with no bone structure to support its shape.

My knee bumped the side of the freezer, making the body wobble in a life-sized Jell-O mold. I was certain that if I touched it—and I sure as hell wasn't—the skin would cave in and sink to the bottom.

Then there was the smell, that noxious, acidic rank that clung to the back of my throat, no doubt stuck to my clothes, and would ruin my appetite for the next few weeks.

I wasn't Tobias's biggest fan, but this was cruel and unusual punishment that I wouldn't wish on anyone. I couldn't blame him for wanting vengeance. I would want the same thing if the tables were turned. Caleb, however, didn't share my compassion.

I was so horrified at the sight that I hadn't noticed Caleb pulling out his phone. Using both hands, he tilted the phone for a good angle. "Marvelous, darling. Work it, work it, work it. Make love to ze camera. Fabulous," Caleb coached in a really bad French accent.

"What are you doing?" I asked, covering my mouth.

"He's gonna want proof that we're not bluffing," he answered, twiddling with his phone.

"Why the photo? Aren't we going to just give it to him?"

He made a face at me like I'd lost my mind. "Hell no. We're gonna make a deal."

"What sort of deal? Caleb, we can't—" Whatever I was going to say had been interrupted by movement in the freezer.

I screamed, jumped away, and almost knocked Caleb down. I held on to him, snatching at his body for safety, comfort, reason, anything. I hadn't imagined it, and the horror-struck look on Caleb's face confirmed what I saw.

Swallowing my heart back down, I slunk toward the box again, inch by agonizing inch. My plan was to close it and by no means look inside, but it didn't work. I saw it, and worst of all, it saw me. The eyelids had opened and revealed a milky white film over the eyes where color should've been. Nothing else on the body moved but those blank sockets, which followed me from left to right.

Having seen enough, Caleb slammed the lid shut and hooked the front clasp.

"All right, that's it. I'm out." I went to the door. A hand caught mine and I jumped, ready to swing.

"Sam, wait," Caleb said. "He can't move. He's paralyzed, remember? He's harmless."

"He?" I said incredulously. "You telling me that Campbell's cup-o-demon over there is alive? I mean really alive? How can Tobias be in two places at once?"

"I don't know, but that's why he wants it. He's still attached to it, more than we realize." Caleb looked back to the freezer. "If so, then he can't truly inhabit another person's body unless this one is destroyed."

I didn't like the crazy look on his face, the wide-eyed mania of a mad scientist. "Whatever you're thinking—don't. Dougie is still—"

He held my arms to keep me from swinging at him. "You need to trust me. If all goes well, Doug and Mia will get out alive." He slipped past me and into the hall. He returned moments later with the strangest-looking jack I'd ever seen.

"What is that?"

"It's a pallet jack. Found it by the elevator. Good for lifting heavy objects, like freight." He aimed the two prongs directly under the wooden pallet under the freezer. When it was secure, he pumped the handle until the entire load lifted an inch off the ground.

"Come on." He dragged the haul out of the unit and into the hallway.

I had to use the strength in my legs to close the door and it locked automatically when it connected with the wall.

Getting the freezer down the hallway was a bit trickier than we thought. I could see Caleb strain to tow the box along and my added strength didn't make much of a difference. Tobias had mentioned once that he was heavy, some crap about cloud density, but damn.

Once inside the elevator, I asked, "How are we going to get this onto the truck?"

He tossed me a smile as if I were the cutest wittle thing

he had ever seen. "The rental truck has a lift gate in the back, Sam. Let's just hope it holds."

Not wanting that look tossed at me again, I didn't ask what a lift gate was. That could wait until we got outside and I could see for myself.

It was dark by the time we got out of the building and the temperature had dropped twenty degrees in minutes. We hurried as best we could toward the rental truck without being noticed.

Caleb started the engine, then came around the back of the truck and pulled down the tailpiece. With a flip of a switch on the side, the metal flap lowered to the ground, and I was introduced to the aforementioned lift gate. Caleb rolled the load onto the plank and flipped the switch again. He and the cargo elevated onto the truck bed with an audible strain that made it clear that Caleb wasn't going to get a return on his rental deposit. The tires sank into the dirt, but it was safe enough for us to drive.

Caleb searched the area for witnesses. "We need to hurry; this place closes in a few minutes."

"What about your Jeep?" I hitched my thumb to the vehicle behind us.

He slammed the flap shut when a pair of high beams glared from the path entry. Before I could get a good look at the vehicle, Caleb grabbed a fistful of my coat and pulled me down behind the truck. I turned to him and he pressed a finger to his lips. I rose slowly, allowing the freezer to shield me as I risked a peek at the black van that pulled up in front of the warehouse.

Four men leapt out of the van before it could come to a complete stop. I couldn't see their faces but each man was dressed in black shirts and jeans. They moved together in a stiff collective formation that spoke of some sort of militant training. Their dark heads looked from left to right, searching the parking lot, and we ducked when they turned our way.

"Shit. They're here," Caleb whispered, squatting low with his back against the truck.

I wasn't following. "Who?"

"Ruiz's men. They know about the storage unit."

I peeked over the truck to the men talking to one another and then crouched back down. "Do they know the code to get in?"

"Doubt it. They're probably gonna guard it or try to break in later. We have to get out of here." He pulled his keys from his pocket. "Once they go inside, I want you to take my Jeep and follow me out of here. Keep your phone on so I can call you. Don't answer the phone unless it's me, okay?" He dropped the keys in my hand.

We looked to the men hovering in front of the building. One by one, they passed through the sliding doors toward the freight elevator. I quickly backtracked what we'd done that might have given us away: the odor in the hallway, the smeared streaks of oil on the floor. There was no time to worry about it now; the main thing was to be gone before they came out again.

"Go!" Caleb sprang up and went around the driver's side of the truck. I got to my feet and ran to the Jeep three cars down. By the time I got in, gunned the engine, and put the Jeep in reverse, Caleb was rolling out of the lot. I was right behind him. We passed the front gate and were on the main road leading back to the parkway.

I kept my eyes on the road and my mission clear. However, my mind veered off course more times than what would be deemed safe while operating heavy machinery. My foot eased off the gas so I wasn't dry humping Caleb's taillights, but I stayed close enough that no cars could cut between us.

As instructed, I turned my phone back on, but no sooner than my thumb pushed the POWER button, I got bum rushed with calls from Angie and Mom. The longer I drove, the harder it got to ignore the buzzing sound and my cell skittering across the passenger's seat. I finally gave in and answered the call.

"Samara! Where are you?" Mom didn't sound happy.

I clamped the phone between my ear and shoulder. "I'm with Caleb."

"Why aren't you home? Do you not know the meaning of grounded?"

Thankfully, my groan was drowned out by the engine. Did Wonder Woman or Buffy have to worry about parents blowing up their phone while they were trying to save the world? Hell no! That's what voicemail was for. "Mom, I promise I'll get back home as soon as I finish."

"Finish what? And what are you doing near Jamestown?" she yelled.

My neck straightened, but I caught the phone before it slipped from my shoulder. "How do you know where I am?"

"Your bracelet, or have you forgotten? I want you home right now. You hear me, Samara Nicole? Now!"

I cringed at the rise in volume and pissedivity shooting through the line. "Mom, if I come home right now, Mia's going to die," I said. "I'm sorry, but I can't let him hurt her. I have to save her. I promise I'll be careful. I'll call you when it's over."

"Let who hurt Mia? Samara, what is going—"

I hung up. I loved Mom, but my blood pressure could only handle one crisis at a time.

But the conversation introduced another problem. My bracelet. The same tool Angie used to trace Olivia would lead the police, and whoever else Mom called, right to the drop zone. That might spook Tobias and he might hurt Mia. Oh yeah, this thing had to go, but I hated ruining my new chain, plus the bolt cutter was in the truck with Caleb.

The party line continued with an incoming call from Dougie's cell. Before I could part my lips with a greeting, Tobias asked, "Where are you taking my body?"

Time to play dumb. "What do you mean?" I asked.

"It's been moved. I can feel it. Are you trying to back out of our deal?"

I shook my head, and then I remembered that he couldn't see me. But then again, I wasn't totally confident about that. "No. I'm delivering it. I-I'm on my way to the rec park now."

"So soon?" He sounded surprised, jubilant even. "I'd underestimated you. We'll be there shortly."

"Let me talk to Mia!" I demanded.

"It's Sam," he said to someone close to him.

There was rustling on the phone, then I heard Mia's voice, watery and hoarse with signs of crying. "Sam, what's going on? Why is everyone acting weird?" she asked.

"Mia I—"

"Be there in fifteen minutes." Tobias ended the call.

I almost swerved off the road as every Mafia movie popped in my head. Did he rough her up; smack her around, or worse? Trying not to dwell on the "worse," I called Caleb with this latest bombshell. "Change in plans. He knows the body's been moved. He wants to meet up in fifteen," I reported.

"Damn! Guess we'll have to take care of it there."

"Take care of what? Caleb, we can't destroy it, and Mom and the National Guard are tracking my location from my bracelet. I need you to stop so we can remove it."

"No time. The bracelet might be a good thing. If something bad happens, we need someone to know where we are. Just follow me."

There were at least four ways to get to the park, but Caleb thought it best to avoid as many stop signs as possible and kept to the highways. We transferred to I-64 then got off at the army base exit toward our ultimate destination: the recreational park on Airport Road. The wide bends, the lack of street lights, and the suicidal deer made the two-mile strip a daredevil drag race. I had no fondness for that particular area, but when your best friend is being held captive by her demon-possessed boyfriend, haggling over meeting spots was a moot point.

Through my window, I could see bales of hay on open fields like giant cinnamon rolls and a family of deer scampered around for food. On the opposite side lay miles of forest where the park and a few biking trails tucked deep in its belly.

Red taillights glowed ahead and the truck rolled to a stop. On the left was the entry to the park, which was guarded by a short metal gate chained together and a sign saying CLOSED UNTIL SPRING in bold letters.

I expected Caleb to ram through the rickety gate, but he parked, got out with the bolt cutters, and cut the chains. He swung the gate open wide, got back in his vehicle, and kept on truckin'.

Under a steeple ceiling of trees, a dirt path led us to a large square posing as a parking lot. Bald patches of earth bordered by logs, gravel, and mulch parted the forest bed. I parked next to Caleb at the far end of the lot, where we had the most light.

Moonlight bounced off corner surfaces, but the trees drenched the park in deep pockets of shadows. Across the lot, the foliage thinned out and scattered, revealing a picturesque view of the lake. The absence of lampposts allowed the night to show off its star power, stretching the cloudless sky like spilt diamonds on a velvet cloth. Picnic benches huddled near the trees and tied-up canoes were stacked on a rack near the guest services station.

A lot had changed since my summer afternoons of duck feeding as a kid, and I certainly didn't recall ever being this nervous. The dark will do that to you. Everything looked blue, cold, and sinister; a realm where things that weren't alive would walk. The whole scene was slasher-flick spooky and I kept my eyes peeled for anyone wearing a hockey mask.

The slam of a door ripped me out of my daydream and my pulse skipped. With trusty duffel bag slung over his shoulder, Caleb went around to the truck and climbed inside the back. He opened the freezer and then gripped the side of the truck bed as the odor from the ice box cold cocked him in the face.

I watched him work diligently and got out of the Jeep to join him. "What are you doing?"

"Getting ready. We only have a few minutes to get this right," he replied, holding the gallon can of kerosene over the freezer. "The olive oil has already purified the body, so all we have to do is wait for him to jump back into it and poof. Barbeque."

Cold air stung my cheeks and my hair tangled around my face in a spider web of curls. The fumes caught on the wind and I realized that was a dead giveaway of a double-cross. We would have to keep Tobias away from the freezer until the body swap. I had a bad feeling about this whole thing. The risks were too high for this to fail.

I had little time to consider it when headlights appeared from the dirt path to our left. Caleb was coiling the rope around his arm and elbow when he perked up at the approaching vehicle. He hid behind the freezer and pulled the kerosene can out of view.

It was too late for me to duck seeing as I was standing in plain sight. The vehicle parked at the end of the make-shift lot and the brights cut off.

Doors slammed and gravel crunched underfoot. Finally, two figures dark as shadow drifted closer. I could tell that the shorter one was Mia, who clung to the taller one's arms for warmth. Moonlight outlined their heads and shoulders, cutting them into sharp contrasting lines.

I met them halfway, taking my time and deliberating my next move. Lilith twisted and slithered up the length of my back, stretching her legs, if she had them. A family of ants curled under the skin too deep to scratch. This turn of events seemed to have gotten her attention and she was getting into position. The stage had been set, all the players were assembled, and with the soft quarter moon as our spotlight, we began the final act.

20

Silence strained between us and threatened to break at any minute.

The tension was thick and too heavy to hold it in any longer. It began to spread throughout our surroundings, interfering with nature to where it, too, wanted to see how this would end. The trees stopped rustling, the leaves slowed their dance around my feet and the night held its breath. We stood in the middle of the parking lot, facing each other with hands at our sides, ready for the quick draw.

Tobias tipped his head in a slight bow. "Samara."

"Tobias," I returned bitterly. I had to keep cool and not give away any reaction he could use against me.

Mia looked at both of us. "Who's Tobias?"

"Ask Dougie." I tipped my chin in his direction. "I have your precious cargo, now let Mia go."

"Where's your other half? There's no way you could've gotten the body out by yourself, and he wouldn't let you come here alone." His fiery gaze drifted toward the truck. "Come out, *Cake Boy*! I know you're out here!" Tobias called out in a mocking tone.

"I'm here." Caleb appeared from the shadows and approached us slowly, but Tobias stopped him.

"Show me your hands," Tobias ordered and stepped in front of Mia.

"No arrows. No guns. The vessel's in the truck." Caleb joined my side and I looked at him, but more directly, the wet string of rope that he dropped by his foot.

The wind picked up and the odor of kerosene floated around me, tickling my nostrils and throat. I knew Tobias could smell it. I wondered if he even cared, and would take the body no matter its condition. Ever since this whole ordeal began he seemed desperate, not his usual suave, flirtatious deviance. Now it was all about survival, self-preservation and he was willing to kill to stay alive.

"Then why don't we have a look, shall we?" Tobias took a step, but Caleb crossed his path.

"Let Mia go first," he demanded.

"You see, there's a problem with that. My body is all the way over there and I'm over here and you stand between us."

"Will someone tell me what the hell is going on?" Mia finally spoke, her head volleying between the two of us. "What body? This is all freaking me out. Sam, can you take me back to my car? I left it at school." She stepped forward, but Tobias caught her by the crook of her elbow.

He yanked her back to him so hard, her neck whipped back, sending wavy strands of her hair into flight. "Don't move," he growled.

Mia pushed against his chest with her free arm. "Dougie, stop! Let me go. Please!" Mia cried.

Tobias flinched, and if anyone blinked, they would

have missed it, but I hadn't. "Dougie? Dougie are you there?" I asked.

At the name, his body began to quiver and struggle for balance.

Thinking fast, I said, "Mia, call to Dougie. He'll listen to you. Cry out, scream so he can hear you."

Though I couldn't see her face, she seemed to understand the gravity of the situation; more so as Tobias grabbed her by the throat. Mia held the hand around her neck, fighting to break free, but he was too strong. She tried to scream, but it came out in a broken gasp.

"Be. Quiet," he commanded in a deep, guttural roar that not even the deaf could mistake for human. His eyes were ablaze, causing Mia to stop struggling and look on with helpless wonder as most women would while under the spell. Any strength to resist left her and her hands slipped from his arm and fell limp at her sides.

"No!" I moved forward, but Caleb held firm to my arm.

"Dougie, please," Mia rasped. "You're hurting me."

The name or maybe the sound of Mia's voice seemed to have caused a short circuit in Dougie's brain, and the angry brilliance inside dimmed from a bad fuse. I understood enough to know that Dougie was scrambling the signal and fighting for control, but he wasn't strong enough.

He drew Mia closer to him and squeezed so hard that I feared he'd crush her. His mouth hovered mere inches from hers, but didn't move any further. He shook so bad; both of their bodies trembled. With what sounded like another roar, he pushed her away. "Go, Mia, Now!"

She lost her footing and tumbled into the dirt. Not letting that stop her, she crab-walked away, keeping enough distance between them to get to her feet.

Caleb knelt down with the lighter in his hand and aimed it toward the wet rope on the ground.

I touched his shoulder. "Not yet. He's still in there. Wait!"

"He's trying to push Tobias out." Caleb pointed to the couple across the lot.

Doubled over, Dougie grabbed both sides of his head and jerked as though trying to remove it from his neck. I could hear Dougie's voice and felt his fear and pain spill out of his scream. He threw his head up and howled at the sky, his neck corded with veins. He looked every bit the werewolf at a full moon fighting the transition.

"Mia, run!" I yelled.

Dougie's head jerked up and looked to her. Tobias had gained control and didn't seem too happy about his hostage getting away. He sprung to his feet as I broke into a run.

Mia ran from the parking area in the direction of the path leading out of the park. Tobias was fast behind her, and I was right behind him.

I saw his hand stretch out, his fingers sinking into the flying strands of her hair. Before he could manage a grip, I jumped on his back, my nails scratching at his face. I didn't want to hurt Dougie—he would survive a few cuts and bruises—but it might be a different story if something happened to Mia.

Dougie's arms flailed in a wide, sweeping motion and he stumbled backward toward the road again. I had to get him away from Mia, away from the denser part of the woods where all kinds of murderous mayhem could ensue. He threw me off his shoulder and I landed on my back against sharp rocks in the cold dirt. I knew they would leave a mark, but I didn't feel pain right away. I was too wired to feel anything until this was over.

Tobias turned and towered over me with the moon at his back. He was a flat black silhouette cut out of the landscape; his eyes were two candles in the dark. He resembled the monster I knew him to be, and in that moment I was able to feel something. Hate.

"This will end badly and more will die before it's over. Just know that if I go, I'm taking him with me." He stooped down and extended his hand for me.

Whether he was planning to choke me or help me up, I didn't know, because Caleb swooped in from the left and tackled him by the waist. The two rolled to the ground and tumbled toward the grass in a swirl of dark fabric. The sounds of hard blows against flesh and ripping of clothing rent the air until there was nothing but heavy breathing.

I couldn't see any of it, because I was caught in the middle of a supernatural beat down. Hands grabbed the collar of my coat and pulled me to the ground. A fist collided with my jaw and I could taste blood in my mouth. A punch struck my stomach and knocked the wind out of me and pushed everything inside toward my throat.

Every attempt to get up from the ground was foiled by another blow. I shielded my face with my arms but that didn't help. This wasn't my fight; this wasn't my body under attack. It was Caleb's. There was another strike and lightning sharp pain spilled over my right eye, making me see double. I tried to scream, but I had no air to push it out. Something heavy pressed down on my neck, crushing the windpipe.

Tears filled my eyes, blurring the night around me in a watery smudge, but there was no one above me, no one holding me down. It was an illusion, a phantom presence playing tricks on the mind. Our connection was a double-edged sword that could penetrate either way. If I owned Caleb's pain then he owned my health, my strength. I clung to that truth, held on to that little piece of myself that I could control and crawled out of Caleb's mind. Higher and higher I climbed out of the pit until I could see light again and take in the first lungful of air.

Once the dust cleared, and my vision improved, I found Tobias pinning Caleb to the ground by the neck.

"Dougie!" Mia screamed, still standing in the middle of the dirt road. Moonlight hit her as she drew closer, showcasing a tear-stained ghost peering behind a curtain of dark hair.

The sound of her voice stopped Tobias, and he looked up. Though she wasn't like us, it appeared she had a type of draw of her own, one that only Dougie was susceptible to. It was brief, but effective.

Gaining an open window of attack, Caleb tucked his knees to his chest and kicked out, hitting Tobias in the midsection. Tobias sailed across the grass toward the picnic area, where a tree interrupted his flight with a loud crack. His limp body slipped down its trunk and he landed onto his knees. He curled over, wrapped his arm around his stomach, then stumbled to his feet again.

By the time he got a second wind, Caleb was on his feet, ready to go another round. Hot steam shooting from his nose and mouth, he was an angry bull seeing red.

Caleb ran toward the tree where Tobias now stood, picking up speed to where there was nothing but a violet ray marking his trajectory. He was stronger, faster, and there was no doubt in my mind that Capone had come out to play. I could feel him rising from the depths, riding the beast of rage into battle.

Tobias charged toward him as well. They were two trains running headlong, parting the air in gold and purple streaks.

I got to my feet, stumbled then limped toward them,

but I was too far away to block the path of the missile. I could see the devastation, feel the pain that would come before it happened, and there was no preparation for it.

The two collided in an atomic blast of pure power. Light, brilliant and nebulous, circled the two men and fanned out in a wide ring, sweeping leaves, picnic benches, and logs out of its path.

There was no time to run or scream. All I could do was cover my eyes and duck. The force hit me like a crashing tide, knocking me completely off my feet and pressing me face-down in the dirt. It rolled over my body in warm currents and howled in my ears. As quickly as it began, it slowed to a gentle breeze over my skin.

I sat up to see Mia at the far end of the lot near the path. She crawled to her knees and pressed a shaky hand to her head, checking for blood. Straight ahead toward the lake, Caleb hunched over Dougie's body with his hands around the enemy's neck.

I stumbled to my feet, and the rush made me see double. Headlights swam through the trees and after I shook the fog from my head, they were still there. Those were *real* lights from *real* cars, coming *real* close. Whether it was the cops or Ruiz's crew, I didn't know nor care. I had to get to Caleb.

I ate up the distance between us on wobbly legs. Caleb was still strangling Dougie, and in turn Dougie held his neck in a vise. Caleb seemed to have the advantage and not even Dougie's best wrestling move could outmaneuver a pissed off Cambion.

"Not so strong now without your body, huh, demon?" Caleb growled, his expression too composed to be involved in anything that physical. No rage or hatred, but a cold, impersonal response reserved for sociopaths. He'd shut down again and that was when he was at his most lethal.

Dougie's face was turning scarlet and the veins along his forehead rose under his skin. He stretched his free arm across the dirt, reaching for aid and came up empty handed.

"Stop! Caleb, he's down!" I pulled at his shoulder, but he wouldn't budge.

Light streamed into the camp ground, and Mia and I took the pose of startled deer. A van and that familiar black sedan stopped at the mouth of the path. Blood pounded in my ears, making me dizzy as too much of everything happened at once. Men were talking in the background. Doors slammed. Mia was screaming and crying, and Caleb spat curses at the boy he was about to kill.

"Get out! Get out of him now!" Caleb bellowed, shaking Dougie by the neck. "Your body is waiting, you evil shit! Go get it!"

I didn't need an empathic link to know he was dead serious. He was going to kill Dougie to get Tobias out and to hell with anyone who stood in the way. I pulled harder on his shoulder, I screamed in his ear, I clawed at his jacket, but it was no use.

Slowly, Dougie's body stopped fighting and his hand slipped from Caleb's shoulders. His eyes rolled back in his head, showing only the whites.

"Caleb, stop!" I pounded Caleb's arm.

When he saw that Dougie had stopped moving, Caleb finally pulled away. Mia screamed, squatted to the ground, and knocked me out of the way for a better look. "Dougie!"

Caleb scooped Mia by the waist and got her to her feet, but she kicked and fought him the whole time. "No, Mia, stay back. He's coming out. Get back."

"You tried to kill him! What the hell is wrong with you?" Mia screamed and wailed at Caleb's head.

"I was forcing the demon out. Get back!"

I returned my attention to Dougie then tumbled away, only now understanding what he meant.

Dougie's lips parted, his chest and stomach undulated in a strange belly dance. Just like the last time, that black, fluid-like mist leaked from his mouth. The dark miasma hovered over our heads, churning and gathering power. Then I saw that beautiful, amber gleam in the center, and I knew Tobias had escaped. I had no idea what would happen when it reunited with the body in the freezer, but it coasted above me with malicious intent.

"Don't anyone move. Stay right where you are!" Ruiz ordered, followed by racing footsteps.

"He's leaving the body!" Caleb yelled at the men then removed his coat and gave it to Mia to use. "Cover your mouth. Don't breathe any of the air until I say."

"Caleb, do it now!" I yelled.

He dashed back toward the parking area. Ruiz raced after him, but he was a bit out of his element, because the one thing Cake Boy could do well was run. Caleb stopped a few feet from the truck and knelt down to the ground as if to tie his shoe. A fire ignited instantly to the rope that lay by his feet. The fire ate at the line in seconds, snaked its way toward the truck and climbed up the side of the freezer. The flame erupted in a radiant ball, illuminating the entire campground.

The inferno reached up to the trees and twirled coils of black smoke at its fingertips. The sound coming out of the fire echoed in a cacophony of screams and wails of torment. It could have been the distance, but the sound seemed to pale in comparison to the noise over my head.

The black cloud had spread wide, reaching at least five yards in diameter. It didn't move or fly away, but flared up and stirred into itself, like an evil spell backfiring onto its caster. The wind slapped my face and blinded me, and the thunderous grind of metal and hellish cries made my blood congeal. This thing, this soul, this life was dying in the worst way imaginable.

"Everyone cover your mouths, now!" Ruiz ordered his crew.

I stole a glance at the four other men with aqua blue flashes in their eyes. They must have been Cambion siblings. That was a good thing. The only person we had to worry about was Ruiz. He was the only male non-Cambion in company. But he seemed to know the score, because he also covered his mouth.

The rumbling grew and sent the ground around us into a tremor. The cloud above expanded and bloated as a real cloud would as it collects water. It became so solid that if I touched it, it would burst. The gold beacon, the nucleus of the organism, had ruptured and sent cracks zigzagging through the darkness. The squiggling gold veins divided the cloud into fractions and pulled apart the pieces with what sounded like torn fabric. With one last inhuman howl, the mist began to dissolve and the sky and its host of stars revealed themselves again. Silence reigned over the park for a full minute while my ears tried to adjust to the noise level.

The twitching body near my foot drew my attention back to important matters. I knelt next to Dougie and held his head in my hands. He was cold and his skin was drying out from the drops of life seeping from his body.

"No! No, Dougie, please stay here. Dougie!" Mia's screams were nothing more than delayed echoes in the background, along with the ringing in my ears. I held Dougie's twitching body as the spasms began to subside.

Behind fluttering lashes, his red, unfocused eyes rolled up to meet Mia's. He seemed to recognize her, and for a second he looked as though he were about to smile. But it never came and his eyes slid closed. He wasn't twitching anymore. He was very still, getting heavier in my arms like dead weight. No, not dead. Not Dougie. Not yet.

There was no time, no second-guessing, and no guarantee that this would work, but I had to try. Against my better judgment, I needed to cast my animosity aside and trust Lilith. She owed me. I wanted my pound of flesh and I was ready to collect. We would be even, all debts paid, if she saved my friend.

Lilith. You have screwed me over raw and you know it. If you have any intention of redeeming yourself, I need you to help me and do as I say.

My plan might've been crazy, maybe suicidal, but not impossible. I did it with Caleb while he was in a coma, but never this far. If what Olivia said was true, that giving energy would've saved Nadine, then I would make atonement through Dougie. It was a good theory, and the only way to learn was through trial and error.

I shook my shoulders loose, let out a breath, and lowered my mouth to Dougie's. His lips felt cold and dry, devoid of the gentle vibration that came with each living being.

"Sam, what are you doing?" Mia called out behind me.

I centered my concentration on Lilith and allowed the energy to flow out of me in a warm gush. I hadn't realized how tense I was until my body uncoiled and loosened under the release. The energy escaped and with it, live green wires pulsed behind my eyelids.

"Sam, don't!" Caleb yelled somewhere in the distance. "No. Let me go! She'll die! Dammit get off me! Samara!" There were sounds of a struggle and sprinting feet, but I tuned it out.

Heaviness overwhelmed me and I was losing feeling in my legs and arms. It could've been from the cold, but something more than warmth bled from me. The numbness started on my left arm then channeled up my shoulder to my chest. The sharp, stabbing pain just under my ribs told me what was happening. It was what happened for most donors when too much energy was taken. An iron hand had gripped my heart in a fist.

"Samara, stop!" Someone had yelled.

I could feel the tears leaking down my face and across the bridge of my nose, but I gave all that I could. I would give more until there was nothing left.

Screams rode the air and arms pulled at me, but I held on. I clung tight to Dougie's waist until there was no more strength in my arms and I had no choice but to let go. My lips broke from his, and with it, the last bit of my energy passed into his mouth. Slowly as if in a dream, Dougie's chest jerked, sending a rolling motion up his body until a gasp escaped his mouth in a fog. His eyes, wide and free of ethereal light, gaped in stunned terror at the stars.

I could no longer hold myself up. I knew death was coming to make another surprise visit and I didn't have the strength to fight. I felt my body falling, but I didn't hit the ground. I looked up and saw Caleb staring back at me, his eyes wild and swimming with tears. Flashing blue lights speared through the trees, but all I saw was the sad boy in front of me.

"Samara, please." I could see his mouth forming the words, but I lay deaf, dumb, and paralyzed in his arms. Caleb's lips met mine, but I had no feeling left to enjoy it fully. Turmoil and firelight grew around us while we found refuge in a place made of violet and emerald hues. But even they too faded, and the darkness came to swallow the world, and take me with it.

21

As I'd said before, these blackouts that I kept having were getting worse. Much, much worse.

What happened between 8 P.M. and 3:07 A.M. was wiped from memory. Instead of the war zone of the rec park, I was now at home, in my room, lying on my side in bed. Thankfully, I wasn't glued to the ceiling this time and my bracelet was still on my wrist. However, there was an addition to this scene and it snored softly next to my ear.

I turned my head as far as I could. Caleb lay behind me in a spooning position, breathing into my hair. His arm draped over my stomach with the slightest of pressure. I wasn't sure why, but moving wasn't a good idea. It was as if I were magnetized, surgically stitched to his body, and pulling away too far would cause tearing.

"You're awake," a voice called from the doorway.

I found Mom standing in the entryway, holding a glass of juice. As expected, she looked torn up and sleepless. Her freckled face was free of makeup, heavy gray bags hung under her eyes, and her hair fell loose in a soft fro of brown curls.

"How did I get here?" I asked.

She stepped into the room to place the glass on the nightstand. "David and his men brought you here. They said there was no need for you to go to the hospital as long as you two weren't separated." The glass shook in her hands as her stare drifted between me and Caleb. "I have no idea what that means, but whenever we tried . . . I, um . . . It's just better that he stays with you tonight."

And she was cool with that? Something was wrong. I looked down at her shaking hands and then to the dark red blotches in the shape of fingers around her forearm. "Mom, what happened? Did someone hurt you?"

Julie Marshall was a woman of many looks, all of them honest and animated. And of all of them, this one made my heart clench. There was nothing I could say or do to take the fear out of her eyes.

"She's made it clear that you two need each other to heal, so I . . . it's best that you do whatever it is you do."

She? "Lilith did that?" Her silence was all the confirmation I needed. Mom had heard about my roommate, had the details explained ad nauseam, but she never had a formal introduction. It was clear the meeting didn't go well and had Mom scared to death. I couldn't believe Lilith broke loose again. Why would she hurt Mom, of all people? "I'm so sorry. I didn't . . ."

"I know. I shouldn't have tried to pull you apart. She warned me, but I didn't understand." Her gaze drifted past me, past the room, past her comprehension. "You're bound to each other now, aren't you? That's why she didn't want you to separate. That's how you're still alive even after killing Tobias."

"Yeah," I replied. "Being bound together trumps anything else, I guess, like rock beats scissors."

She lifted her head, her glistening eyes met mine with a look so broken that it made my own eyes prickle. "Too soon. It's too soon," she mumbled over and over. "I tried to keep you from making the same mistakes as I did, but you're as stubborn as I was at your age. One careless night will affect the rest of your life."

"I'm so sorry. The last thing I'd ever do is hurt you. You believe me, right?"

I could tell she was having trouble accepting my apology. I couldn't blame her. I had aged this woman fifty years in the span of six months and every minute of it showed through her watery blue eyes. That wall she built to keep the monsters at bay had come crashing down, and the burden of our situation was more real, more present.

She was quiet, but a tangle of emotion crawled under her skin. "I understand. I don't like it, but I understand. I just wish there was another way. I can't protect you from this and I hate it."

I reached my hand as far as it could go for hers. She took it and squeezed, and the fear seemed to run down her arm and up mine. The sensation made my lips quiver and tears leaked down my temple. "I shouldn't have told you. Any of it. What I was, or what was happening."

"And have me go through this blind? No. You did the right thing. I may not like what I know, but at least I know what I'm facing."

"Did you call Dad?" I asked, bracing myself for the answer.

Mom sighed and slumped her shoulders as if the thought of Dad crippled her strength. "It's better that he doesn't know about this. He would not even begin to tolerate it. I thought it was best that he knew, but after what I saw tonight, I don't think so. Your father would kill Caleb, and that might be a problem."

I nodded and rested my head on the pillow. "Are Dougie and Mia safe?"

"Yeah. Douglas went to the hospital and Mia's at home. Ruiz is trying to get everything sorted out with the park and removing the remains. He wants to keep you two out of trouble with the police, so he got you out of there first."

"Tobias is really gone? It worked, right?"

She nodded and I had no idea why that made me sad. Or maybe it was just a by-product of Lilith's grief. I realized that I wasn't the only one who almost died. In a way, a part of her did die. She was very still now, most of her weight spread evenly along my back and skull. I thought it best not to confront her now.

"Get some rest. We can talk later." Mom kissed my forehead then reached over to turn off the lamp, but I caught her hand.

"Leave the light on, please."

She didn't question me and backed out of the room, leaving the door cracked.

"Is she gone?" Caleb whispered in my ear.

Wrapped in his arms, I rolled over to see him fully. He looked like a ghoul with pale hollow cheeks and dark circles under his eyes. A huge, multi-colored bruise covered the entire left side of his face and a dark red gash split his lip. "You look like hell," I said.

As he closed his eyes, the corners of his mouth curled upward, but he was too weak to form a complete smile. "You're no super model either. How are you?" he asked, his voice hoarse with sleep.

"Ask me tomorrow," I grumbled. "It turns out our mission was accomplished. Dougie's alive and Williamsburg faces another dawn free of demons." When he nodded, I asked, "I gave Dougie almost all of my energy. How were you able to save me?"

"We're bonded, Sam. We keep each other alive. Even when you're on the brink of death, Lilith will cling to Capone for help. That's how I survived my coma; why not return the favor." His shoulder twitched in a light shrug. "My eating disorder came in handy tonight. I had enough for us both."

"Yeah well, I still want you to cut back. I don't want you bingeing anymore."

"I know. I think things'll be better now. I won't have to compensate. We'll still have to feed on others, but not as often."

"What do you mean?"

"You didn't feel it in my room the other night?" he asked.

"I felt a lot of things that night; you might wanna be more specific," I replied.

He chuckled, then sucked in a sharp breath in a hiss. Almost instantly, soreness flared in my chest.

"Don't make me laugh; it hurts too much," he said. "Our spirits feed off energy and respond to the emotion of others. The purest, most concentrated form is sexual energy. Think about it; it's where life originates, right? There's power behind it that I won't even try to understand. Incubi and succubi thrive on it and their method of feeding is what's made them famous for centuries."

I tried to follow, but I wasn't doing a good job. "So we don't need other people's energy as much because . . ."

"We can make our own," he finished.

"Is this your elaborate way to get me to sleep with you again?"

His eyebrows rose and he lifted his head from the pillow with apparent interest. "Why, is it working?"

"No."

His head fell back onto the pillow. "You always say that, but I end up getting my way. You said I'd never feed from you; I did. You said I'd never kiss you again; I did. You said that I'd never have to fight you off me; now look at you." He actually smiled this time.

I made a face at him, and though his eyes were closed, I knew he could feel my angry glare. "No matter what, it always comes down to us getting it on. Maybe it's a sign."

"I don't believe in signs or some fate written in the stars. Soul mate is an action not a title; it's not what you are but what you become. I wasn't born in this exact point in time just to meet you, but I'd die to keep you with me." He kissed my nose and with elegance to rival all love sonnets, he said, "Put out that light. I'm sleepy."

The thought of being in the dark made my skin tingle. "Would it bother you if I left it on?"

"It's okay, Sam. There's nothing waiting for you in the dark but me. I won't let anything happen to you. I've got you."

At his statement, my skin really did tingle, but for an entirely different reason. When I reached over the side of the bed to click off the light, I saw a white index card propped against the lamp. Immediately I knew who it came from. This message was shorter with even messier handwriting than the last one. The ink bled from each line and dragged across the paper, giving the impression of spastic hands and scrambled thoughts. But I could make out the letters enough to read what it said.

Samara,
You got your pound of flesh.
We're even.
                    Lilith

I knew it was hard for her to sit back and watch her old mate die. And there was a small ounce of pity still left inside me, stored away in case of emergencies. I closed my eyes, centered on Lilith for any response, and offered my condolences if she needed it. But there was no movement inside, which meant "No." That was fine by me. She had said her piece, and I was too tired to respond anyway.

I dropped the card back on the table, clicked off the light, then rolled back into Caleb's arms. Out of some subconscious reflex, he trapped me in his arms and squeezed his favorite pillow.

The hallway light leaked into the room and I was somewhat thankful that Mom had left the door open, but I was sure she did it for other reasons. Even if it was locked with no one home, we were too beat down to do anything but snuggle. And it was just as satisfying. There was peace there that had been missing for months, lost for so long that I'd forgotten it was ever there. I was his security blanket, the familiar face that kept the beast calm and made the voices go quiet. Stability.

"Yeah, you've got me all right," I replied in the dark, but he was already asleep.

22

The downside of secrets was keeping your lies straight. Lies were the seas that separated the land, ensuring that neither coast would touch.

The only way to keep from drowning in the gulf was to confess. I knew I couldn't keep this secret anymore and why I kept it for this long was a testament to my gullibility and pride. Honesty wasn't as easy as it sounded, but it was a quick indicator to tell who your friends really were, who had your back and who didn't. It was a relief to lay it all on the table, and if I was to do that, I'd best do it right so I wouldn't have to repeat myself.

Dougie's mom decided that this meeting should take place outside in their Zen-friendly backyard, where her son could get some fresh air. He'd been cooped up in his room for a week since he'd been released from the hospital and he was just now accepting company. The twenty-degree weather was worth it to see him, to know for myself that he was alive.

Dougie appeared to be his usual wise-cracking, thug-tastic self, but there was a vacancy behind his eyes where mischief and humor used to live. Something haunted them now, something dark and inexplicable that only slept in the daytime, which likely contributed to his insomnia.

He claimed he had little recollection of what had happened to him, or at least that's what he told his parents and the police who visited him in the hospital. Detective Ruiz had done a good job covering the evidence, removing the vehicles and burnt remains, but not the memory of us being there. Dougie was aware that something evil had happened to him and he knew that Caleb and I were connected in some way, but not enough to stitch together a patchy police report.

Caleb came for moral support and, if necessary, to apologize for beating the living crap out of Dougie. I found it funny that we stood in the same place he taught Caleb how to fight off the wanton women in the area. No one expected the teacher to get schooled by the pupil and not in such a brutal manner. Judging by how Dougie narrowed the one eye that wasn't swollen shut, I was pretty sure he could at least remember that part. He took the defensive pose, but it was hard to look tough with an upper-body cast and neck brace.

The doctor said he would be fine in six weeks, but his wrestling career would have to wait until then, which rightly, was another reason Dougie had his panties in a twist. He sat quiet in the bamboo lawn chair under a blanket, his face swollen and placid as I spat my tale.

Mia sat at his side in the twin chair, holding a can of Sprite for him to drink through a straw. One good thing to come out of this was their newfound appreciation for each other, even if it came at the cost of our friendship.

Mia had returned to giving me the silent treatment in

school, not even bothering to look at me, but held enough compassion not to rat out anyone to the police. She had seen what came out of Dougie's mouth and heard the demon's cry, but none of the events that night could be explained without the aid of Mulder and Scully. Curiosity had won out and she had agreed to this meeting, wanting to collect on that promise that I would tell her everything.

I talked better on my feet, so I paced the patio area and recapped everything since last summer, from the Fourth of July party to Nadine, to Caleb's coma, to Malik Davis, to the three-way link, ending with, "And then a demon jumped into your body."

The two kept quiet to the end, their jaws slacked the whole time I revealed the details of the incredible story.

Mia's reactions were the textbook stages of grief, starting with incredulity. "You're joking, right? Quit playing." Then the last-minute attempt at logic. "Oh yeah? You sure you're not just bipolar?" Followed by overdramatized panic. "Oh my God! You're a monster!" Finally, awkward resignation. "So, what happens now?"

"I go on with my life, if that's all right with you," I replied. "I'm still me. It's just me with a little bit extra."

Dougie scowled at me, struggling to process my explanation. "You say that you're Cambodian now? You're not even Asian."

"Cambion, Dougie. Cambion," I said.

Mia's body shifted along the chair and she tucked her scarf tighter around her neck. "I thought that was fried squid."

"That's calamari. Okay, guys, say it with me now. Cam-bi-on," I pronounced the word slowly.

Dougie turned to Mia, revealing the right side of his face, which had bloomed into a big maroon-colored blister. The two judges leaned close, conferring with each other for the next panel question.

"How do you get rid of it?" Dougie asked.

"You have to die," Caleb said from one of the patio chairs behind me. He'd been quiet all this time, letting me do all the talking.

The two stared at Caleb, surprised at his comment, too wrapped up in my story to remember he was still there.

"And you say you were like this all your life?" Dougie asked him.

Caleb nodded and blew hot air into his chilly hands. "But Sam's new to our world. She acquired a spirit with Nadine's death."

"That's why your eyes look like that." Dougie studied me with new understanding. "And Olivia is one too?"

I gave a small nod.

"Who's Olivia?" Mia asked, her voice edged with accusation.

"A memory." Dougie leaned over and kissed Mia's cheek, then asked me, "How can you be cool with this?"

"Because spazzing out is counterproductive," I said and smiled to Caleb. "I just wanted you to know because you're the closest people in my life aside from my family. You wanted the truth; there it is and I'm sorry that you don't like what you're hearing. What you saw that night was what happens when these things get out of control, when we as human hosts lose sight of who we are. And if we hadn't stopped it, it would have killed you both. It had no humanity, but we do. And I'm holding on to mine for as long as I can."

When I got no objection, I continued. "So there you have it, the reason why I've been acting weird, why all the boys love me and all the girls hate me, why I have to wear these painful contacts, and why I've signed up for therapy. There are things in this life that are far scarier than school, and you only had a taste of what I've had to deal with. Welcome to my world."

I turned to leave, but Dougie's voice stopped me. "Wait. I ain't sayin' you're a bad person, Sam. It's just this is too weird for me, you know? Demons? My folks don't believe that one-religion stuff, but damn, I'm ready to go to church." He dropped his gaze to the ground in deep thought, his brows knitting together. "These dreams, man, they keep buggin' me. I keep seeing that thing— what it wanted to do. Can't even breathe air now and not think of what's in it. And all these people in my head. I can hear them screaming. I just need to think about it, you know? Get my head right."

When I nodded, he asked, "Malik Davis is dead, isn't he?" but it didn't sound like a question. He knew the answer and just wanted me to say it.

"Yeah." I stared at my feet and kicked leaves off the clay tiles of the deck.

The hype over Malik had died down in school and the search had been pushed aside to more important matters, as happens with most cold cases. It may sound cruel, but I cared more about his family than the boy himself. The dead didn't have any problems, but the living were riddled with them. They needed peace, and a reason to stop searching and release the hope that was never there. Between the fear of being exposed and the lack of solid evidence, none of us could give it to them. In fact, I was certain that this conversation would go no further than the four of us. As Hamlet said, "Thus conscience does make cowards of us all."

"What happens now?" Mia asked, her voice small and timid as she hugged her arms.

"We move on and celebrate life while we've got it.

Other than that, I gotta get back home. I was only allowed an hour out." I went to the picnic bench and grabbed my shoulder bag. "So are we cool?" I asked.

"I really don't know, Sam," Mia said. "Can we get back to you on that?"

"Yeah. I'm not going anywhere. I'll catch you later." I left the patio and went around the side of the house with Caleb right behind me.

"Don't let it get to you, Sam. They're scared and need time to figure all this out. They'll come around. You did." He bumped my arm. "Your mom was serious about you being grounded until you're eighteen?"

"Yeah, but it's cool. It's only a month." I was lucky to get off so easy. I'd put my mom through hell, and I was once again thankful for Ruiz's manner of distraction. He had been in New York for weeks, but called Mom every day, which made her smile and forget her own name at times.

Ruiz told me that the remains along with the photos Caleb took on his phone were enough to sate the Santiagos' bloodlust. Brodie was released from Santiago custody and flew back to England with a belligerent Michael in tow. Our participation had guaranteed a pardon for any persecution, and the family looked forward to meeting me in person. A cold day in hell came to mind. I'm sorry, but threatening to kill me and my boyfriend's family wasn't water under the bridge for me.

Angie left for Poland and promised to return in March after her art exhibit. She had somehow found inspiration through this whole ordeal. She made a comment about using Tobias's ashes for pigment for a piece she was working on, but I hoped to God she was kidding.

Speaking of morbid, I got a package from Olivia last week with the book she bought about the serial killer boyfriend. It was actually a good read, good enough to recommend in our next book meeting at work. Olivia and I still weren't bosom buddies, but it was a start.

The repairs on Caleb's town house were complete, and not a day too soon given the fact that he and his brothers were politely evicted from their lavish hotel room. Haden was staying with Caleb until he recovered from his bullet wound and from how Caleb puts it, milking his injury to keep from helping with the move.

Now with everything settled, all I had to worry about was passing trig and devising ways to sneak off with Caleb to feed. This Cambion soul mate stuff was bigger than either of us signed up for, that was for sure. But as Caleb said, there was nothing easy about us. I will say, it's very entertaining what love will make people do. It's a great way to start your year.

"Did you want to get something to eat?" I asked as he walked me to my car.

"Naw. I gotta finish moving my stuff back. But I'll call you later tonight." He pecked my lips, cheek and neck, successfully making me shiver from more than just the cold.

Finally, he pulled away. "I'll see you around, Miss Marshall."

"I know."

He was halfway to his Jeep before he rushed back across the front lawn for another kiss. This one was quick but with more meaning than the first. A cold, flat disk passed from his mouth to mine. The invasion startled me, but the soft clink against my teeth made his motive clear. We pulled away and stared at each other, examining our fate mapped in front of us.

I've seen this face a hundred times, but the image seemed new to me. This wasn't Caleb, the guy in the music department at work, or Caleb, the Cambion, or Caleb, my boyfriend. This was my future, my matter of life and death, calm and very aware of his effect on me.

Without another word, he walked away, taking another piece of my heart with him. I watched him drive away before I pulled the quarter from my mouth, hoping against hope that he washed it beforehand. Tucking the coin in my back pocket, I realized at this rate, I was going to need a bigger jar.

The Cambion Chronicles

On sale now

Book 1: *Living Violet*

He's persuasive, charming, and way too mysterious. And for Samara Marshall, her co-worker is everything she wants most—and everything she most fears . . .

Book 2: *Burning Emerald*

Dating the most popular guy in school is every girl's fantasy. But to Samara Marshall, he's a dangerous force come to rekindle their tangled past. Only it's not *her* past . . .

Turn the page for an excerpt from these exciting novels . . .

Living Violet

Love indulged the masochist.

Truer words have never been spoken, if I do say so myself. It's a philosophy that has kept me sane for as long as I can remember and helped me survive the weirdest summer of my life. On the flip side, it's very entertaining what love will make people do. It's a great way to spend your lunch break.

Sitting on my car hood, sucking down a Big Gulp, I watched the pinnacle of love unfold before my eyes. My best friend, Mia, and her on-again off-again boyfriend, Dougie, squared-off like prize fighters in the middle of the outlet center parking lot.

This week's drama included props. Dougie pivoted along the concrete, ducking and avoiding death by the finest designer handbag money could buy. Through the litany of screams, cusses, and purse swinging, I figured Mia had caught Dougie hanging out with another girl. Mia could be a little high-strung sometimes, but when it came to her man, she advanced to straight head case.

That jealous insanity went both ways, depending on the day, and much amusement awaited all who watched.

"God, you're such a liar! How could you do this to me?" she raved.

"Chill, baby! She was my cousin!" Dougie escaped the oncoming blow from Mia's handbag by an inch.

"You lying piece of crap! I've met all of your relatives, Douglas. She never came to your house before."

Dougie ran in circles around her, the blood rush turning his face beet red. "She just came into town! I swear, baby."

"Why didn't you introduce me, huh?" Mia wiped her sweaty brown hair from her forehead. "What, are you ashamed of me?"

He paused, clearly hurt at the suggestion. "No! Why would you say that?"

"Liar!" Her purse swung at his head, but missed.

Dougie grabbed one of the straps, and the two began a full tug-of-war in the middle of the parking lot. Weekend shoppers watched in horror, covering the ears of their children from the curses flying in the air. At any moment, someone would definitely call security, so I decided to leave the lovebirds to their own devices.

"Hey, guys," I yelled behind me. "I gotta get back to work, but I'll see y'all later, okay?"

"Okay, I'll call ya!" Mia yelled back before shoving Dougie in the chest.

I dumped my cup in the trash, then entered the side door of Buncha Books. The air-conditioning slapped me in the face and pushed the June heat back outside. Mellow jazz rang through the speakers in a chronic loop from the satellite radio. Tourists and townies overran the floor in a slow, indecisive dance around the bookshelves.

I strolled through the main aisles, past the kiosk of new releases and bestsellers toward the customer service desk in the center of the store. Working at Buncha Books since sophomore year taught me a few tricks of the trade, namely to never get caught on the actual book floor. I also discovered that if I didn't make eye contact with the customers, they wouldn't talk to me. That policy remained tucked in my back pocket until my shift started. Casting a wary glance over my shoulder, I singled out an empty computer and clocked back in.

Stealth infiltration and quick reflexes allowed me to reach the other end of the store without incident. When I breezed by the magazine aisle, I caught something odd in my peripheral, a scene disturbing enough to break my stride. I stopped, blinked a few times, and then backtracked to the Home & Garden section to confirm what I just saw.

Caleb Baker, the assistant manager in the music department, held some redhead in a devastating lip-lock. She didn't seem to have a problem with the public tonsillectomy, but this wasn't the type of customer service the managers urged us to practice.

Just as I turned to leave, his gaze met mine.

Caleb's looks would never stop traffic, but he was worth a second glance with his deep dimples, and the most intense violet eyes I had ever seen. Despite his claim of authenticity, eyes that color shouldn't exist in nature— eyes that now reflected every purple tone of the color wheel.

Light brown strands draped over his face as the two continued to slob each other down. If they didn't come up for air soon, Caleb would no doubt suck the life out of her. From what I hear, cheap hotel rooms existed for such an occasion, and there were plenty in the area to choose from.

Of the year and a half I worked here, that kid weirded me out in one way or another. Not to mention the number of women who chased after him on a regular basis. This fact went unnoticed and unaddressed by everyone in the store, including the managers, which disgusted me even more. Having seen enough, I walked away toward my station before my lunch came back up.

Cuppa-Joe was a coffee shop in the back of the bookstore, the place where people kicked back and talked trash about everyone; the cesspool of company gossip and customer-bashing.

I closed tonight with my weekend partner in crime, Nadine Petrovsky, a Polish exchange student at The College of William & Mary, and one of the most cynical people I ever had the pleasure of meeting. Guys came to the café just to hear her exotic accent and watch her work. One glimpse of her explained why.

Model scouts would salivate over her European beauty: her long wheat-colored hair that reached her butt, and her freaky green cat eyes. Too bad none of the attention interested her. Having no time for the BS left the girl cutthroat and caustic. She was just too focused to let a guy or anyone else slow her down.

Nadine stood in front of the barista machine, rinsing the steam wand, when she caught me in the corner of her eye.

"You're late," she noted without looking up.

"Sorry. Mia and Dougie were having it out in the parking lot again." I tied my hair into a bun and grabbed my apron from the back kitchen.

"Oh yeah?" She craned her neck, straining to see the front of the store. "Their fights are good. They need their own sitcom."

"I told them that."

Worry lines etched her forehead as she shook her head in disapproval. "Their relationship isn't healthy, Sam."

"What relationship is?" I tightened my apron, then went to the sink to wash my hands.

"The sane kind."

"Well, as soon as I see one of those, I'll let you know what I think."

While drying my hands, the second reason why I hated customers approached the counter. A kid dressed in all black with a dog collar leered at me.

Nadine kept herself conveniently busy, so I made my way to the register. "Can I help you?"

"I'd like an iced chai latté," the boy said, deadpan. It was hard to tell if the kid was high or half-asleep, or whether he was, in fact, a boy. His parachute jeans dragged the floor like a prom gown, the cuffs frayed and dirty, hiding the clown boots underneath.

I rang up his order and shot Nadine a look, which she mirrored perfectly. After he left, I leaned against the counter and laughed.

Nadine didn't smile, no matter how hilarious the joke, which I'm sure made her a real delight during the weekdays when she babysat preschoolers in daycare. Instead, she wiped down the work area with aggravated swipes.

"I hate those Elmo goth kids," she griped. "What self-respecting sociopath drinks chai anyway? What do they know about real torment? Let them survive a concentration camp and then they can complain."

"It's called 'emo,'" I corrected her. "And your great grandparents didn't even get to the camp before the U.S. troops came in."

Nadine moved to the back counter and checked the timers on the coffeepots. "It's still torment. And if you say 'emo,' I say 'Elmo' because they are equally childish."

Shaking my head, I watched her in amusement. "You don't know what his home life is like."

"*Everyone* knows what his home life is like. He doesn't get along with his parents. He stays in his room and whines and writes bad poems about being a vampire."

Laughing, I stepped to the espresso machine and stole a shot.

"Hey, it's your turn to wipe the tables." Nadine tossed me a rag. "And don't forget to put back those magazines."

Groaning, I dragged my feet to the sitting area and gathered the discarded cups and straw wrappers. Seeing no one else in line, I took a moment to return the magazines to the racks. When I had finished, I turned around and met Caleb, still as idle and unproductive as when I last saw him.

He sat on a reading bench by the window, holding his head in his hands. Afternoon light showered his back and crowned his dark hair in a golden halo. Normally, I would've ignored him were it not for the slight tremors that rocked his body. Was he crying? Did he and his new arm candy have a falling-out? It was just off-putting to see a guy cry, but no tears fell and none were wiped away by his hand. His body teetered back and forth, and I half expected him to start begging for spare change. How long was his break anyway?

I went over to him and tapped his shoulder. "Hey, Caleb. You okay?"

"Yeah," he mumbled from under his hands. Thankfully, I didn't smell any alcohol on him, but he definitely wore the hungover look. Then again, he always looked like that.

One hand reached for the sunglasses hooked on his collar, while the other shielded his eyes—whether from shame or the glaring lights, I wasn't sure. I also wasn't sure about the source of the purple rays leaking between his fingers.

For a split second, a cast of purple flooded his eyes, swelling in a fluorescent glow. Caleb quickly turned his head, leaving a streak of color dragging through the air in a residual haze. That was an interesting trick for someone who supposedly didn't wear contacts.

He rose from his seat and paused at the shocked look on my face. He shifted his feet and messed with his hair, trying to play it off as if he'd been caught with his fly open. However, the only things I caught were vision problems and a bad vibe.

I took a step back. "You sure you're okay? Are you sick?"

My question made him laugh, but it sounded dry and full of bitterness. "You have no idea," he said before marching back to his end of the store.

My mom taught me not to judge people, but damn, that kid was out there. I didn't know much about him, but that only made the fact that much more tangible. Something told me that ignorance was bliss when it came to Caleb Baker, so I went back to work, hoping for a distraction. But the damage was done. My curiosity had been piqued, and that hungry creature wouldn't let me rest until I fed it.

Burning Emerald

When you're a Cambion, balance is paramount. Never lose control, never allow emotions to run wild, and never, ever forget who you are and what lives within you. Such discipline requires a sound mind, a thick skin, and a high tolerance for all things weird, because one wrong move and it's over. No matter how tempting it is at first, in the end there's nothing more tragic, more excruciating, than losing yourself.

Well, except maybe high school.

I swam against the rough current of swinging backpacks, sharp elbows, and whipping ponytails, all in hopes of reaching the auditorium in one piece. The corridors overflowed with foot traffic, disorganized chatter, and the rowdy boom of slamming lockers. The floor rumbled from the stampede fleeing the fourth class of the day.

The varsity team hooted victory chants to the trophy gods behind the glass case in front of the main office. Teenyboppers huddled together in tight clusters, sharing magazines and gushing over the latest fad. Straight ahead lay the obstacle course of shameless make-out bandits who needed to rent a hotel room and stop blocking the hallway. The only thing missing was the cheesy pop soundtrack and the CW logo in the bottom corner. TV high school looked a lot cleaner though, and I bet it didn't reek of bleach and dried ketchup.

I hid my face behind my compact mirror while trying to ignore the dagger stares aimed in my direction, especially if the owners of those eyes had a boyfriend nearby. Even Lilith, my "internal roommate," bristled at the laser beam of hate that shot my way.

My peers had dubbed me the freak of James City High School, not because of the red and white stripe in my hair or my butterball figure, but because of the avid attention from the males who crossed my path. 'Twas the curse of the dreaded possession, I'm afraid.

I wouldn't have been able to explain what a Cambion was three months ago, or known such a thing as human-demon hybrids existed. But now I knew from firsthand experience what it meant to have a soul of a succubus inside me, draining my energy, and luring unsuspecting males to their death to get more. Nothing much I could do about the long, hungry glances and the not-so-subtle whispers. All I could do was avoid eye contact, stay out of trouble, and pray for June to come quickly. I only had eight months to go.

Flashing lights attacked my retinas as soon as I entered the auditorium. Two murky gray backdrops were stationed in the center of the stage, where hired photographers captured our final year for posterity. Two lines ran at opposite ends of the platform steps and leaked into the aisles.

I trotted down the steep incline where teachers directed students to the photo table. I found my name on the list, grabbed my ticket and one of those cheap plastic combs nurses use to check for head lice, and then got in line. A good number of students stood ahead of me, fixing their hair and retouching their makeup. The rest sat in the rows of seats, in no rush to go to class.

Not even a moment after I stood in line, my best friend rested her head on my shoulder, her whole body trembling with laughter. "Girl, did you see what Courtney G. is wearing? It's what you would call 'a piping-hot mess.' "

I blotted my nose and chin. "Now, now, Mia. Be nice. We all can't be a fashionista like you."

"Of course not, but I expect the basic principles of coordination. I mean, really?" Mia shook her head, her whiskey-brown eyes widened in dismay. "Another thing, when are these kids gonna learn that you don't keep wearing your new clothes the first few weeks of school? You slowly blend it into your existing wardrobe."

There was the fashion police and there was the one-man Gestapo called Mia Moralez. How she passed dress code with the getups she wore was the magic trick of the century. And today's eye-popping number was no exception. She showed more breast and thigh than an eight-piece combo meal, yet never got called to the office. How did that work? I envied her bravery and her slim physique, but as of late, I envied her ability to ace pre-cal without breaking a sweat. The girl was a walking Pentium chip with expensive taste.

"Ohmigod! What happened to your face?" She spun me around and pinched my cheeks between her fingers. "Sam, who did this?"

Why do people feel the need to poke and prod at a victim's injuries? Ducking her curious fingers, I answered, "Stray dodgeball to the dome." I took a deep breath, knowing I wouldn't get two feet without telling her the whole story.

Female aggression had reached critical mass today when

the girls in third period gym decided to use me for target practice. A simple game of dodgeball had led to a thirty-minute death match, and even the gym teacher had turned a blind eye to the ambush.

Caleb, my main squeeze and fellow Cambion, had experienced his share of rabid females. He'd warned me about our powerful allure and told me to expect hostility from other girls, especially the insecure ones. But oh no, I had to be hardheaded and shrug it off. The daily dose of haterade was bitter and hard to swallow, leaving my thirst for female camaraderie unquenched.

Well, almost.

"Those evil bitches!" Mia shrieked again after hearing my tale of woe. "Of all the days to get a black eye—Picture Day! These are our senior pictures, the ones that are going into the yearbook, for the world to see. Now look at you, a shell of what you once were. Don't worry, I'll take 'em down." She searched around the auditorium as if one of my attackers lurked in the shadows.

And the award for best actress in an over-dramatization goes to . . .

It wasn't that bad, nothing a little concealer couldn't fix, and the swelling had gone down considerably—a little puffiness near my cheekbone. "Forget it. I can take care of myself," I assured.

"I know, but they can't just—"

"Let it go, Mia. I don't want any more trouble. I want to survive the year without further bloodshed."

It took a few minutes, but she finally let the subject drop. Folding her arms, she studied me from head to toe. Her long, dark locks rested over her right shoulder in one enormous curl, accenting her exotic, island features. "You're not gonna wear those contacts for your picture, are you? It would add a little flare to the aesthetics, but it might draw more attention to your shiner."

I froze mid primp. I knew I'd forgotten to do something when I left the house this morning, but I'd been running late and pretending to be normal took a lot of prep work. For the sake of appearances, I'd had to order a lifetime supply of brown contacts to pass as my old color, thanks to the sentient being living inside me. Lilith's occupancy made my eyes extremely sensitive, and she hated weird window dressing obstructing her view. To give her peace, I switched up every few days and I took them out as soon as I got home. As far as anyone knew, my emerald-green eyes were fake, not the other way around.

"Well, I wanted to make my mark," I replied with a bit of sass.

"Suit yourself. I'm out. Catch you later," she said just as I caught Malik Davis entering the auditorium from over her shoulder. I knew as soon as he saw me, he would try to spark a conversation.

I turned to Mia in a rush of panic. "You're done?"

"I was the first in line. Had to get it over and done with. It's hard work to look this good all day." Mia sauntered away before I could grab her and use her as a shield.

Normally, I wouldn't be so clingy, but I so didn't feel like having another run-in with Malik. It was bad enough my black eye would be immortalized in eight-by-ten gloss; I didn't need him rubbing it in.

Malik Davis, a senior and my new shadow, fueled the wet dreams of every girl in school. As if he needed more attention, Malik had become an overnight celebrity when his truck wrapped around a tree last month and he walked away without a scratch, a heroic tale that he never grew sick of telling. Who wouldn't want to hang on the arm of the sexy basketball captain who cheated death? Oh yeah, that would be me.

"How you doin', Shorty?" he drawled in that smooth, magnolia tone that could melt butter. The solid wall of his body brushed my back.

The nickname grated my ears and made my skin crawl. True, the top of my head barely reached to his shoulders, but I wasn't a garden gnome, and pointing out someone's faults was not a good way to spark a conversation.

"Great, thanks. And yourself?" I stepped away as the line moved forward.

"It's a good day, especially after seeing you," Malik whispered in my ear.

"You give me too much credit. You shouldn't need a girl to make you happy. If so, you have plenty to choose from."

"Maybe so, but you've got my undivided attention, girl. I don't know why I never noticed you before; we've got a bunch of classes together and all that. But I like light-skinned girls, and your contacts are hot. They look so real."

Here we go. If I had a quarter for every time someone mentioned my eye color—

"Let me ask you something. What's a fine sistah like you doing with that white boy? You know he's using you, right?"

I stopped. "For what?"

His gaze slid down my body at leisure. "What you think?"

I wasn't even going to dignify that with an answer, but it served to remind me why I couldn't stand him in the first place. Since tenth grade, Malik had made my mixed race a subject of ridicule, judging my choice of friends, my vocabulary, my taste in music, and now my boyfriend. The words *sellout*, *Oreo*, and *zebra* were commonly used in our brief exchanges. "Fine sistah" had never been included, but was a new moniker, courtesy of my roommate's influence, no doubt.

"I don't mean no harm by it," he said. "I just—"

"Just what, Malik? 'Cause I don't like your tone."

"That Caleb guy will never take you seriously, Samara. He's just gonna take what he wants, then leave."

"And let me guess, you're so much better for me, because we all know you would never get with a girl and leave her high and dry," I bit back.

The photographer's perky assistant yelled for the next pair to approach the stage, which was Malik and me.

After handing the assistant his ticket, the cause of my growing headache turned to me. "Look, I'm just watching out for you. How could you even stomach being with somebody like that?"

That did it. Evidently, people didn't get anywhere in life by being polite in this school. Turning on the balls of my feet, I glared up at him. He looked amused, but that didn't last long.

"Look here, there's no nice way to put this, so I won't even try. It's none of your damn business what I do with my boyfriend. I'm sure it eats you up inside that I'm not sniffing behind you like the rest of the herd, or that you will never in life get to sample any of this luscious I got going on, but seriously, you need to get off my ass, or else I'll break my foot off in yours." I strolled to the stage, leaving Malik standing with a stunned look on his face.

The assistant directed me to the stool and ordered me to sit up straight. Malik sat in the station to my left, his stare burning at my profile, but I wouldn't give him the satisfaction of caring.

There was just something about him that didn't sit well with me, even more than usual. An air of danger loomed around him, an unnatural aura that gave me the willies.

Lilith felt it as well, voicing her disquiet with sharp tingles up my spinal cord, and worrying the network of nerves lining my midsection. While the photographer arranged my chin and shoulders in the right position, I snuck a glance at Malik.

He was good-looking, hotter than my boyfriend, though I would never whisper that to a living soul. It shamed me to admit that I'd had a few fantasies of him, most involving a hot tub and a vat of cookie dough ice cream, but that secret will follow me to the grave. Besides, looks meant nothing if you were an asshole, a self-righteous tool who turned into a skeleton in sharp lighting.

Wait, what the—?

I blinked and spun my stool completely in Malik's direction. Did I just see what I thought I did? As soon as the camera flashed, his clothes, skin, and all external material vanished, leaving a framework of bones sitting on the stool. The weird X-ray vision only lasted a second, but that was enough to freak me out.

When the photographer finished, Malik rose to his feet and strolled to the opposite side of the stage. He spared me a fleeting glance and smiled with more humor than the occasion called for. A quick glint of gold flickered in his dark brown eyes, then disappeared.

"Face this way, hon. Shoulders straight." The voice of my own photographer snapped me back to attention.

My heart tapped Morse code against my ribs as I tried in vain to make sense of what I'd just seen. Forcing the worst smile in history, I waited for the camera flash.

Nothing outside of the natural surprised me anymore, but my curiosity would never die. The events of the summer had taught me well never to ignore those feelings, but to embrace them and expect the unexpected. Maybe I wasn't the only freak getting their learn on at James City

High School. Perhaps it was a new power I had acquired that I was just now tapping into, an ability to foresee danger, like in those *Final Destination* movies. More than likely, it was my overactive mind running wild, something that happened a lot lately.

I only knew that this was a warning of some sort, a whisper too faint to make out the words.